Not Over It

Margaret G. Cahill

Margaret G. Cahill

Copyright 2014 by Margaret G. Cahill

ISBN 978-1501068317

For Edward

Chapter One

He stopped in front of the New York City 26th Precinct on the upper Westside. *I'm not sure I can do this.* He walked a little farther, sighed, gathered all his strength and pressed on. At the door he wiped the moisture from his palm on his pants. With a hard swallow he stepped inside.

The front desk sergeant jumped up. "Good to see you, Peter. Sorry for your loss."

"Thanks." Detective Peter Hajek dreaded the litanies of 'sorry for your loss' that faced him more than he worried about being assigned desk duty. He knew when he took leave to care for his wife that his cases were distributed to other detectives. *I hope I won't be given cold cases.*

As he made his way through the busy precinct to Captain Wilcox's office, co-workers offered condolences. He nodded, shook hands, and accepted shoulder hugs.

"Peter, wait." Nick Kostas walked toward him. "Welcome back. I hoped I'd see you before I left for patrol."

"I'm on my way to find out what cases the captain has for me—I'm looking forward to getting back on the job."

"Ease into it. You haven't given yourself much time."

"I've been away from work for three months."

"I know but Francine died only eight days ago."

"I've no reason not to be back. Nick, thanks for everything. You and Camille were a lifeline for me these past months. I really appreciate it."

"Camille told me to tell you that you have an open invitation for dinner with us whenever it works for you." Kostas tapped his arm. "Gotta run."

1

When first with NYPD, Hajek logged many hours with Kostas in a patrol car. Kostas, two years Hajek's senior, choose to continue as a patrol officer while Hajek became a detective.

Hajek continued to his boss' office. A man with a round face, brown eyes and graying hair at the temples hung up the phone. Captain Henry Wilcox stood to meet his young detective.

"Beautiful service, Peter. I loved the story of how you met your wife. You thought she crashed the party."

"That's the truth." Hajek smiled at the memory of the fundraiser at the Metropolitan Museum of Art. It was his good fortune that she landed in the chair next to him.

Wilcox interrupted Hajek's replaying in his mind the conversation that led to his asking her out. "Only married four years. I can't imagine your loss. How are you doing?"

He shrugged. "I'm glad to be back at work."

Grabbing his jacket Wilcox said, "Come with me. I want to check in with the team that's been at Grant's Tomb for hours."

"What?"

"Didn't you hear?"

"I never turned on the radio or TV this morning."

"Early this morning there was an explosion at Grant's tomb. Looks like a terrorist attack."

"Strange." Hajek, thankful for a focus, considered the former President's burial site an odd target.

They walked to a cruiser. "Ever been inside Grant's tomb?" Wilcox asked.

"Not exactly, but the museum for sure."

2

Wilcox laughed. Of course you've been there, you history buff. Tell me about it."

Sounding like a park ranger presenting to visitors, Hajek gave a thumbnail sketch. "The official name is The General Grant National Memorial. The setting initially overlooked the Hudson. Decades of development now block the river view. Murals, mosaics, embroidered tapestries and displays in the exhibit space commemorate Grant's life and accomplishments as a General and United States President."

At 122nd Street and Riverside Drive, Wilcox pulled the cruiser up on the sidewalk behind three TV vans. The men navigated around a *Closed Today* sign. Curious bystanders gathered at the perimeter. An officer lifted the crime scene tape for them to walk under it.

Detective Dorgan approached. "Good morning, Captain… Peter."

"What do you have so far?" Wilcox asked.

"The bomb went off shortly after 4:00A.M. ATF's preliminary sweep revealed no other bombs. They're still checking. So far there's no evidence of radiation or biotech agents."

"Any confirmed dead?" Wilcox asked.

"No. And no one injured."

"Any leads?"

"If the FBI has any they haven't shared. They mostly want our guys to keep reporters and onlookers away. We're doing the usual photographing of the crowd, canvassing the area and directing traffic."

Hajek went directly to the monument for a closer look. Ironically etched in stone above the entrance was the phrase *Let us have Peace.* Soot coated a wide area of the main door and the wall to the right. Strange that someone chose early morning and not when people were around. The blast appeared more smoky than

3

powerful. The smell reminded Hajek of the pungent odor of the illegal firecrackers that he had played with as a kid. The old-fashioned device surprised him. It dirtied the front entrance but caused no destruction. He took a photo.

"I'll send someone," Wilcox said into his cell phone and then clicked it off. "Peter, the Police Commissioner and FBI are convening a task force this afternoon to look into the explosion."

"Who's in charge?" Hajek looked again at the doorway.

"Usual haggling. FBI believes it's a terrorist attack."

"Most terrorist strike busy places, not empty buildings," Hajek walked with Wilcox.

"You're my guy for the two o'clock meeting this afternoon at Javits."

"Okay."

"Nothing much we can do here. Let's go."

Stopped at a traffic light Wilcox turned to his detective. "Peter, I'll assign you a partner as soon as I can. This morning settle into your desk and give some thought to the upcoming meeting downtown."

***

At 1:45, Hajek wandered into the Javits Federal Office Building at 26 Federal Plaza in lower Manhattan. After the tedium of the last few hours, the meeting gave him something to do. He cleared security, found the small conference room for the task force meeting, and leaned his five foot ten-inch frame against the back wall of a packed room. Looking around he recognized two men from the NYC Counterterrorism Bureau, noticed representatives from Homeland Security, and various Federal government agencies. In the crowd of males there were very few women.

The FBI agent chairing the meeting opened with the known facts and then announced their plan for a two-prong investigation. His agency would canvas area high schools to determine if this was a senior prank. Agents would also question those on their terrorist list.

Another agent suggested investigating everyone who worked at Grant's Tomb, particularly anyone who recently left employment. A senior manager from The National Parks of New York Harbor offered to review recent requests for special access to the Memorial's research library.

"Has anyone taken credit for this explosion?" a park ranger asked.

"So far a couple dozen calls and emails--nothing credible—all came after the explosion," an FBI agent replied. "Chemical analysis will be done at the main FBI lab in DC and will take days"

Hajek listened to suggestions of increasing security at other monuments. When someone mentioned the birthplace of President Teddy Roosevelt on 20th street, Hajek had heard enough. Why not Hyde Park or Clinton's office in Harlem? Hajek regarded staying any longer as wasted time. He glanced around the room and noted that everyone seemed much older than he. Thirty-three did not command respect in this business. The guys, in their fifties, wearing dark suits, were considered the experts.

Back at the police station, Hajek wondered how he could add to the FBI investigation. I need to find something out of the ordinary. He looked at the photo of the soot on the memorial. For the next twenty minutes he searched for information on small but dirty explosives. Firecrackers did not typically coat a nearby surface.

Still wondering what device was used, he decided to look at surveillance video of vehicles leaving the city between the hours of 3:00 and 6:00 A.M. He would have liked access to anything on security cameras from buildings in the area near Grant's Tomb but he knew the FBI would have already taken possession of those pictures. Of the many bridges and tunnels into Manhattan, Hajek decided to review cars crossing the George Washington Bridge and those heading into the Lincoln Tunnel. There were many good reasons someone drove out of the city in predawn hours. Without rush hour volume; he hoped to find something unusual and useful.

For hours, he scanned two of several major exits from Manhattan. At six his cell phone rang.

"Where are you?" Kostas asked.

Hajek hesitated.

"You're at work. I heard about the blast at Grant's Tomb. Is that yours? "

"Yeah me, the Bureau, and about ten other agencies."

"Sounds fun. Tomorrow's another day. Go home."

"Soon. I promise."

Around 8P.M., the vehicles started to blur and he had trouble concentrating.

Hajek took a cab to the 7th Avenue station and caught a direct subway to the Astoria section of Queens. Family and friends teased him about living in his childhood neighborhood but in this borough he felt close to his parents, especially his father who died seven years ago. Peter loved to listen to his stories about Astoria's history.

At the apartment door, his chest tightened. He hesitated and then walked inside. Francine's absence hit him with every step. Just inside the front door hung the framed photo of the original Yankee Stadium, his birthday gift for her twenty-eighth birthday. A hand-painted, porcelain vase that had been her grandmother's sat on a curio cabinet. He took a few more steps, stopped, and gazed at the Shelter Island Ferry watercolor, a reminder of a fun weekend on Long Island.

In his bedroom he paused and picked up the bowl-shaped urn. The colorful piece of raku pottery held Francine's ashes.

6

Francine, Talk to me! Remember when we found this apartment. I never thought you'd leave the West Village. I was so happy you were willing to live in Queens and didn't think I was crazy to want to stay in the neighborhood I grew up in…

After placing the urn back on a night table, Hajek emptied the contents of his pockets on his dresser, locked his gun in its safe and gazed at their wedding photo. *How can I go on without you?* Wilcox liked the story of how they met. And so did Peter. He continued to stare at his bride and replayed their first encounter. Peter met Francine because his mother was not able to use the ticket she bought for a Metropolitan of Art Museum fundraiser. She asked him to take her place. His mother made it clear that she counted on him to notice everything and give her a full report.

Recounting the evening a few days later, he did not tell his mother about the woman he met and asked out before the end of the evening. Wandering near his table, Francine, in a perfectly fitted, teal blue dress, grabbed his attention. Only briefly did he admire her looks. Her movement convinced him that she slipped in without a ticket. Then he overheard Francine ask about an empty seat at his table and a woman replied, "You're welcome to sit here. My husband's stuck in an airport. He'll not be needing it." Only later did he learn that Francine had a seat at a prominent table, one purchased by her employer, The New York Yankees. She happily sat in the back to avoid sitting near the disgraced governor. *"You were such fun. How could you leave me?"*

His home phone rang. Seeing it was his brother Roland, he picked up.

"How'd the first day back at work go for you?"

"Okay. It's strange after being away so long. In fact everything's strange. Did you have any trouble getting home yesterday?"

"No I was lucky. Only an hour delay getting into Chicago and I still made connections for the Seattle flight. I won't keep you I know it's late. Think about a trip to the Pacific Northwest."

"I will. Talk with you next week."

Peter put a frozen chicken potpie in the microwave. In the living room he turned on the TV. The first image was of an FBI spokesperson informing reporters of the status of the bombing investigation. As he listened to the agent, "We have a task force and a plan of action." Peter shouted, *And so did General Custer*!

He hit mute, surfed through repetitive news stories and numerous commercials. Hearing the beeps from the kitchen he retrieved his meal. Unable to sit at the table where he and Francine usually dined, he returned to the living room, switched to the weather channel, and ate while storm chasers tracked an Oklahoma tornado.

Finished with his food, he clicked off the TV and grabbed his iPod. After shuffling through playlists, he selected Francine's favorite jazz moments. Stan Getz saxophone, Hajek remembered as romantic. Tonight his playing of "Desafinado" sounded like a funeral dirge. He hit next.

In a recliner with his feet up, he gave into the flood of feelings. At first tears trickled, and then built to wrenching sobs. This was forever. He would never again hear her say 'this music's beautiful'. He would never again glide on a dance floor with her in his arms.

At 3:30A.M. Peter woke still in the chair. Once he managed to stand, he made his way to his bedroom, undressed and set the alarm for six. *I need to look at other exit routes out of the city.*

Chapter 2

Hajek woke the next day thinking about the explosion at Grant's Tomb and eager to get to work. He wondered if the April 9 date had significance. Believing that the bomber left Manhattan, Hajek considered the quickest way to leave the city from Grant's Tomb. By the time he dressed, he settled on Route 9 North as the logical choice.

At his desk at 7:30A.M., he focused his searching to cars traveling north on Route 9. The traffic slowed at the tollbooth. He watched big rigs, limos, and a variety of cars before stopping at a picture of a red pickup truck with a Virginia tag. Rewinding he zoomed in on the back bumper. A sticker on the left side of the bumper proclaimed 'Rebel to the End'. In the center was a symbol, red background, blue X with white stars. Hajek first thought it was a confederate flag. A closer view showed the logo for Sons of Confederate Veterans with the year 1896 on the bottom. He jotted down the plate number.

With his police access to motor vehicle records, Hajek identified the truck owner as John B. Gordon, a Petersburg, Virginia resident. The driver's license photo showed a Caucasian man with dark hair, a mustache and several inches of scruffy beard. His date of birth indicated he was fifty-three. Further checking revealed no criminal record for Gordon.

What is this southerner doing in greater New York City, Hajek wondered. He entered John B. Gordon in a search engine. *Oh yeah, he's our guy.* Hajek smiled as he scrolled down the returned hits. He read about Robert E. Lee's trusted General, John B. Gordon, who led the last charge of the Army of Northern Virginia at Appomattox.

After clicking the link for Sons of Confederate Soldiers, Hajek sat back in his chair and listened to the website message. A man in the gray uniform

9

championed the citizen-soldiers who fought for the Confederacy and personified the best qualities of America. The soldier called the conflict the *Second American Revolution*. The website included membership information and photos.

Pausing at another link that piqued his interest, a John B. Gordon owned a souvenir store in Petersburg, Virginia, Hajek noted the name and phone number. Next, he examined the shop's website with its reminders of a war fought 150 years ago. There were bullets, buttons and belt buckles. There were pistols, rifles and swords. There were pictures of generals and packets of confederate money. He called the number listed for the store.

"Genuine War Artifacts," the man announced in a drawl familiar to Hajek from his student days at the University of Virginia.

"John B, please," Hajek said as if they were the best of friends.

"Not here. Can I help you?" the man asked.

"Oh, that's too bad. I was hoping to see him after work," Hajek said.

"Sorry. He's going to be out all week."

"That so."

"Yeah some trip north."

Chapter 3

Hajek issued a Bulletin on the truck's license plate and John B. Gordon. This guy would stay around long enough to hear the news reports and gloat.

Captain Wilcox walked over to Hajek's desk. "How's the task force proceeding?"

"Away from the target, I'm afraid. I'm following up on a hunch and should know more soon."

Wilcox raised an eyebrow and tilted his head like a teacher waiting for a student to come clean about who really wrote his assignment.

"It's not the work of a Middle Eastern terrorist. The motive's disrespect," Hajek said.

"Don't tread on FBI turf, Peter. Be a team player. I don't want any trouble."

"Just trying to solve this case." Hajek smiled. Wilcox walked away.

Hajek pulled his ringing cell phone from his jacket pocket. "Detective Hajek."

"Beacon Police Chief Sloane, here. The pickup truck you're looking for is parked alongside the river near the Newburgh-Beacon Bridge. One of our patrol cars called it in. The driver's asleep."

"You guys are fast."

"What's he wanted for?"

"He's a person of interest in an explosion."

"Fatalities."

"No."

"How dangerous is this for my men?"

11

"Hard to know. I'm betting he has a gun but doesn't want to use it. Follow protocol and bring him to your station for questioning. It should be interesting to meet him. I'm on my way. I'll call when I get closer to Beacon."

***

Hajek traveled across the George Washington Bridge and headed north on the Palisades Parkway. Driving in view of the Hudson triggered many pleasant childhood memories. His Boy Scout troop had annual camping trips to Bear Mountain. For a boy from New York City, this area was remote and wild. He laughed remembering tours of West Point and his transition from aspiring to be a cadet to gratitude that he had skipped the marching in formation in perfectly polished shoes.

Passing a sign for Cold Spring, he felt nausea building in the pit of his stomach. His wife loved poking around the shops in this historic village, stopping for lunch, and then walking the path along the river. He doubted he would ever return to that town.

His cell phone rang. He pushed the speaker button on his phone.

"Hajek."

"We have one angry man here. Can you hear him?"

"Yes." Hajek could not make out all the words but he recognized the southern accent of a man yelling in the background.

"Cursing, calling us Yankees and yelling about our blue uniforms."

Hajek moved to the far right lane. "Tell him someone who lived in Charlottesville, Virginia would like to talk with him."

Sloane repeated Hajek's words to Mr. Gordon.

"That seemed to help. How far away are you?"

"Twenty minutes tops. I assume he's not asking for a lawyer," Hajek said.

12

"Right," Sloane said.

For the remaining minutes of his drive to Beacon, Hajek thought about his days at the University of Virginia. He initially planned to be a lawyer. By sophomore year, Hajek shifted his career goal from the courthouse, to New York City streets as a police officer. Front line law enforcement fitted his personality. He never looked back or regretted his choice and had quickly progressed to detective.

In Charlottesville, Hajek's education included learning nuances of southern culture, especially the lingering resentments for northerners and the hero worship of Southern Civil War generals, particularly Robert E. Lee, the commanding general of the Confederate Army. Idolizing losers mystified Hajek. New Yorkers liked winners. When he told family and friends back in New York City about a January celebration south of the Mason Dixon line they accused him of exaggerating.

He smiled remembering his first southern barbecue. Hundreds showed up to celebrate the beloved General Lee's birthday. Small town festivals held look-alike contests of the general with *Dixie* and *When Johnny Comes Marching Home* blaring in the background. No one mentioned that Lee graduated from West Point and took an oath to the USA and its constitution before the Civil War. Hajek kept that detail to himself. Guests of every age enjoyed the food prepared according to favorite family recipes. Church hall tables were jam-packed with fried chicken, barbecued pork, biscuits, okra, coleslaw, macaroni and cheese, banana pudding, and assorted pies and cakes. Hajek asked a classmate where the hot dogs or hamburgers were and endured a quick rebuke. In time, he improved his skills and did not question things he found bewildering. Restraint served him well in the city of Richmond. He did not ask why there were so many monuments to second place. Today he would need self-discipline when speaking with John B. Gordon.

13

Chapter 4

Thinking about meeting the possible bomber, Hajek continued past exit signs for West Point and Cornwall-on-the-Hudson to the one for downtown Beacon. He made his way to the municipal complex that included the police station, drove up a steep incline, and found a parking space.

An officer sitting in a glass booth greeted him. "Good Afternoon."

Hajek responded into a speaker. "I'm Detective Peter Hajek. I'm here to see Captain Sloane."

A medium built man in his fifties, dressed in formal police uniform complete with a tie approached. His hair floated from his temples in soft waves. "Thanks for coming. I'm Captain Darren Sloane."

"Pleased to meet you. I'm Peter Hajek. How's our guy?"

"Very unhappy."

"Objects to your hospitality?"

"An odd one for sure. Calls us aggressors, even invaders… My officers did not find a weapon on him or in his vehicle."

They stopped outside the interrogation room. Hajek looked through the glass at a man straddling a chair and clinging to the table, as one would grip a raft out of control in whitewater rapids. He was thin and his six-foot plus frame was obvious. He parted his dark hair on the right side and slicked it back behind his ear. Neatly cut in the back it curled to the nape of his neck. His mustache merged with a beard that covered his chin and extended to his chest. His appearance reminded Hajek of an earlier time. It would be difficult to tell the difference from this man's picture and some civil war generals in history books.

"How about coffee?" Sloane asked.

"Water would be great. I would like this recorded," Hajek said to Sloane.

14

"No problem. I'll turn it on."

Hajek continued to watch Gordon until Sloane returned.

Handing over a bottle of water, Sloane opened the door for Hajek to enter.

"Hi, Mr. Gordon," Hajek greeted the man in police custody. "I'm Detective Peter Hajek. How are you today?"

"Terrible. I'm treated like a prisoner of war." The man looked directly at Hajek.

"Would you like coffee or water?"

"No."

"New York's a strange place, isn't it?"

"Yeah."

"What brings you here?"

"Trying to understand why you guys head south so much."

"The University of Virginia lured me," Hajek said.

"You went there? You sound like a Yankee." A hint of surprise in his voice.

"Studied there four years."

"Seems there are enough southerners to educate without you northerners."

Hajek resisted mentioning his scholarship. No need to kick the man. "I found the people in Charlottesville very welcoming. I enjoyed my college years."

"No one brought you to the police station in handcuffs, I bet."

Hajek laughed. "You're right. Do you live in Charlottesville?"

"No, Petersburg. Ever been there?" Gordon's hands released their grip on the chair.

"I did the tourist stuff. Interesting history. What do you do there?" Hajek asked in a tone that conveyed genuine interest.

Gordon looked directly at the detective. "I own a store."

"Tell me about it."

"I have real, genuine, historic artifacts from the war between the states including an early edition of John Gordon's book *Reminiscences of the Civil War.* My great-great-great grandfather fought for the Confederacy at Petersburg. He was General John B. Gordon. Ever hear of him?" Gordon asked.

"Of course. He was with General Lee at Appomattox Court House on April 9, 1865," Hajek replied. "Any connection with that meeting and you visiting New York?"

"Maybe."

"General Grant humiliated your ancestor, didn't he?" Without waiting for an answer Hajek continued, "Heavy burden to have his name."

"It's an honor. I like that I look like General Gordon. A college in Georgia is named after him. In Atlanta, on the state capitol grounds, stands a statue of General Gordon on horseback."

"You want your ancestor to be remembered respectfully, don't you?"

"I'm a proud Son of Confederate Veterans," Gordon straightened his back. "I wear the uniform in reenactments to honor the Confederacy. He was a better man than that butcher Grant. and a better soldier." Gordon spit the words more than spoke them.

"So you came to New York to square things on the anniversary of Lee's surrender."

"I don't know."

"I think you do. You wanted to get even. You trashed Grant's tomb to show your disrespect."

Gordon smiled but remained silent.

"That's why you came to New York City."

"He doesn't deserve to be ensconced in a big monument. Tax money from good southerners helps maintain it. I blackened Grant's tomb so people would know he was no good."

***

Hajek left the interrogation room at 4:35P.M.

Sloane stood looking through the one way mirror at Gordon. "He admitted to the bombing. Congratulations."

"Thanks for taping it. I'll call my precinct."

"I'll make you a copy." Sloane walked toward the room with the recording equipment.

Watching Gordon staring into space, Hajek called Wilcox in Manhattan. "Captain, I have a confession from our bomber."

"Is the FBI with you?" Wilcox asked.

"No. The man's in custody in Beacon, New York."

"Are you sure he's the bomber?"

"I've a video-taped confession."

"Airtight?"

"Unquestionable. Captain Sloane here observed and taped the interview."

"That's great, Peter. "I'll let the Commissioner know. He'll inform the FBI and the mayor. We'll coordinate with Beacon PD to bring Gordon to Manhattan," Wilcox said.

"Is one copy enough?" Sloane handed Hajek a disk in a clear case.

"That will do."

From the hallway Sloane and Hajek watched Gordon sitting ramrod straight and staring at some spot in front of him.

17

Sloane stepped closer to the one-way mirror. "Hard to understand. What did he accomplish?"

"He settled a personal vendetta," Hajek said.

"One that will cost him. Do you think he realizes that?"

Hajek nodded. "I think he does. I think he believes whatever the price, he has honored his namesake and that makes everything worthwhile."

"I'll be right back."

Sloane returned with Officer Voit who entered the interrogation room, approached Gordon and gently asked him to come with him. Gordon rose from his chair and silently followed Voit back to his cell.

"You called your captain?"

"Yes. He's calling our commissioner who'll contact the FBI. I expect you'll get a call within the hour with instructions for the transfer of custody." Hajek laughed.

"Of course. It's the fed's case. Let's go to my office and do the paperwork."

Hajek sat opposite Sloane.

"I better call my wife. I told her I'd be home early."

Hajek's jaw tightened dreading the inevitable question. "I need a break. I'll be right back."

After taking more time than necessary, he returned and immediately asked Sloane about a framed picture hanging in his office.

"Northern Lights over Juneau, Alaska. A gift from a friend. Ever been?"

"Not yet."

"My wife and I went there a few years ago. Spectacular beauty. When people say it's the last frontier they're not kidding."

18

Hajek listened as Sloane recounted highlights of the Alaskan cruise. He nodded and smiled while his own thoughts wandered among the list of places he and Francine planned to visit. She knew he wanted to see Pearl Harbor and in her final months she insisted he get there some day. Ignoring his protests that he could not enjoy travel without her, she would say, *Please go. I'll be with you in spirit.*

Sloane described glaciers and bald eagles. When he started on the salmon he was stopped short.

A petite woman appeared in the doorway. "You're making this man hungry. When you told me you'd be late I decided to bring dinner here. She placed an insulated container and a brown bag on Sloane's desk.

"Honey, this is Detective Peter Hajek from Manhattan," Sloane turned to Peter. "Meet Claire, my better half."

Hajek stood and shook Mrs. Sloane's hand. Her short hair with blonde highlights gave her the appearance of a woman in her early forties. Hajek guessed she was at least ten years older.

"I hope you like roast pork."

"I do. Thank you."

"In a couple of hours the traffic will be lighter. Celebrate the success of your day and let Darren extol on Beacon. You can eat a second dinner when you get home." Turning to her husband, Claire said, "Melissa called. Her sister's here from D.C. I'm going to stop over at her house. I'll be home by ten." She kissed him goodbye and left.

Hajek looked away and took a deep breath.

Sloane moved a pile of papers clearing a surface for Hajek s plate. He pulled out the prepared plates of food, silverware, napkins, and bottled water.

"Smells delicious." Hajek opened a bottle of water.

Sloane uncovered the food. "Does your wife cook?"

19

"Not anymore." He looked at the gold wedding band on his left hand. "She died."

"I'm sorry."

"Let's eat. Are you a Yankee fan, Darren?"

Before he could answer, Hajek's phone rang. "My captain. Hajek here."

"Peter, how soon can you be back? The Mayor plans to announce the capture of the bomber at Gracie Mansion tonight. He wants you there."

Chapter 5

The next morning Hajek arrived at work with renewed energy and none of the uncertainty of just a couple of days ago. The lobby area had several people waiting to talk with the desk sergeant. Three police officers near the stairs leading to Hajek's area were looking at a newspaper. One looked up and seeing Hajek, greeted him. "Barely back on the job and stealing the limelight."

He held up the New York Post and showed Peter the front-page photo of him standing with Police Commissioner Sullivan and Mayor Lockhardt in front of the Mayor's residence.

"Nice photo," an officer said.

"You really impressed the mayor." An officer read from the article: "Detective Peter Hajek, deserves most of the credit for cracking this case in record time. His cooperation with Beacon Police Captain Sloane resulted in Gordon's arrest."

Hajek shrugged. "I got lucky."

"Promotion soon to follow," someone announced from across the room.

"Congratulations, Peter. You bring pride to our precinct," Captain Wilcox extended his hand.

"Thanks."

Co-workers got up from their desks to praise Hajek. Several shared how much they loved NYPD getting the credit over the Bureau.

"Wilcox—phone," an officer at the front desk shouted. "It's the mayor. I'll transfer it to your office."

Wilcox smiled. "I'll take it here." He picked up the phone. "Good morning, Mayor Lockhardt. Yes, he's right here." Wilcox listened without saying a word. His expression changed from enthusiastic to blank. Then he said, "Of course, whatever you need." He handed the phone back to the desk sergeant.

"Not all our cases are solved. Back to work," Wilcox said to the gathering. He turned to Hajek. "I need to speak with you in my office."

They walked silently the short distance to Wilcox's office. Hajek closed the door and remained standing.

Wilcox sat at his desk drumming his fingers. "A young woman was found dead in her upper east side apartment this morning. Her father is personally connected with Mayor Lockhardt. The mayor wants you to take the case."

"Upper eastside is not in our precinct." Hajek stood with his back against the door.

"I know. It's hardly standard protocol for the mayor to assign cases. Cracking the Grant case in less than forty-eight hours impressed him." Wilcox shifted in his chair.

"Is this okay with you?" Hajek transferred his weight to his left leg.

"He's the mayor and he cleared it with the police commissioner. A car will pick you up in about ten minutes to take you to the scene."

The mayor's driver and Hajek exchanged cursory greetings. Unaccustomed to someone holding the door for him, Hajek clumsily climbed into the back seat of the Town Car. Briefly, he thought about Francine's reaction and then remembered he would never have another conversation with his wife about day-to-day happenings or anything else. Hajek sat in silence as they made their way to the upper eastside address. He swallowed hard acknowledging there would be many more events that he would not share with Francine.

Workers removed boxes of tile from a van parked in front of the high-rise apartment building on 3rd Avenue. Two police cruisers and a Crime Scene Investigation vehicle lined up behind the van.

"Busy place. Double park and I'll jump out," Hajek said.

"Do you want me to wait?" the driver asked.

"No. I'll find my way back." He exited the vehicle and identified himself to the doorman.

"Detective Peter Hajek, you're expected…Apartment 9D." He pointed to the elevator at the back of the lobby.

Hajek noted the craftsmanship of the 1940-era elevator. No one today would bother with brass panels and a tile floor. The unique lighting fixture looked more like one carefully selected for a well-appointed room. He pushed button 9.

A uniformed police officer stood at the open door of the victim's apartment.

"Don't think we can blame this crime on a civil war descendant. Some sicko for sure." The officer stepped aside.

Hajek walked into the apartment. A large oil painting labeled Nea Moni, an 11th century monastery on the Greek Island of Chios, immediately caught his eye. Crime scene investigators were dusting for prints and there were open boxes of collected evidence on the kitchen floor.

A man in a suit approached. "I'm Detective Rafferty. I heard you were coming and I understand you're taking over this case. All of us in this precinct will cooperate."

"Thanks. What do we know?"

"Ms. Hanson appears to have been strangled. There were nasty marks on her neck. It looked like her attacker struck as soon as she entered the apartment. Her purse landed on the floor inches inside the door." He pointed to a Louis Vuitton bag.

"Any evidence of forced entry?"

"No. May have come in with her."

23

"Or already inside," Hajek suggested. "Any marks around the lock?"

"No." Rafferty said.

"Robbery?" Hajek examined the door lock.

"The purse was still closed. Cash and credit cards are inside. The rest of the place looks undisturbed."

"Who found her?"

"A cleaning woman. She's very distraught. One of our female officers took her to the precinct." He took a notebook from his pocket and read "Her name's Beatrice Allen."

"She let herself in?"

"Yeah. She's here on Wednesdays to do laundry, housekeeping and grocery shopping. The other four days she works for the victim's parents."

"A potential suspect?" Hajek asked.

"No. The parents know her well. She called 911 first and then the girl's father, Clifford Hanson. He arrived soon after the first responders."

"Is he still here?"

"No. He insisted we remove the body and then he left."

"The body's gone?"

"Nothing about this one's routine," Rafferty said. "Hanson called the mayor's personal cell phone and Lockhardt said to work with him."

"They're friends." Hajek looked around.

"Yeah, I'm told they both serve on the Board for The Metropolitan Museum of Art and have vacation homes in The Hamptons. We ignored standard procedure and took the body out."

"I understand. I hope you have pictures."

"Yeah. Not pretty... naked victim, possible sexual assault."

"I'll need copies of the photos."

24

"Sure."

"Did the deceased have a job?"

"Something with a building preservation group."

"Hardly a job to finance this place." Hajek surveyed the spacious apartment decorated with sculptures, oil paintings and oriental rugs.

"I'd guess dad pays the bills."

Looking at a rope on the floor, Hajek asked, "Who untied it?"

"911 responder, I assume," Rafferty said.

"This rope doesn't belong in this apartment. It looks very old." He bent over the thick braided twine with frayed ends knotted to prevent further unraveling.

"Killer brought it with him is my guess." Rafferty shrugged.

"Weird."

"No crime of passion," Rafferty said.

"Passion maybe, but not spontaneous. Unlikely there are any prints on the rope but maybe the killer's DNA."

"I'll bag it if you're finished, detective," a crime investigator said.

Hajek nodded. "How would a killer get into this secure building?"

"For now we're assuming the victim knew her attacker. No need to scare residents by indicating it was a chance encounter," Rafferty said.

"You spoke with the doorman?" Hajek asked.

"Yes. His shift began at seven this morning. First he knew of any problem in the building was when the 911 responders arrived. He did say the night doorman Carlos, did not report anything out of the ordinary."

"I'll look around the rest of the apartment," Hajek said.

"Even without the extra pressure of our mayor, the crime scene team does an excellent job. They'll scrutinize this place. They've already gathered samples of fluids on and near the body. I doubt they'll miss a stray hair on a pillow or clothing."

"I'd like to snap a photo of the victim with my phone. Is this her with her parents?" Hajek held a silver framed photo.

"That's definitely her father and a much better picture of his daughter."

Hajek took a couple of pictures. "Do we know who the building manager is?"

"Yes, a Mr. Howe. I contacted him and he will be here soon with the doorman who worked last evening."

"Good. Give my cell number to Howe. I want to talk with him." He handed him the number.

"Will do, Detective."

"I assume the police removed last week's surveillance records. Can you get me copies?"

Rafferty nodded. "I'll have the tapes and crime scene photos delivered to your precinct before noon."

"Thanks for your help. I'll take a look around the building."

Chapter 6

Hajek went to the stairwell and walked down several flights. On the third floor, he heard hammering and sawing. The sounds led him to 3E. He pushed in the slightly ajar door. A man bent over a sawhorse trimming a board with a power saw. When the noise stopped, Hajek showed his badge and introduced himself.

The worker jumped back knocking the wood to the floor. He put his tool down.

Reading his name tag Hajek said, "Tony, I'm sorry to disturb you. I need to speak with the Project Manager."

Tony pointed to a man standing with his back to them talking to a worker across the room.

Hajek introduced himself. "I understand you're in charge."

He put his clipboard under his left arm and extended his right hand, "Jeff Grier. What's the problem, Detective?"

"A woman was murdered in this building last night. I'd like to know more about the workers on this job. How many are there and who is their employer?"

"Most days I have five to eight guys with me. We work for BH Classic Renovation out of the Bronx. Some days I have subcontractors."

"Have you had subs in recent days?"

"Most days for the past three weeks there have been three or four."

"About how many different men have been involved in this project?"

"Maybe two dozen."

"I'll need the names and contact information for everyone."

"I can get that for you."

Hajek and Grier exchanged business cards.

"Thanks. Call me if you think of anything."

Hajek walked to the far end of the third floor and descended the stairs into the basement. There was no door to the outside. The primary access was through the front door. Once in the building, tenants used the elevator or stairs.

He returned to the first floor and found a door that exited to a side street. It had an alarm and a camera. There was no evidence of a doorstop or any material to indicate that this door had been temporarily propped open. Hajek's phone rang.

"I'm Mr. Howe the building manager. Detective Rafferty tells me you're in charge. I'm on my way over. I called last night's doorman Carlos. He will be there soon."

Hajek walked to the front door and chatted with Louis, the man currently tending the door. Louis liked his job of seven years and could not recall any crime during his tenure. Other 911 calls were for medical emergencies. He did not know anything specific about Courtney Hanson, the woman who lived in 9D.

A man, sixtyish wearing a sport jacket and tweed cap approached the building. "Good morning Detective, I'm Marvin Howe, building manager."

"Thank you for responding promptly."

"I recognize you from the photo with the mayor. Glad you're on the job," Howe said.

Another man, about mid-thirties dressed in jeans and a navy sweater entered.

"Carlos I hated to wake you. Thanks for coming by. This is Detective Hajek."

"Hi Carlos, what can you tell me about Courtney Hanson?"

"She was always pleasant."

"Can you remember anyone entering the building with her?"

"No. She was usually by herself."

"Did you notice anything unusual during your shift yesterday?" Hajek asked.

"No, sir."

"Anyone approach the door that appeared anxious or looked out of place?"

"No, sir."

"In the last few days did you notice the same person in the area, maybe casing the place?"

"I don't recall seeing anyone suspicious," Carlos answered.

"Do visitors sign in each time they enter?" Hajek addressed both doormen.

"Yes," Carlos said.

"Do they sign out?"

"No only in," Louis answered.

"How familiar are you with the construction crew?" Hajek asked.

"They have been here each workday for a couple of weeks. No problem. They come in around 8A.M. and usually leave by four in the afternoon," Louis said.

"Do they sign in?"

"No. Only the lead guy from each subcontractor."

"The project manager told me there have been many different workers. How do you keep'em straight?" Hajek asked.

"They always have a badge with their company identification on it."

"How about lunchtime, do they leave?"

"Sometimes they run out but most often they bring their lunch. Food's expensive in this neighborhood."

"I'd like your sign-in log for the last month."

29

Louis removed several pages from a drawer in his desk and a half-filled page on a clipboard. "Here's from mid-February." He handed the list to Hajek.

"Thanks, Louis. Here's my card if you think of anything else. I appreciate your cooperation." He handed a card to each man.

"Can I go home?" Carlos asked.

Howe looked to Hajek. "Any more questions for Carlos?"

"No. I appreciate your cooperation, Carlos."

"Mr. Howe I have a few more questions for you."

"Let's go inside." They walked toward the elevator.

"Did the police take the security tapes for the back door?"

"That's what I was told."

"Have you had any recent trouble with employees?"

"No. This group has been stable for a few years now. It's a good assignment."

"I'll need a list of residents. And the names of all your employees."

"Certainly, Detective. I'll fax that as soon as I return to my office."

"Thanks for your time, Mr. Howe."

"I hope you get the killer."

Hajek hailed a cab and returned to his precinct. He went directly to Captain Wilcox to brief him on the Hanson case.

When he finished the Captain said, "Hanson's top priority but I have another case for you."

"That's fine. Give it to me. Only in the town of Mayberry or on TV shows does a detective work on just one thing."

"A man died three weeks ago. The routine blood work came back to the medical examiner and he flagged it as a possible suspicious death. Here's what we know." He handed Hajek a file.

30

"I'm on it." Hajek went to the fax machine and picked up the list of residents and employees that Mr. Howe had promised. At the front desk, he found a padded envelope with his name. He climbed the stairs to the second-floor room with the DVD player. He opened the package and popped in the disc. Once he determined if he had anything worthwhile, he would look at what made the medical examiner skeptical about a man who had been dead for weeks.

He cued to a frame with the time stamp of 5AM that morning. The camera angle was from just inside the front door. Hajek watched a couple of people exit the apartment building before six. Around seven, a steady stream of well-dressed men and women headed off to work. He opened the photo of the victim on his phone and placed it on the desk. As described by the project manager he had met earlier, the construction crew entered carrying toolboxes and supplies. He recognized the men working at the third floor job site. A young woman, possibly the one in 9D, exited talking on her cell phone. He jotted down the time, 8:32 and added cell phone records to his need-to-obtain list. He fast-forwarded through blank lobby scenes stopping only when a person appeared in the frame.

At 4:13P.M., tradesmen carried out what looked like trash. For the next ten minutes, they were back and forth lugging debris from their worksite. One carried a toolbox into the building. The pace of traffic picked up during the next two hours. Residents greeted the doorman and everyone entering seemed to belong. A vivacious, attractive woman entered the building at 6:50P.M. Hajek looked again at the photo on his phone. He cringed realizing her father saw her dead on the floor of her apartment. She returned home alone.

Thinking it odd that someone had brought in a toolbox at the end of the day, Hajek looked again at the pictures starting at four o'clock and stopped at one that concerned him. The man wore gloves. He enlarged the frame. The man's face turned away from the camera and his cap blocked Hajek from getting a clear view.

31

Hajek zoomed in and saw the letter M or N on the cap followed by a couple more letters that Hajek could not identify. He did not wear a badge. Slowly he reviewed the next fifteen minutes. This man did not leave with the other workers. He did not appear in the surveillance for the next three hours indicating he remained inside the apartment building when the victim returned.

Hajek examined two more hours. No cap wearing, toolbox-toting man showed up. A man wearing a sport coat with patches on the elbows walked out at 9:21P.M. The back view gave Hajek little to work with but the height and build looked similar to the man with the toolbox and he was sure no current resident wore this outdated jacket.

Chapter 7

Returning to his desk, Hajek thought about the man who posed as a construction worker. He sat for a moment and glanced at the closed file the Captain had given him on his new case. He needed to look at it. *Soon, he promised.* First, he had to confirm a gut feeling.

Hajek exited the precinct building, flagged a cab, and crossed town to 3rd Avenue. Watching a bike messenger zip along at a good clip while he made little progress, he remembered preferring his mountain bike for transportation. In his early days with NYPD, he pedaled from Queens to the upper Westside police station. He loved the views from the Queensboro Bridge as he crossed over the East River.

He gave up biking to work after marrying Francine. She feared an accident would make her a widow. Sitting in traffic, he realized that any lull in his pace brought her to the forefront of his thoughts. He missed her. How would he ever cope with the endless days ahead without his loving wife?

"Right or left on 3rd?" The cabby asked.

"This is fine." Hajek paid the driver, exited the cab and crossed the street. "Hi Carlos, back on the job so soon."

Carlos smiled.

"I need to take a look around 9D."

"Sure, Detective. An officer's onsite. Go on up."

A uniformed officer sat on a chair outside the door reading the Daily News. Hajek introduced himself.

"I recognize you, Detective. What brings you here this late?"

"A hunch."

"Be my guest. Let me know if you need anything." The officer folded his paper.

Hajek pulled on gloves and went into the apartment. He opened closets, looked mostly on the floor, and closed them again. He checked under the living room couch, even though he gauged the height as too low. In the kitchen under the sink with detergent and two vases, he found a toolbox. The hinges were rusted. He flipped open the older style latch and removed the upper tray exposing scratches on inside walls and the bottom. Hajek guessed there had been enough space for a rolled jacket. He left the cabinet door open and returned to the police officer.

"That was fast."

"I found what I was looking for."

Hajek called the crime scene unit, "I need more testing." He requested analysis of the toolbox under the kitchen sink in the Hanson unit. "Please tell me everything you can about this as soon as possible."

Once assured that the crime scene unit would pick up the toolkit in the morning, he took the elevator to the lobby. Leaving the building, Hajek wished Carlos a good evening. Famished and not finished for the day, he decided to get takeout. Rationalizing a way to delay going home, he told himself that first thing tomorrow Captain Wilcox would want his impressions of both the Hanson and Stover cases.

At a market near the 125th Street precinct, Hajek made several selections from the extensive steam table and salad bar and walked the short distance to his office. He wondered if the dead woman knew her killer. Was he a former lover? Did he have a key?

At his desk, he reluctantly turned his attention to the new simple case. That is how Wilcox described it--simple. After a couple mouthfuls of brown rice, he scanned the file. Mr. Nathan Stover, thirty, of Westport, Connecticut collapsed at an alumni event in New York City at Columbia University. The man sitting next to him reported that Nathan arrived sweating and looking ill. When he asked about his health, Stover's response was dismissive—"I'm fine. I've been rushing around today." Stover worked as an account executive at Lamar & Stover Advertising Agency.

Without an obvious cause of death, the medical examiner ordered an autopsy. Hajek read the comprehensive report quickly. This man had no known medical condition, yet he dropped dead. Standard blood work results triggered the suspicion of possible foul play and a referral to the police. Hajek's medical knowledge did not include the toxins listed in the toxicology report. *Bad street drugs?*

At his computer, Hajek entered clostridium botulinum. After glancing at medical terms that he could not decipher, he decided a conversation tomorrow with the medical examiner would be a better use of his time. Next he searched on Nathan Stover, obituary, Westport, Connecticut. He read that Stover's wife Joan, parents and three daughters survived him. The only thing simple about this case was its few details. He needed to speak with people at Stover's office, his family, and the medical examiner. Tonight he could not do any of those tasks.

Returning to the Hanson case, he glanced at the list of people to question. He would start with Courtney Hanson's father. Looking at a phone number on his notepad, he dialed Mr. Hanson. Noting the time --9:10 P.M.--he cancelled the call. He's certainly not sleeping, Hajek thought and hit redial.

"Mr. Hanson?"

"Yes."

"I am Detective Hajek. I apologize for this late call but I'd like to meet with you tomorrow morning."

"I've been expecting your call. What time, Detective?"

"How about nine tomorrow morning at your place?"

"Fine. Let me give you our address."

Hajek left the office at 10:00 P.M., troubled by the calculated planning of the man who carried a toolbox into Courtney Hanson's building. He must have picked the lock to her apartment door and then waited for her to come home, Hajek thought. His scrutiny of the door had revealed no telltale signs of something other than a key opening the door. This man was very good. He left no trace. Convinced this was not a random killing, Hajek wondered about motive. If he could figure that out, it would lead to the perpetrator. He hoped talking with the victim's parents would generate some clues.

Chapter 8

The next morning, Hajek walked along Amsterdam Avenue from the subway under cloudy skies. A half block from the precinct, he spotted Wilcox and waited for him at the entrance.

"Morning, Captain."

"Took my daughter to school." He shook his head.

"How's Jill doing?"

"She cut a few classes last week and I had to speak with the Principal. Whoever said girls are harder to raise was so right. How are things with you?"

"When I reviewed the surveillance tape from the victim's apartment building, I noticed a man walking in with a toolbox late afternoon. There is a construction crew on site but they leave at that time. In later frames I think I saw the same guy leaving without the box. I found it last evening. CSI is checking for fingerprints and DNA. If we're lucky there might be some clues in a toolbox the killer left."

"I'll follow up with forensics."

"I've an appointment with the victim's parents. Maybe they'll have ideas of possible suspects."

"Keep me posted, Peter."

Hajek stopped at his desk long enough to organize his thoughts on this morning's interviews. He looked again at the Stover autopsy and put it in his jacket pocket.

Just before nine, he arrived at the Hanson apartment building. Mr. Hanson responded to the door attendant's announcement of Hajek's arrival and stated he would meet him at the elevator on the top floor. Dressed in neatly pressed khaki pants and a crisp denim shirt, Mr. Hanson greeted Hajek, "I'm glad you're on the case. My friend, the mayor, holds you in high regard."

Hajek noted Hanson's handsome features in spite of eyes that showed lack of sleep. Standing six feet with no extra weight and a full head of brown hair he appeared to be in his forties rather than sixties.

"I'm sorry for your loss, Mr. Hanson."

Hanson swallowed and blinked. "We can talk in here." He led Hajek to an enormous room with a wall of windows providing a panoramic view of Central Park. In a prominent spot a baby grand piano stood with a vase of fresh flowers. Hanson moved to a sitting area at the far end of the room.

"Detective, please have a seat."

Hajek settled into one of the four leather club chairs and Hanson sat in another. "My wife's sedated. She was hysterical and her physician prescribed something to help her sleep."

"I can speak with your wife at another time. Tell me about Courtney."

"Courtney was our only child. She was a dear and very precious to us." He paused. "I can't imagine anyone harming her."

Figuring an all business approach would be best, Hajek said, "Mr. Hanson, I'd like the names of your daughter's friends, particularly any that may have visited her apartment."

"She had many friends."

"A boyfriend?"

"No one in particular this past year. She dated a classmate from NYU but he took a job in Singapore and I'm not sure how much contact they still have."

"And co-workers—do you know anyone from the agency that Courtney may have spent time with outside of work?"

"My wife would know that. I'll get that information for you."

38

"Did your daughter ever speak of anyone threatening her or anyone she was afraid of?" Hajek asked.

"Never." Hanson turned and looked out the window.

Both men remained silent. Hajek's eyes welled up, his own loss so fresh.

"Did you say something, Detective?" Hanson straightened his back into a military style posture and faced Hajek.

"Anyone come to mind that might want to harm you or your family?"

"I can't think of anyone. I try hard to make friends, not enemies. Aren't some crimes just senseless? They defy reason. A robbery gone bad is possible," Hanson said.

"Of course we want to consider every possibility." Hajek proceeded to inquire about close associates, extended family members, community involvement, and network of friends. He listed Hanson's responses in his notepad.

Hanson crossed his leg and sat back into the chair. His hands rested lightly on the chair arms. "Some years ago our friend's daughter was murdered. I hadn't thought much about that until today."

"Did they catch the killer?"

"No."

"Here in New York?"

"No, Connecticut. I forget the town. My wife will remember." The sound of a door closing stopped their conversation. "Angela's up. I'll ask her to join us." He exited the living room. Hajek browsed several shelves. The numerous framed photos included Clifford Hanson fishing from a yacht and a sepia tone picture of an elderly couple who looked like his parents, given the resemblance in the eyes and chin.

Hanson returned with his wife leaning on his arm. "Angela, meet Detective Hajek."

"Sorry to bother you this early in the morning, Mrs. Hanson."

She nodded, shuffled across the room, and sat down without saying a word.

"Dear, the detective offered to come back if you're not up to answering his questions today."

"It's okay."

"Mrs. Hanson When did you last speak with Courtney?" Hajek asked.

"Wednesday. She called me from a cab on her way home."

"The time?"

"I'd guess around six. Clifford and I were going to an early dinner and then the Philharmonic at Lincoln Center. Courtney wished me a Happy Birthday and reminded me of our plans to see the new exhibit at the Guggenheim next weekend."

"Wednesday was your birthday?"

"Yes."

"Anything unusual about the call?"

"No. Courtney was in good spirits. Her agency succeeded in saving a building scheduled to be destroyed. She told me where it's located, but I forgot. She loves her work."

"Mrs. Hanson. Can you think of anyone that might want to harm your daughter?"

"No." She wiped her eyes.

"I'd like a list of the names of Courtney's friends."

"Of course. We'll put it together," Mr. Hanson put his hand on his wife's shoulder.

"Whenever you can is fine."

"Your husband mentioned a friend of yours also lost a daughter."

"Yes, Teresa. I forget exactly when, a few years ago."

"She was murdered?" Hajek asked.

"Yes."

"Who killed her?"

"The case was never solved."

"You keep in touch?"

"She's on our answering machine. She heard about Courtney on the news. I couldn't talk. I'll call her later or tomorrow."

"What's Teresa's last name?"

"Jenkins."

"And the town she lives in?"

"Fairfield, Connecticut."

"Was her daughter killed in Fairfield?"

"No. Bethel, Connecticut."

"Her daughter's name?" Hajek asked.

"Maura Santori."

"I'd like Teresa's phone number."

"Sure. Clifford can you bring my address book? It's on my desk."

He returned carrying a spiral notebook with a Monet painting on the cover. "You're welcome to any information, Detective." He showed Hajek Teresa's number and he jotted it into his notebook. "Should Angela tell Teresa to expect your call?"

"Yes. When you have a list of Courtney's friends, call me and I'll stop back. Thanks for your time."

"Detective. I'll walk you out." Hanson stood.

Mrs. Hanson remained seated.

As he opened the door for Hajek to exit, Hanson said, "Find the killer, Detective."

Chapter 9

After leaving the Hansons, Hajek walked along the edge of Central Park toward Columbus Circle. He sat on an empty bench to regroup. Although he had talked with relatives of murder victims before, today was different. Seeing Mr. Hanson struggling to stay composed, he saw himself. Untimely death is dreadful for survivors. There is no good way to spin it. Well intended people insisted it was good he had time to say goodbye to Francine. The real agony of their final days together tortured Hajek. He detested that she suffered so long. The Hansons wrenching separation from their daughter had the same result, incredible loss.

An elderly couple smiled hello as they passed. Hajek's next destination was twenty blocks south. He decided to walk. Cutting across 53rd street in midtown, Hajek entered Paley Park, his favorite Manhattan pocket park. Cool April temperatures vacated an otherwise popular place, providing him privacy. He sat at an umbrella-covered table and called the medical examiner's office. Hajek took the autopsy report from his inside jacket pocket and waited for Dr. Perkins.

"Perkins, here."

"Dr. Perkins, I'm Detective Hajek. I've been assigned the Stover case and would like to know more about the toxins found in Mr. Stover."

"Clostridium botulinum usually results from improperly processed canned goods. It can be fatal but not necessarily."

"Accidental food poisoning happens all the time, but you flagged this as suspicious. How come?"

"Stover also had Escherichia coli 0157:H7 in his system."

"Several nasty E.coli contamination cases have occurred in recent years. I remember hamburger, tomatoes, lettuce, and spinach, just to mention a few," Hajek said.

"This guy had both Clostridium botulinum and Escherichia coli 0157:H7."

"That's unusual?"

"Never saw these quantities or combination before," Perkins said.

"What's your hunch?"

"Deliberate. No accident. His body should not have had both microorganisms. It's not like he worked at a research lab or a hospital," Perkins said.

"Doubt there are petri dishes at his ad office. I'm on the way there."

"I expect this stuff made him sick for hours, if not days before he died. I asked the health department in Connecticut to check Stover's home to make sure there was not any contaminated food that others might consume. The report was negative. Good luck, Detective."

"Thanks, Dr. Perkins."

Hajek closed his phone, 10:35. He had enough time for a conversation before workers left for lunch. Wondering who had the means and opportunity, he jotted down some notes from his call before continuing to Lamar & Stover Advertising Agency on Madison Avenue.

A standard corporate entranceway greeted Hajek. He nodded to the two uniformed security guards, crossed an expanse of marble flooring, and approached the reception desk. Hajek showed his badge and asked to see Nathan Stover's boss.

"I feel terrible about Mr. Stover. He was nice…always called me by name, so young and his family…three little girls without a father. I'm sorry. I'll call." She dialed an extension, spoke softly and said, "Okay." She turned to Hajek. "Mr. Bradshaw will be right down."

44

Hajek looked at the oversized paintings of Manhattan city scenes from at least a hundred years ago. A gentle gurgle sound drew his eyes to a water feature nestled among vegetation.

Looking around, he wondered what it was like to be in such surroundings day after day. Did one come to believe in a perfectly polished world? A young man in a blue suit with a bold multicolored striped shirt and lime green tie stepped off a middle elevator in a bank of six.

"I'm Jeremy Bradshaw, Nathan Stover's administrative assistant. The senior Mr. Stover is out of the building. He will join us as soon as he can."

"Peter Hajek, NYPD."

"How can I help you?"

"Mr. Stover's untimely death triggered a referral to NYPD. I'd like to ask you a few questions."

Bradshaw's head jerked to the right, "I thought he had a heart attack. Let's go upstairs."

Hajek moved to the back of the elevator. "How long did you work for Mr. Stover?"

"Eight years. Now I'm training the assistant for Nathan's replacement. Next week I'm history. I can't believe this place." Bradshaw motioned to the right when the elevator doors opened.

They walked down a hallway of cubicles and into a small office.

"This was Stover's office. The new guy's out for a few hours. We can talk here."

Bradshaw pointed to a chair.

"Did someone want Stover's job?" Hajek sat down.

"I doubt it. The firm's reorganizing and downsizing."

"You're being let go?"

45

"We lost a few accounts. Like many companies today we have to do more with less." Bradshaw ran his fingers through his hair. "Allen's not happy about taking over for Nathan. This is not a promotion for him and he still has most of his old job responsibilities. When he insisted on keeping his assistant, Nathan's father agreed."

"Did you get along with Stover?"

"Yeah, he was all right. I'm sorry he's dead."

"Tell me his schedule the day he died."

At the computer, Bradshaw pulled up the electronic calendar the two shared and reconstructed Stover's day.

"He took a late morning train into the city from his home in Connecticut, arriving in time for a 1:30 appointment that afternoon with a client here at the office." Bradshaw scrolled down. "He had another appointment at 4P.M. on 10th avenue near 57th Street. Both accounts had longevity. As best I know those ad campaigns were going smoothly, no conflicts or dissatisfaction."

"Did he often come to work so late?"

"Not often. Maybe a couple of time a year. Usually when he had an evening event."

"Anything about lunch?" Hajek asked.

"No."

"Where do you think he ate?"

"I don't know." Bradshaw sat back.

"I'd like a printout with his client names and numbers. Please highlight the two he met the day he died."

"Mr. Stover would need to authorize giving you any confidential information. He should be here soon."

"Did Nathan get along with co-workers?"

"Stover was a very vanilla guy. He did his job and mostly kept to himself."

A woman dressed in black slacks, a print top, and fuchsia jacket appeared in the doorway. "Hey Jeremy, when you have a minute I'd like to review some accounts." She walked away without waiting for a response.

"My replacement." Bradshaw grimaced.

"Did Stover have any personal items in his office?" Hajek looked around.

"There wasn't much, a couple of pictures, his diploma and his attaché case. I gave them to his father. Detective, do you suspect foul play?"

"It's routine for police to investigate when there is no clear cause of death."

"I heard it was a heart attack."

"Do you think your boss took drugs?" Hajek asked.

"I doubt it. His behavior was consistent, never erratic."

"What about affairs?"

"That's trickier to know for sure but I have no reason to believe he fooled around," Bradshaw said.

A man wearing a well-tailored suit rushed in. He extended his hand. "Rodney Stover, sorry to keep you waiting, Detective."

Hajek stood. "Peter Hajek, pleased to meet you. Sorry about your son."

"Thank you. It's tough to believe he's gone." He looked around the room. "This was my son's office."

"Call me if I can assist, Mr. Stover." Bradshaw exited.

"Mr. Stover, can you give me the names of the clients your son had appointments with in the days leading up to his death?" Hajek asked.

"Detective, you can't think our clients had anything to do with Nathan's death."

47

"It's important that I talk with the people he met on the day he died and the day before."

"Isn't there some other way? We safeguard our clients' business information."

"Mr. Stover, there's a lot we don't know about your son's death. I need to speak with anyone that he spent time with in his final hours."

"I don't understand the need for a homicide detective to be involved. There have been many problems with our food. It comes from all over the world. Isn't it possible my son ate some tainted vegetables or meat?"

"We need to be certain."

Mr. Stover took a deep breath. "I doubt the answer is with my son's accounts but you have my full cooperation. I'll have Bradshaw give you the names and contact information for Nathan's appointments on the two days you want."

"Thank you. How's his wife doing?"

"It's hard. He has three daughters. My daughter-in-law's a good mother." He went to the window and looked out. "Their 10th anniversary is next month."

"When did you last speak with your son, Mr. Stover?"

"The day he died. He stopped by my office. He seemed fine. He looked forward to his evening at Columbia University."

"Tell me about the event."

"A gathering of Columbia Alumni for networking and socializing. Nathan often attended," Stover said.

"Anything strange about his late arrival the day he died?" Hajek asked.

"No. It wasn't unusual for him to come in late if he had an evening event."

"How about lunch? Favorite places? A regular anywhere?"

"Sometimes he dined with clients. Other days he picked up a sandwich at a deli," Stover replied.

"Any idea where he ate lunch the day he died?"

"No."

"Was he allergic to anything?"

"I don't think so."

"Mr. Stover, I appreciate your assistance. If I could have that client information, I'll be on my way."

"I'll get Bradshaw."

"Here's my card if you think of anything that might help."

Bradshaw returned and opened a spreadsheet with the information Hajek wanted, hit print, and handed Hajek the page from the printer.

"Thanks." Hajek extended his hand. "Good luck to you."

Chapter 10

Hajek hailed a cab. The slow traffic pace that usually irritated him provided time to absorb the information he gathered this morning and consider his next steps. He asked the driver to stop at a deli a block beyond the precinct. Hajek picked up a sandwich, chocolate chip cookies, a soda, and returned to the station. He left the food on his desk and went to check in with his captain.

Wilcox waved him in as he finished his phone conversation. "Peter, that was forensics. They assure me that we'll have some crime scene investigation results from the Hanson case in a couple of days."

"Good. This morning I met with the victim's parents. I'll be following up with some leads they identified. Long shots but I'll work with what I have."

"Let's hope we get a break with the crime scene unit info," Wilcox said.

Although Wilcox showed more interest in the Hanson case, Hajek shared the medical examiner's concern about Stover and summarized his interview at the ad agency.

"I'm sorry a partner is not available for you right now. I planned for you to have a slower pace coming back."

"I understand. I'm fine." Until four months ago, Otto Snyder had been his partner, a skilled professional fifteen years his senior. Hajek liked working with him. They got along fine, but unlike with Kostas, they did not socialize outside of work.

"Let me know as soon as something breaks. I need to keep the commissioner happy," Wilcox said.

Hajek left the office. He blanked on the name of the police officer approaching him.

"Nice to see you back. Can I buy you a beer after work?"

50

"I'll take a rain check on the beer. I have some research to do."

"Later."

Hajek continued to his desk and opened the deli bag. His style of investigating called for more exploration. At his computer, he accessed the police database and browsed while eating his lunch. First, he followed his curiosity about Mrs. Hanson's friend and found newspaper reports of her daughter Maura Santori's murder in Bethel, Connecticut. Her license photo in a police database showed an attractive, brown-haired woman. Wanting more details of the crime, he wrote down the number of the Bethel Police.

Hajek's next search generated dozens of murders that involved a rope in New York City. Two were hangings. In three, the rope was described as nylon, each of a different color. There were no other similarities with his Manhattan victim case. Most of the murderers were convicted and serving life sentences. Two of them were dead.

Looking at more unsolved cases, Hajek found none to pursue. He pulled a mug from the lower drawer and went to the break area to make tea. Thinking about a next step, he decided to schedule both his interview with Stover's wife and Mrs. Hanson's friend in Fairfield, Connecticut on Monday. Before arranging those meetings, he contacted the medical examiner.

"News already?" Perkins said as he picked up the call.

"More questions. On the day before he died, Stover's co-workers did not see any symptoms of illness."

"I'm surprised," Perkins said.

"Stover's assistant stated that he seemed fine for his 1:30 appointment. I called that client and he reported that Stover was with him about an hour and fifteen minutes. He did not appear ill."

"He should have."

"I left a message for the client Stover met later in the afternoon. Maybe he noticed something peculiar."

Perkins continued, "Initially I worried about the strange combination of Clostridium Botulinum and Escherichia coli 0157:H7. What I thought had happened was that he had an upset stomach from bad food and then was sick for a couple of days. I assumed the high level of toxins developed over time. Once the bacteria was in his system, it would multiply over time."

"Now you're thinking he ingested large quantities of these toxins the day he died," Hajek said.

"Right. That would explain the high levels in his bloodstream and organs in a matter of hours instead of days. This was a fast death."

"Where can a person get high levels of these organisms?"

"Certain biological research laboratories might have them. They are not available to the average person. Call me if I can be of further assistance," Perkins said.

"Thanks. I will."

Hajek punched in the home number for Mrs. Stover. After a few rings a message played. He identified himself, indicated he wanted to stop by, and had started to leave his number when a woman picked up.

"Detective, this is Mrs. Stover."

"I'm sorry for your loss, Mrs. Stover. I'm assigned to look into your husband's death."

"Yes. My father-in-law told me that police were involved."

"Can we meet at ten Monday morning?"

"That's fine."

"You're on Greens Farms Road, right?"

"Yes, right off the Connecticut Turnpike at Exit 18."

"I'll find it."

"See you then, Detective."

Next, Hajek shifted to the Hanson case. He flipped his notepad to the page with the phone number for Teresa Jenkins, Mrs. Hanson's friend.

A woman answered. "Hello."

"Mrs. Jenkins, I'm Detective Peter Hajek."

"Angela told me to expect your call. I hope you can help my friend. I can't believe someone murdered Courtney." She stopped and sniffled. "No parent should have to go through this."

"I will be in Connecticut Monday. Any chance I could stop by around one?" Hajek asked.

"That would be fine. I should warn you that I'm getting over shingles. My doctor said to avoid young children. I don't think you'll be in any danger."

"Sorry to hear that. I understand it's very painful." Hajek confirmed her address and the exit to take from the highway.

At six, he left the precinct, opened his phone while walking, then stopped. For years he had called Francine to let her know he was on his way home. With the phone back in his pocket, he opted to continue past the first subway station and delay getting to his empty apartment.

Chapter 11

On Friday morning Hajek picked up the information he requested from the Hansons on business associates, community work, and their network of friends including access to Courtney's Facebook page. He started with Courtney. Search engine hits included links to her friends' Facebook pages, notices of employment and promotions, and several wedding announcements. He logged on to Courtney's page. Recent postings on her timeline included photos of a friend Lori's new puppy, a link to Megan's vacation photos and NYU's alumnae newsletter. He followed up on the former boyfriend. His last message was a generic holiday greeting. Hajek read comments on *Argo*, *Breakin Bad*, and *House of Cards*. Reviewing the hits for the male friends on the list nothing appeared unusual.

He moved on to Mr. Hanson's connections. His circle of friends were CEOs, corporate attorneys, and individuals well known in New York City arts and politics. A stockbroker would have angry clients Hajek thought. He decided to ask Hanson about any accounts that lost big money recently and any phone calls from upset investors.

Mrs. Hanson had several friends and associates involved with her volunteer work at Covenant House, Infinite Family and New York Literacy. Her connections might provide a lead to a killer. He needed to follow up with them. He scanned the websites for the three volunteer organizations. He would call each to find out the names of individuals with whom Mrs. Hanson had direct contact.

When Mrs. Hanson told him about her last conversation with her daughter, she mentioned a recent success saving a building. Maybe an unhappy property owner or a builder had turned violent. Hajek added contact the landmarks preservation commission and get Courtney's cell phone records on his to do list.

Captain Wilcox stopped at Hajek's desk. "I got a call from forensics. The toolbox is pre-1980 and they can't trace where it was purchased. There are no fingerprints or DNA. It appears to be wiped clean. The rope is really old and not made anymore. Any finger prints on it are smudged and useless. I'll forward you the report when I receive."

Hajek frowned. "What do you think about having them zero in on the surveillance video of the suspect entering with the toolbox. The writing on the cap could be a useful clue."

"Worth a try. I'll get on it."

"I'm off to Courtney Hanson's workplace. Monday I'm interviewing Mrs. Stover in Connecticut."

"The dead ad guy?" Wilcox asked.

"Right."

Hajek grabbed his jacket, put his notebook in his pocket and left the precinct.

***

Later that evening, at home he took his bike from the hook over the washer and dryer to prepare for his morning ride with Nick Kostas. It seemed strange not to be reminded to spread a cloth under the bike. "It's easier to keep grease off the floor than to clean it," Francine would say. One completely flat tire required a patch job or a new tube. He missed hearing her say, "For a non-handy man you mastered bike repair." He remembered impressing her when he told her he fixed a flat with a dollar bill after getting a puncture. To break the silence and cut short his downward spiral, he turned on his television.

He had not touched his bike in months and it needing attention did not surprise him. With an ad for European river cruises droning in the background he found a new tube in the cabinet where he kept cycling stuff. He removed the back tire and replaced the old tube. Before putting the wheel back in place he inflated the tire. Then he added air to the front tire. Hajek tightened the stem bolt for the handlebars, cleaned the chain, and made sure the brake pads contacted the wheel rims when he applied the brakes.

Fifteen minutes later his phone rang. He muted the TV.

"How'd your week go?" Roland asked.

"It's been busy."

"Anything new with Mom?"

"No. I'll see her Sunday."

"I told Diane of your plans for Francine's ashes. If you're serious about waiting until the summer we can all come out when the kids finish school."

"I'd like that, Roland. Thanks."

The brothers chatted for a few more minutes. After the call ended, Peter sat in front of his silent TV remembering Francine articulating her wishes. "You need to listen to me…" That's how she began. He dreaded those words. A request, a direction or something he did not want to hear always followed. She told him what music she wanted at her funeral and asked him to scatter her ashes in the Hudson River. Most painful for him was Francine's insistence that he not take too long in getting on with his life. "You're so young. You can't mourn me forever."

Early the next morning, after a mostly sleepless night, he met Kostas at the subway station and together they rode a train to Battery Park. Some Saturdays they hit the streets and bike paths of Queens but their favorite was an early ride along the Hudson. A half-hour into the mostly level ride, Hajek felt winded and signaled for Kostas to stop.

"What's up?"

"More than a little out of shape I'd say. Last night I tuned up the bike but didn't think about the effect not riding for months had on me."

"Four months off the trail is a lot. Want to stop?"

"No. I'll slow my pace and be fine."

"Are you sure? Your face is pretty red." Kostas straddled his bike.

"Last night I kept waking up. I'm tired but let's keep going."

The men rode at a leisurely pace, commenting on the barges on the Hudson and enjoying the cool spring day. At Riverside Park, they took city streets to a favorite bagel place. Hajek ordered his usual two cinnamon bagels with cream cheese, a large tea, and water. Kostas chose an everything bagel with cream cheese, a sundried tomato bagel with butter, a large coffee, and water. They settled at an outside table with their bikes propped against the building. "Tough first week back." Kostas took a sip of water.

"Nonstop which is fine with me. Two cases without any clear leads."

"They can't all be like Grant's Tomb. That was amazing work. What possessed you?"

"Sometimes I get lucky." Hajek took another bite of a bagel.

"You really showed up the Bureau."

"That wasn't my plan. Just wanted to solve the case," Hajek said.

"What you working on now?"

Hajek filled Kostas in on his murder case and the autopsy that triggered a police referral. He told Kostas about his visit to the owner of a townhouse on West End Avenue, a gamble that led nowhere. The man resented the hoops the preservation agency placed on him regarding any renovations to his property but he was no murderer and had no connection with the victim. Hajek planned to do more work on associates of Mr. and Mrs. Hanson.

Back in Queens, Kostas said, "Sorry I have to rush off. Our cousin's wedding is tonight in Rhinebeck. What are you up to?"

"Resting my sore muscles."

57

Kostas laughed. "See ya."

Hajek hung his bike on its hook in the laundry room. He put his gear in a crate on the floor, tossed his biking clothes in the washing machine, and took a long shower. Feeling fatigued he stretched out on his bed. Three hours later, he woke surprised that he had slept soundly.

He opened the blinds and gazed at the shadows twilight created in the East River. The tightness in his thigh muscles reminded him of his earlier bike ride. Turning on his phone, he retrieved a message from Francine's sister, Veronica. She sounded like Francine. He turned it off again. Francine's family meant well and he liked them but they were a painful reminder of her absence. He would call Veronica tomorrow. No he wouldn't. He turned his phone back on and texted her to let her know he was fine and that work was very time consuming.

After wandering from one room to another he settled in front of his computer. He googled Clifford Hanson. The search generated several hits. He read six articles. From numerous client testimonials, it appeared that Hanson had a good track record for picking winning stocks and had no obvious enemies. When Hajek had asked, Hanson did not recall even one hostile phone call. Next week he would provide Hajek with names of his clients who had significant losses in the market, insisting that it would be a short list.

Hajek got up from his computer, walked to the TV in the living room, and picked up the remote. He clicked it on, looked at a few channels, and flipped the remote on a chair. Back in the kitchen he opened a beer. Standing, staring at nothing in particular he drank from the bottle. After several minutes he returned to the computer and looked up the Lamar & Stover Advertising Agency.

Its history showed steady growth until four years ago. Two business reports linked decreased revenue with a failure to offer innovative placements and a lack of strategic vision. Hajek decided to revisit the senior Stover and find out more about clients' negative comments.

Still thinking about his cases, Hajek left his home around nine to find dinner. A neighborhood bistro, that he and Francine ate at often, had an extensive to-go menu. The restaurant owner came over to the take-out area and greeted him. "Nice to see you, Mr. Hajek."

He wished he had thought to call ahead. Hajek ordered the soup of the day, lentil, and the pork tenderloin dinner with oven roasted potatoes, vegetable medley, and applesauce.

"I'll be right back," Hajek said to the hostess. He walked a few blocks rather than stay in a place flooded with pleasant memories of dining with his wife. Fifteen minutes later he returned, paid for his meal and started home.

Back at Burnham Tower he checked his mail box. Dreading more sympathy cards, he had put off doing this mundane task. He pulled out grocery flyers, catalogues for clothing and household gadgets addressed to Francine, and many card-size envelopes. After the funeral his sister-in-law offered to send out the required acknowledgements when he was ready. He would call her and accept her help but not tonight. In the kitchen, he spread his meal containers on a counter and ate standing.

***

The next morning, Hajek dressed for church. An uneasy feeling began in his stomach and gradually his throat tightened. Deciding he could not face the empathetic people in his parish, he skipped it. He picked up his copy of the *New York Times* in the lobby, returned to his apartment, and settled into a comfortable chair.

That afternoon, Hajek visited his mother in a nursing home in nearby Forest Hills. Before entering the large community room, he watched her from a distance. She sat with several other residents, all in wheelchairs, oblivious to their surroundings. He sighed, squared his shoulders and walked up to his mother.

"Hi, Mom." He kissed her and held her hand.

She smiled.

The brightness in her eyes countered the unpleasantness of dementia. Although he resented that this disease deprived him of conversation, the lack of any physical suffering consoled him, and her cheerfulness raised his spirits.

Over the years, he had enjoyed his mother's sharp wit and often sought her insight. Now he had only memories of when they shared world events, commented on books and reminisced about family members. As difficult as he found sitting with his mother, he could not imagine staying away. Three years ago Roland moved for a new job and found it hard to be so far way. He regularly thanked Peter for attending to their mother's needs.

Chapter 12

After briefly checking into the precinct Monday morning, he drove onto the Westside Highway and watched the sunlight dancing on ripples in the Hudson. Once on I-95 he felt like the quintessential commuter only in reverse direction. He drove north in light traffic. High-rise buildings and warehouses comprised the view while in New York. Once in Connecticut he saw more trees and open space. A few towns into the state, he entered Westport with its well-kept homes that echoed prosperity. He parked in the driveway of a large colonial, walked to the front door, and rang the bell.

If he had an image of a typical Westport wife, Joan Stover did not fit it. A clip on the crown of her head gathered her dark hair and pulled it back from her face. Dressed in a plum athletic suit she wore little or no make-up.

"Come in, Detective. I made coffee. Would you like a cup?"

"Would tea be too much trouble?"

"Not at all."

"Thanks."

She led him to the kitchen passing three girls drawing at a table.

"These are my daughters, Rebecca-nine, Emily-six, and Tanya-four." Joan pointed to the oldest first, than the middle one and finally the youngest. "Girls, this is Mr. Hajek from New York. He needs to speak with me."

The girls looked up from their coloring, but showed little interest in their mother's visitor.

"I'm sorry Mrs. Stover. I thought I chose a time your daughters would be in school."

"Usually they are but they seem to be coming down with colds and I thought I'd save myself the trip to pick them up when the nurse called."

As Mrs. Stover filled a kettle and put it on the stove to heat, Hajek commented on the children's artwork. "Nice colors. Wish I your talent." They smiled without saying anything.

Joan set her mug of coffee on the island, pulled up a stool, and motioned to one for Hajek.

He sat down.

"The tea won't take long."

"They're beautiful girls. It must be hard for all of you."

"We're adjusting."

"Do you have family nearby?"

"Nathan's parents are in Greenwich. The girls are their only grandchildren. They see them often."

"And your family?"

"My parents live on Staten Island. They have busy work schedules and visit when they can."

"Have you seen the medical examiner's report?"

"No. My father-in-law told me about it." Joan glanced toward the stove.

"Was Nathan sick in recent weeks?"

"No. In fact, he's hardly ever been sick in our years together. Some minor colds, a couple of bouts of the flu. Nothing out of the ordinary."

"How about allergies? Are you aware of any?"

"Cats. The girls begged him for a cat but his eyes water and puff up with the slightest contact."

"Nothing food related?" Hajek asked.

"Can't think of anything."

"What do you know about clostridium botulinum?"

62

"I don't know anything. My father-in-law told me some bacteria killed him."

"It appears your husband ingested unusual doses of toxins. Can you tell me what he ate the day he died?"

"Do you know how many meals I've made since then?"

"That morning he went to work late. His routine was different. Can you remember anything?"

"He liked eggs in the morning when he had extra time. I may have cooked him a couple."

"Other than eggs you have no idea what Nathan ate the day he died?"

"He was in New York most of that day. That was weeks ago. The Health Department checked our kitchen. Let me get your tea." She went to the stove, poured boiling water into the mug and placed the tea in front of Hajek.

"Thanks." He added cream from a pitcher and took a sip. "When was the health examiner here?"

"Two days after he died."

"Tell me about that."

"The inspector asked if I did canning, had any homemade food gifts in the house, and how long ago I opened the jar of mayo."

"Did he take anything to analyze?"

"An open jar of peanut butter and the mayo. Oh, and he wanted to know how long some items had been in the freezer," Joan said.

"The inspector concluded that nothing in the home made your husband sick?" Hajek asked.

"As far as I know."

"Mommy, can we go outside?" The oldest daughter appeared at Joan's side.

"No, Honey." She touched her daughter's cheek.

"Please. I haven't coughed or sneezed. I feel fine."

"It's better if you do quiet things today. How about a game or puzzle?" Joan stroked the little girl's hair and smiled.

Emily came over. "Rebecca, let's do that puzzle grandpa brought us yesterday. I bet I'll fit more pieces than you."

"Not a chance. Let's go."

"Me too." Tanya got up and followed her older sisters out of the kitchen.

Pleased to have them out of earshot, Hajek asked, "How are the children doing?"

"They're managing fine."

Hajek waited for Joan to elaborate but she did not.

"What did you think when you were told your husband had bacterial pathogens in his system?"

Joan shrugged. "I thought what lousy protection we have for our food. It's scary to think how easy it is to eat bad food. Life's unfair."

"This is hard but I have to ask. Would you say that you and Nathan were happily married?"

"About the same as most people." Joan picked a hair off of her sleeve.

"Meaning?"

"We got along. We were content."

"Did you ever think he might have someone else?" Hajek asked.

"No."

"How about you?"

She snickered. "Definitely no. The mother of three is not usually sought after."

"How did you and Nathan meet?"

"I worked at a pizza restaurant that was popular with Columbia students."

"Were you also a student?"

"Yeah, but not at Columbia, CUNY."

"What was your major?"

"I never finished." She took a sip of her coffee. Hajek heard disappointment.

"Did Nathan study business?"

"No. He wanted nothing to do with business and had no intentions of working for his father. He studied art."

"With hopes of doing what?"

"Drawing cartoons. He loved art but I think his motivation was mostly to annoy his father."

"They didn't get along?"

"Nathan rebelled by doing exactly the opposite of what would please his father. He particularly objected that his father wanted him to marry one of his business associates' daughter." She sat straighter in her chair.

"So when did he join Lamar & Stover?"

"Right after college."

"Really."

Joan sighed. "I got pregnant and that changed everything."

"So he's always worked at his father's firm."

"Yes. We married during his last semester of college. I was a sophomore. I dropped out to take care of Rebecca, and then Emily and Tanya. His parents were not thrilled but they financially supported us so he could finish his degree."

"The grandchildren brought peace."

She nodded. "Slowly, but yes. His parents love their granddaughters."

"Did your husband have a home office?" Hajek asked.

"Yeah."

"May I see it?"

"I guess that would be all right. It was off limits for all of us. Doesn't matter now."

"Off limits?"

"Yeah. He was secretive about his stuff. No one could use his computer. Usually he locked his office. I can show it to you."

She placed the empty mugs in the sink and started walking out of the kitchen. The girls were busy with a puzzle. As they passed bookshelves in the living room, Hajek glanced at family photos.

Hajek pointed to one. "Where's this ?"

"Provincetown."

"When did you vacation on the Cape?"

"We go most years for the 4th of July. That picture was taken after a whale watch excursion."

"Looks like a fun day."

"It was. The girls loved it. They have friends that return to Chatham each year. My husband spent summers there when he was a boy."

"How about you?"

"I had a different childhood. Not bad, just different from his. My family went to the public beach when we could. We didn't have money to rent a cottage. Initially I think Nathan liked our differences. Later it seemed to me he really enjoyed irritating his parents by dating someone below their status. If I hadn't gotten pregnant, we probably never would have married."

On an upper shelf, Hajek spotted an award with Nathan's name. He examined it. "Your husband volunteered at a church here in Westport?"

"Yes, he helped the pastor set up the church bulletin layout."

"I'll want to talk with the pastor and any other friends in the community."

"I'm sure they'll be happy to speak with you. Here's Nathan's office. I'll leave you to have a look around. I'll be with the girls when you're done." Joan walked away.

The room had a desk and a black leather swivel chair on a plastic mat. Hajek turned on Nathan's computer and waited for it to power up. A laminated poster by Norman Rockwell hung on the wall across from the desk. 'Carefree Days Ahead' depicted children still dressed in school clothes running, climbing on benches, tossing a ball and jumping rope. Three framed pictures on the side wall looked like early Disney hand paintings for animation. This man really wanted an art career.

Looking back at the computer, he saw the password box. He tried his usual tricks to bypass that screen without any luck. He would take the tower for NYPD's computer experts to look into what Nathan guarded on his hard drive.

Before returning to the kitchen, Hajek thought about Joan. For a single mother of three with less than a month of experience as a widow, she presented herself as coping. Protective of her daughters, she accepted her husband's fate as unlucky. Some women he knew would be railing against the Food and Drug Administration. Others would barely function, unable to say her husband's name without bursting into tears.

Who was he to judge Joan? Nothing about his demeanor revealed him as a new widower. People do what they have to do. She took care of her kids and their home.

Walking back through the living room he slowed his pace and observed Joan and her daughters looking intently at puzzle pieces on a table in the living room. The scene touched Hajek. He glanced around. He saw a fieldstone fireplace, oriental rugs, and plush chairs, furnishings consistent with an affluent home. In the far corner of the room stood an aquarium. Colorful fishes darted among plants. Hajek had a good feeling about this woman and her daughters.

"Mrs. Stover, any chance you have Nathan's password?"

"No. I never used his computer."

"I'd like to take the tower with me."

"Help yourself. It's of no use to me."

"Did he have a laptop?"

"Yes. He had a company one. It must still be at the office."

"What about his cell phone?"

"The hospital gave it to me."

"I'd like that also."

Joan opened a cupboard, retrieved a cell and handed it to Hajek.

"Could you give me the pastor's name?"

"I have a church bulletin in the kitchen. I'll get it."

Hajek watched the girls move pieces of blue, creating a cove with boats. Joan returned and gave him a paper.

"Our pastor's name, phone and email are all here."

"Thank you. Here's my card." He handed it to Joan. "Bye, girls."

They waved and returned their focus to the puzzle.

"Thanks for your time, Mrs. Stover. I'll be in touch." Hajek walked to his car, placed the computer tower in the trunk, and hoped an inspection would generate leads on who wanted this man dead.

He backed out of the driveway and drove a short distance to a diner parking lot. A steady flow of customers entered and exited as he reviewed his time in the Stover home. Joan did not offer any details about her husband, she did not relive the circumstances of learning of his death, and she provided no information on the kind of father he was to their daughters. He did notice the children's

68

artwork was colorful and they seemed content. Nothing about Joan's or the girls' behavior indicated that a husband and father had been abruptly taken from them.

A couple of men walked by rehashing Tiger Wood's golf future. He checked the time. His next appointment was not for another hour. He called Teresa Jenkins to see if she could meet with him earlier. She agreed.

Chapter 13

He made his way to the entrance ramp for The Connecticut Turnpike North. The slow pace of Route 95 traffic allowed him to anticipate the woman he was about to meet. It surprised him that Teresa Jenkins did not question why he wanted to speak with her and gave no sign of annoyance. Most people avoided a visit from a detective if possible. Wondering about this high school friend of Angela Hanson, he could not dismiss a possible connection with the murders of their daughters.

At Mill Plain Road, he exited the turnpike and followed the sharp turn of the ramp. An acre of space separated houses in this neighborhood. The flowering shrubs and majestic trees contrasted with his place in Queens. Connecticut had beautiful landscape, but not his style, too pretty, too remote, and too quiet.

A black mailbox had a cluster of wildflowers painted on the side and the number 787 on the front. He pulled into the driveway and parked near a two-car garage. Tall evergreens were visible behind the house. Trees he could not name stood in the front yard with a slight hint of buds. Behind these trees towered four white birches. He walked the curved slate pathway to the front steps, pushed the doorbell, and activated a series of chimes that sounded like a choir of bell ringers.

A woman, about five feet four with short wavy gray hair framing her round face, opened the door. She was casually dressed in jeans and a beige sweatshirt with an embroidered cardinal resting on a snow covered evergreen bough.

He showed her his badge. "Mrs. Jenkins. I'm Peter Hajek with NYPD."

"Come in, Detective. I was having some corn chowder. Can I interest you in a cup?"

"I'd love some."

70

"Don't let my shingles rash scare you. I am not over it yet. She pointed to a red patch on her neck just below her right ear. But I'm not contagious."

He noticed the inflamed skin on her chin, left ear and her neck. "It takes more than a little redness to worry me. Trust me I've seen horrible."

"It's been almost two months."

"Wow. I had no idea it lasted that long."

"It's hard to believe a virus can lie dormant in your system for decades and then cause such unbearable pain. I had chicken pox at age four, a long time ago."

In the kitchen, Teresa motioned for Hajek to take a seat at a table. While Teresa ladled soup, he gazed at a cluster of daffodils and purple crocuses that had already peaked. Forsythia and bright red shrubs lined the back. "You have a gardener?"

"Yeah, me."

"Very nice work."

"Thanks, I've played in the dirt since childhood. Silly, but I enjoy it. I can no longer kneel—arthritis—but I manage."

The microwave timer beeped. Teresa put a bowl in front of Hajek and one at her place.

"Water?"

"Yes, please."

Teresa poured two glasses and left a pitcher within his reach.

Hajek took a spoonful of the chowder. "This is delicious."

"Glad you like it. I find soup soothing. It's a frequent meal for me."

Hajek's mind drifted remembering soups that Francine made and how she tried to convince him that soup could be a meal.

Teresa picked up her spoon. "How can I help you?"

71

"I'm not sure. In my business, every strange association may be significant. I have a habit of checking out my hunches or they nag me relentlessly."

"Courtney's death hit me hard. I find myself thinking about…" She stopped and looked away.

"I'm sorry about your daughter. When Mrs. Hanson told me a friend of hers also had a daughter murdered, I thought maybe there's a connection."

"Unlikely. Maura died years ago. Our daughters weren't friends and didn't know the same people," Teresa said.

"It may be implausible. It's important for me to find out if there's any link. How long have you and Angela been friends?"

"We went to high school together and have been friends ever since."

"Tell me about your daughter."

"Maura? My oldest?" Teresa blinked and straightened her back.

"You have other children?"

"Yes, thank God. My daughter, Kaitlin, lives in Charlotte, North Carolina. I hate that she's so far away."

"Did she move for a job?"

"No. She went to the University of North Carolina in Chapel Hill. She loves the area and took a job in Charlotte."

"There are more jobs there than here," Hajek put his spoon down.

"That's what I tell myself. Eventually I hope she'll find a job in Connecticut."

"My girls were not much alike. Predictable Maura finished college, started teaching and married her longtime boyfriend."

Teresa lifted a spoonful of chowder and put it back without tasting it.

"And settled in a town not far from you."

72

"Yes. Unlike Kaitlin who lives several states away."

"How far is Charlotte from here?"

"Seven hundred and sixty miles. Not a day's drive."

"More independent…"

"For sure. My favorite Kaitlin story is at age three she questioned the preschool teacher who told the children to get in line. With her hands on her hips, she asked 'Why?' I'll never forget it. Maura would have gotten in line without saying a word."

Teresa laughed and Hajek joined her.

"Can I see some photos?"

"I've resisted having a Maura shrine….with difficulty I might add. We have many photos of our girls over the years. They're in the family room. Come with me."

They left the chowder and walked to the back of the house. Teresa pulled out an album. There were photos of Maura the dancer, the flute player, Maura wearing frilly Christmas dresses and Easter finery and Maura in several Halloween costumes. She put the book back. Teresa pointed to a framed collage hanging above a bookcase.

"These are some of my favorite pictures of Maura." Teresa pointed to a collection that included Maura winning an academic award in eighth grade, singing at church, handing out boxes of Girl Scout cookies, and playing soccer and softball.

"Looks like she was an all-around kid." Hajek stepped closer. "And this is Kaitlin?"

"Yes. That's her high school yearbook photo."

"Very attractive."

73

"That she is. Let me show you Maura's wedding photo. You know, everyone has great photos from their weddings but Maura's are exceptional. She could have been a model. I'm, of course, glad that she had no interest in that profession."

They stood in front of a large photo of Maura and her husband on their wedding day.

"Isn't she beautiful?" She wiped a tear from her eye. "I'm boring you, Detective."

"Not at all."

"How could someone kill Maura? We live in a crazy world, don't we?"

"Yes, we do. I know this is a lot to ask but I'd like to hear what you remember from the time around her death."

"She died on my birthday, October third."

"Your birthday."

"My parents named me after St. Teresa, the little flower. Her feast day is the third of October."

Looking at Maura the bride, he thought maybe someone targeted these young women.

"Let's go back to the kitchen, Detective. That chowder must be cold, I'll warm it up." Teresa placed the bowls in the microwave and turned it on.

Hajek returned to his seat.

"To celebrate my birthday, Vincent and I were meeting Maura and her husband Domenic at the Front Street Restaurant in Bethel."

"That's the town they lived in, right?"

"Yes. We were already seated when the police came in and told us that Domenic found Maura on the kitchen floor when he came home from work. They had Domenic at the station for questioning."

"Standard procedure to bring in the spouse."

"It was awful for him."

Teresa blotted her eyes with tissue. After a few moments she continued. "It seems Maura came home from work a little earlier than usual because of our dinner plans and interrupted a robbery."

"Anything taken?"

"Dominic said nothing seemed to be missing. The police interrogating him really upset Dominic. His wife and his dog dead in his home and they're talking to him like he's a murderer." Teresa reached for a tissue.

"I didn't know about the dog."

"Shot in the head on the back porch."

"Was your daughter shot?"

"No…strangled."

Hajek sat silent.

"Tell me about Dominic."

"A real nice guy. He was crazy about Maura. Vincent and I loved him as a son."

"What's his work?"

"Domenic's a chemist. He had worked at Clairol's research lab in Stamford."

"Where's he now?"

"In Houston."

"A transfer?"

"No. A total change from hair dye to oil refining. He did not want to stay in Connecticut. Turns out his job wouldn't have lasted anyhow, Clairol has gone to Mexico."

"How's he doing?"

75

"Okay as far as I know. We don't hear much from him. Keeping a distance is his way of coping, I guess. People talk about closure. Nothing will bring Maura back but I wish they had found the murderer."

"I'd like to speak with Vincent, Kaitlin and Domenic," Hajek said.

"Forget Vincent. He won't speak with you."

"You're certain?"

"He refuses to talk about Maura, even with me. If he had his way all her pictures would be in a box out of sight." Teresa sighed and blinked backed tears.

"For him that must be easier."

"I know there's no one way to cope with loss. It's hard for me. I like to talk about Maura." Teresa swept her hair behind her ear.

"What about your daughter in North Carolina and Maura's husband?" Hajek asked.

"Kaitlin's away until tomorrow evening. I'll check with her and let you know. Domenic I'm afraid, will be more difficult."

Chapter 14

Kaitlin Jenkins exited the Charlotte Douglas Airport. The cool evening air was a welcome contrast to the stifling airplane. A women tottering on high heels rolled a bag into Kaitlin's leg. When Kaitlin regained her balance, she made her way to the line waiting for parking lot shuttles. Cars, hotel vans and limos passed by. After fifteen minutes she boarded a shuttle for Parking Lot One, tossed her bag on the luggage rack, sank into the nearest seat, and pulled her phone from her bag. She spoke with her mother most days but in the last two she had no chance to call. Before she hit the number for Mom, she decided against having an audience for her conversation. Leaning against the back cushion, she noticed the usual post flight tightness in her neck and shoulders extended down her back and into her legs. She closed her eyes for the short distance to her car.

At the shuttle stop with a W on the shed, she got off the van and retrieved her car. With rush hour over, her ten-mile drive to uptown Charlotte had no traffic problems, making the ride quick and painless. After parking near her home in the city's Fourth Ward, Kaitlin opened her front door, kicked the pile of mail to the side, and made her way upstairs to her bedroom. Looking around she told herself she was lucky to have such a nice place, a house-sitting gig. Professor Catherine Watson of the University of North Carolina in Charlotte agreed to teach the Spanish influence in the American Southwest at the University of Madrid for the next two years. A professor friend of Watson's at UNC in Chapel Hill knew Kaitlin had a job offer in Charlotte and recommended her.

Leaving her suitcase unpacked she shed her business suit and pulled on gray Capri pants and a tank top. Comfortable, she returned to the first floor taking her phone to the kitchen. As she poured a glass of juice, she called her mother.

"Hi, Mom."

"Are you home?"

"Yes, finally."

"How was the training?"

"Exhausting 16 hour days…relentless."

"I have some bad news. My friend Angela's daughter, Courtney, is dead. Someone murdered her in her apartment in New York."

Kaitlin did not immediately respond. She shuddered.

"It's horrible." Teresa said.

"The Hansons must be devastated," Kaitlin managed to say. "I remember seeing them at Maura's wedding. Didn't Courtney live in a swanky building?"

"Right. No place is safe these days." Teresa paused. "The detective on the case talked with me today."

"Really. Why?" Kaitlin took a sip of juice and paced.

"I'm not sure. He said he's interviewing family friends."

"The Hansons are well known in the city, aren't they?"

"Yes. They donate to several charities. Mr. Hanson's on the board for the Metropolitan Museum of Art and other community boards. He and the mayor are good friends."

"That might help."

"This detective seems determined," Teresa said.

"I hope he gets the killer. I hate that Maura's got away."

"Kaitlin, he asked a lot of questions about Maura's murder." Kaitlin heard the tremor in her mother's voice.

"He thinks there's a connection?"

"Maybe."

"It's been seven years."

78

"He finds it a strange coincidence that two friends had daughters murdered in their homes."

"What's his name?"

"Peter Hajek."

Kaitlin searched the Internet on her phone. "He's younger than I thought he'd be. I'm looking at his photo with the mayor in the New York newspaper. This guy came to your home yesterday?"

"Yeah."

"The mayor of New York City honored him for cracking a recent case in record time," Kaitlin read to her mother.

"That's right. The paper reported that a man still unhappy about losing a war fought 150 years ago caused the explosion at Grant's tomb. Many law enforcement officials thought a foreign terrorist did it."

"Good for him. I hope he's as fast with Courtney's case."

"He'd like to talk with Dad."

"No chance of that."

"I told him so."

"He'd also like to talk with you."

"What can I do for him?" Kaitlin sat in a rocking chair in the living room.

"Not sure. I told him I'd check with you. Sorry, dear. I know it's a lot to ask."

Kaitlin increased her rocking. "For what it's worth I'll talk with him."

"I'll give him your number. What are your birthday plans?"

"Samantha's coming to visit next week. She regrets taking that job in Omaha, Nebraska."

"Why did she go there? I never understood that move?"

79

"She wanted to experience another state. The job's disappointing, boring actually. I tell her that's why it's called work. Now it isn't easy for her to find another job. Hard to believe we have such pitiful options as college graduates."

"Every generation has its challenges. Mine struggled with the Vietnam War."

"Your work options were more useful."

"For men maybe. Your Dad actually made products people needed. My choices were teacher, social worker, or nurse. I wanted none of those. After my stint in the Peace Corps my four year degree landed me an office job."

"Are you seeing the detective again?"

Theresa laughed. "Your father might object to your word choice. I expect Detective Hajek may phone me again. You must be tired. I'll let you go. Good night, dear."

"Good night, Mom."

Chapter 15

Kaitlin Jenkins turned off her phone, set her iPod for favorite tunes, and started on the usual back-home tasks. Kaitlin picked up the pile of mail she had kicked aside, and scanned for anything first class. Two bills she tossed on a table, and dumped the catalogs and slick advertising postcards in the recycling bin.

Walking upstairs, she stopped on the landing. Staring at Georgia O'Keefe's Easter Sunrise print hanging on the wall, she fantasized traveling to New Mexico. Then she continued to her room, selected an outfit for the next day, and hung it on a hook over the closet door. In the master bath, she adjusted the water temperature to comfortably warm and sprinkled in bath salts. As the oversized Jacuzzi tub filled, she thought again how lucky she was to have this luxury.

Kaitlin switched to a classical music playlist and placed the iPod in its deck on a shelf. She lit a candle, inhaled the pleasant lavender scent, and sank into a soothing soak. The conversation with her mother filled her thoughts as if she hit replay. Tears formed and she let them flow over her cheeks and mix with the bath water. She missed Maura. Often, she cried about the fact that she would never be an aunt and that the children she wanted would never play with their cousins.

Mournful violin strains matched Kaitlin's mood. As a child and teenager, her big sister showered her with kindness. Maura cheered for her as much as her parents did. Kaitlin believed in their adult years, they would be more like peers with the age gap disappearing. The anniversary of Maura's birthday and wedding triggered particularly painful memories but day-to-day pain had lessened with time. What did this detective think he could accomplish?

***

The next morning Kaitlin woke remembering the conversation with her mother. She knew her mother would waste no time in relaying the message to Detective Hajek that she would talk with him. Her eight-block walk to work through Fourth Ward Park brightened her spirits. Charlotte's springtime displays included beds of daffodils dotted with crocuses and clusters of azaleas in white, pink and red. She stopped at a coffee shop for yogurt with fruit, a bagel, and coffee.

At Bank of America on Tryon Street in the center of uptown Charlotte, Kaitlin passed through the security checks and rode an elevator to the 23rd floor.

When she set her breakfast on her desk, Lorraine looked up.

"Early, aren't you? 7:10 is a record."

"Wide awake at 5A.M. … did you miss me?" Kaitlin asked the older woman who sat at the next desk. Neither of them had the status of individual cubicles.

"Of course. How was the training?"

"Just thrilling." Kaitlin laughed.

***

Three hours later a ringing cell phone startled Kaitlin. It flashed 'private number' as the incoming caller. She stepped away from her desk looking for a quiet corner. She saw people gathering in the conference room for a meeting. The hallway by the elevators had people coming and going. With no place for privacy available, Kaitlin pushed talk, "Hello."

"Detective Hajek with NYPD. Your mother gave me your number."

"Yes. She said I'd hear from you. Can you call me back in ten minutes?"

"Sure." The call ended.

Kaitlin walked over to Lorraine and whispered, "I'm taking a break."

Lorraine waved.

82

Outside, Kaitlin walked to nearby Polk Park and stood near the cascading waterfall. This little oasis had a smell of nature amidst concrete and asphalt. Her phone rang.

"Kaitlin, Detective Hajek here again. Did I give you enough time?"

"Yes."

"I appreciate your willingness to talk with me. For the record, you should know that I'm with the NYPD and I am not handling your sister's case. I'm looking into it to see if there's any connection with the Hanson murder."

She sat on a stone bench.

"I'm sure it's not easy to revisit Maura's death," Hajek said.

"Last night after I talked with my mother I kept remembering my sister. She was a good person and her murder was awful. It would be great if you found the killer. I fear he may hurt others."

"Tell me about your relationship with your sister?"

"I was fortunate to have her for a big sister especially because I was an older sister's nightmare." She laughed.

Hajek also laughed. "You were a nightmare?"

"Yes. I wanted to tag along with her and her friends. They were four years older and considered me a nuisance. At home Maura treated me well--helped me with my schoolwork, taught me to ride a bike, swim, and play tennis."

"Tell me what you remember about the day Maura died. Start with the morning."

Kaitlin paused. When she spoke her voice quivered. "I was a student at the University of North Carolina in Chapel Hill. I called Mom before I went to class to wish her a happy birthday."

"Any idea of the time?" Hajek asked.

Kaitlin took a tissue from her pocket and blotted her eyes. "I'm not exactly sure."

"Okay. Go on."

"After we spoke I was in classes for the day. I ate dinner at the student center. I studied at the library before returning to my room. Then my mother called at 11P.M. I remember that. It was unusual for her to call so late. Since I already had spoken with her earlier in the day, I didn't expect good news. Nothing prepared me to hear my mother say, *your sister has been murdered*." Kaitlin sobbed.

"I'm sorry. I'll call back."

She took a deep breath. "No. Give me a minute." Kaitlin wiped her eyes and blew her nose. She inhaled and exhaled slowly.

"Take your time."

Kaitlin stood and paced. "The rest of that conversation with my mother was surreal. She told me the Bethel Police believed the killer got in the house before my sister came home from work. When my brother-in-law came home, he found Maura on the kitchen floor. He called 911. The ambulance and police came. My parents and Dominic spent hours at the police station. I told my mother I'd be home on the first flight I could get. The next morning I was on a US Airways flight to Connecticut."

"Tell me about your brother-in-law."

"Domenic's a real nice guy."

"Do you think Maura was involved with anyone else?"

"Not a chance. Dominic and Maura were a good match."

"Can you think of anyone that she didn't get along with or maybe had a grudge against her?" Hajek asked.

"No."

"What about former boyfriends?"

84

"It's hard to remember anyone before Domenic. They dated a long time," Kaitlin said.

"From your perspective was your sister happy with her husband?"

"Definitely. And very excited about having a baby. Everyone said they'd be great parents. It was terrible the way the police treated Domenic."

"As a suspect?"

"Yeah. If you knew him, you'd understand how unbelievable that was. He was crazy about Maura and would never hurt her."

"Are you in contact with him?"

"Yeah. I call him once in a while. He's working in Houston... The memories of Maura were too intense for him to stay in Connecticut."

"I'd like to speak with him. What are my chances?"

"Not sure. Let me call him first."

"Thanks Kaitlin. I'll call in a couple of days."

In the small city park, Kaitlin stared at the water tumbling over boulders and splashing near her feet. She would like to believe this New York detective could find her sister's killer but she was too much of a realist to hold out much hope. He sounded sincere, not a show-off trying to augment his resume. Although the loss of her sister created a hole in her heart, she functioned and approached her life and future with optimism. This detective came across as compassionate.

Kaitlin walked to the crosswalk at Trade and Tryon Streets. Waiting for the light she looked up at the sculpture of a woman holding a child over her head. The sun glistened on the mother's admiring gaze. Maura would never smile on her child, she thought...a killer stole Maura's future. The light changed ending WALK. Kaitlin waited again for the traffic to stop.

Chapter 16

"NASCAR?" Lorraine asked when Kaitlin returned.

"No." Kaitlin laughed and deflected the conversation to her recent date. A guy she had met in her neighborhood invited her to a race at the nearby Motor Speedway. His office had a block of tickets and he planned to go with several of his co-workers. Three or four of them were bringing a guest. Kaitlin accepted with mixed feelings. He interested her. The attraction of crowds paying to watch cars race laps around an asphalt oval baffled her.

"Once is it for me," Kaitlin answered Lorraine. "He was nice enough and if he suggests dinner, the theater or a concert, I'd be interested. But the car thing-- BORING!"

**

Later that evening, Kaitlin called Domenic. After a brief exchange about the weather, she plunged into the reason for her call. "Domenic, yesterday a NYPD detective talked with my mother about Maura." She stopped. "Today he called me."

Domenic's silence did not surprise Kaitlin. She kept talking, summarizing what she knew about Courtney Hanson's death and reminding him that her mother and Mrs. Hanson were old friends. In a rush to finish, she said, "He'd like to talk with you."

She waited.

"What's the point in dredging everything up? He can talk with the Bethel Police for anything he needs to know," Domenic said.

"He thought Maura was shot. My mother told him that Maura was strangled. He was surprised." Kaitlin's voice cracked.

"Why would that matter?"

"Domenic, I hate reliving this. I know it's much worse for you. It's a long shot but if I can do anything to catch Maura's killer I will. So I talked with him."

"It's hopeless. Too much time has passed. Nothing will come of this," Domenic said. "I've accepted it. You should do the same."

"Check this detective out. His name is Peter Hajek. He just cracked a big New York City case in record time. FBI agents and top brass in NYPD were following what they thought was a terrorist case. Hajek figured out it was a statement of disrespect for General Grant from a descendant of one of Lee's key generals."

Kaitlin realized that she had been pacing between the living room and the kitchen and sat down.

"Give me his name." Domenic said.

"Peter Hajek." She spelled the last name.

"I know it's painful, Domenic, but it's worth a try. No one else is doing anything."

"Okay, Kaitlin, I'll do it for you. Give the detective my number."

"Thanks Domenic. I really appreciate it."

Chapter 17

The next evening after work, Kaitlin parked near her home at 7:30P.M. Drenched in sweat from a Hot Yoga Class, she dashed to the front door conscious of her red face, dripping clothes and matted hair. Dropping her purse and laptop on the bottom step, she bounded upstairs with the bag containing her work clothes. In the bathroom, she peeled off her soggy top and tights, dropped them on the floor, and showered. Wearing pajamas, she sat on the cushioned bench at the foot of her bed, and reflected on how distracted she had been in the yoga class. Kaitlin worried about pinning too much hope on Detective Hajek's skills and feared that she would regret convincing Domenic to speak with him.

Still mulling over recent events, Kaitlin picked up her wet things from the bathroom floor, deposited them in a laundry basket, and went to the refrigerator to find supper. She pulled out leftover salad, opened a can of tuna, dumped it on the greens, added several crackers, and quartered an orange. Kaitlin placed her plate of food on a placemat protecting the lace covered dining room table. Not one to inhale meals, no matter how meager, Kaitlin lit a candle in the crystal candlestick, sat on a carved wooden chair, and ate her food.

She continued to think about the New York City detective. When her mother called and told her about Hajek's interest in Maura's murder, Kaitlin googled 'Peter Hajek NYPD'. His successful resolution of the Grant Tomb explosion case impressed her. Remembering that there were many other hits, Kaitlin decided to find out more about this detective. She placed her dishes in the dishwasher. Then she took her laptop from its case on the stairs and carried it into the living room. She sat on the red velvet chaise lounge and balanced the computer on her knees. After again searching Peter Hajek NYPD, she sorted the results by most recent. One of the first items was an obituary for Francine Hajek, age 31.

Kaitlin checked further. She read that the survivors included her husband, Peter of Queens, parents, Claude and Patricia DeLuca of Tucson, Arizona and a sister and brother-in-law, Veronica and Mike Geffken of St. Louis.

Noting the date of her death was ten days before Hajek cracked the Grant case, Kaitlin thought, how can this man deal with the grieving Hansons, and the loss of his wife? Kaitlin read more. Francine Hajek had worked in the marketing department of the New York Yankees. She grew up in Park Slope Brooklyn, attended local public schools and earned a BA and an MBA at Fordham University. Francine served on several nonprofits that helped children. In lieu of flowers, the family requested donations to the American Cancer Society or any charity.

An article applauded Francine for chairing a successful fundraising event to benefit an after school music program for middle school students. A photo of three couples accompanied it. Looking at Francine and Peter Hajek in the middle, Kaitlin felt sad. They appeared vibrant and happy. Francine, with chin length light brown hair, wore a royal blue dress with a geometric silver pendant at her neck. Hajek's short, curly dark hair gave him a boyish look.

Next, Kaitlin went to the funeral home's online guest book. She read condolences from friends, coworkers, neighbors and some from people touched by Francine or Peter Hajek's community work. One note mentioned his work with youth in Queens—'my son enjoyed biking with you on the Sierra Club nature outings. He is sad about your wife'. Another wrote 'Mr. Hajek's guest lecture in my high school inspired me to pursue a career in law enforcement'.

The phone interrupted Kaitlin's reading. "Hi Kaitlin, I'm psyched about being in Charlotte this weekend."

"It'll be fun. I've tickets for the North Carolina Dance performance Saturday night." Kaitlin moved her computer to a nearby table.

"We could help the NASCAR Hall of Fame attendance stats. Now that you've been to the Speedway I'm sure the museum will interest you."

"No way. You can go without me," Kaitlin said as she walked into the kitchen and poured a glass of seltzer.

"I'm looking forward to catching up with you and just hanging out. My parents want to take us to dinner Sunday before I fly back."

"That sounds good." Kaitlin returned to the living room, took a sip and said, "A New York City detective visited my mother this week to talk about Maura and he called me. I don't know what to make of it. A young woman was murdered in Manhattan. Her mother's a friend of my mother."

"That's terrible. He thinks the deaths are connected?"

"Not sure. He's looking into it."

Kaitlin told Samantha about Domenic and her misgivings about expecting too much. "When you called, I was reading stuff online about the detective."

"Think he can solve Maura's murder?"

"His wife died a couple of weeks ago."

"What?"

"The detective that called me. I just read his wife's obituary."

"Was she murdered?"

"No. Breast cancer."

"How can he do a job that's all about death?"

"I can't imagine. Reading about him makes me think he's a good guy. He took family leave to care for her."

"I hope he can get the murderer. With all this going on, I bet your mother wishes you were back north."

"More than wishes. She's focused on finding me a Connecticut job. She has a neighbor who works at General Electric checking openings. The corporate headquarters is in Fairfield."

"Anything interesting?"

"Banking isn't exciting but tracking minutia related to turbines or locomotives--I don't think so," Kaitlin said.

"Tell your mother you need more experience at Bank of America before making a change. And you're house-sitting-- isn't the professor teaching in Spain for another year?"

"Yes. The truth is I need to be a plane ride away from my parents."

"Let me know about those jobs. I'd leave Omaha in a heartbeat."

"Speaking of your heart, how'd that date go?"

"I hoped you forgot."

"Come on, tell me."

"This one belongs in Dealbreaker, you know the book Tina Fey's character wrote on the 30 Rock TV Show."

"Love it. It's a dealbreaker…'if your boyfriend wears a gold chain…or is over 30 and lives with his mother…' That bad, eh."

"Remember how his mother recruited—rather tricked me into going out with him? Since she's my supervisor it's awkward."

"Weird for sure. Where'd you go?"

"We met at a downtown restaurant that he picked. I expected upscale."

"Had you seen a picture of him to know who you were looking for?"

"No. I told him I'd be wearing a blue suede beret."

"You had no idea what he looked like?"

"His mother described him as good looking, funny and smart. She neglected to tell me his height. As I'm walking up to the front of the restaurant

91

someone yells *Samantha wait*. I turn and saw this five foot nothing guy running toward me."

Kaitlin laughed knowing Samantha liked tall men. "And you said, I'm not Samantha."

"I couldn't dump the hat fast enough, Kaitlin. He reminded me of one of the geeky nerds on the TV Show The Big Bang Theory."

"The most socially inept one?" Kaitlin put her feet up on the chaise.

"He raved about the restaurant's high tech features. Instead of a hostess, a large screen suspended inside the entrance greeted us. He told me the available tables were in green. I just gawked. From the keypad on a stand under the screen, he selected a table in the middle of the room. Immediately the green turned to red."

Kaitlin laughed.

"When we sat down, a robot voice said 'Welcome to Techno Cuisine'. There were no tablecloths or candles. A touch screen embedded in the table top displayed the menu. We ordered by tapping on selections."

"Hooray for Omaha. Never seen that. Do they have robots for wait staff?"

"You'd think since he bragged about cutting edge programming. No a person brought our food. A screen mounted next to the table had several viewing selections, an African Safari, Tropical Birds, sport events and other programs."

"You could have stayed home, watched the National Geographic Channel, and texted him." Kaitlin moved a pillow to her back.

"It was pretty bad. He talked about some network hardware that his company recently bought from Cisco. He had sample diagrams on his iPhone."

"And explained 'em?" Kaitlin asked.

"Oh, yeah, in boring detail."

"Did you make another date?"

"Not a chance. He asked nothing about my interests, my background. Totally self-absorbed."

"You didn't enjoy learning about emerging technology from a pro?"

"I'm not sure why I was there."

"His mother. What did you tell her?" Kaitlin asked.

"Fortunately I haven't seen her. She went to a conference in California and added vacation days. She's back next week. I don't know what I'll say."

"Tell her you're gay."

"Forward me those job openings from your mother."

Chapter 18

"Detective Hajek, this is Gary in the lab. I just spoke with Wilcox. He told me to give you the early results on the Hanson case."

"Great."

"The urine is from a human male probably in his sixties. We ran standard drug tests and did not detect any illegal drugs. The sample showed no recent alcohol consumption. He has early stage diabetes. The kidneys are probably not functioning as well as they should."

"What about the cap?"

"We're still working on that. The video is in black and white and there are shadows on the cap. It looks like there are three or four letters. We have good software that might bring out more detail. We should have that in the next forty eight hours."

"Thanks, Gary." Unlikely the cap identified a company where the guy worked or had his name on it. Still, Hajek wanted to know what it said. Male in his sixties was consistent with the person in the surveillance photo.

Tonight he would call Domenic Santori in Texas. He did not ask Kaitlin how she convinced him; he just thanked her. To prepare, he reviewed his notes from his conversation with Kaitlin. His eyes filled with tears as he read that at one point he heard joy in her voice. This young woman suffered a tragic loss and still sounded light-hearted. Why did this case bother him so much? He questioned people about the circumstances of a loved one's death many times.

Officer Nick Kostas walked up to Hajek's desk. "You're still here? How about we get dinner?"

Hajek turned and looked at his friend. "Can't tonight. I have a call to make,"

"Do you know what time it is?"

"An hour later than Houston. I need to talk with the Connecticut victim's husband. He lives in Texas now."

"I'm worried about the hours you're putting in."

"I'm okay."

"Don't be too late."

"Yeah sure."

"Goodnight." Kostas left.

Hajek looked at his notes from the Santori murder. The killer had a gun. He shot the dog. Why strangle Maura? The Bethel police believed it was a burglary gone bad. Hajek thought the killer targeted Maura. But why? And why on her mother's birthday?

At 8:02 P.M., he called Domenic. "This is Detective Hajek, Thank you for agreeing to speak with me. I know this isn't easy."

"You have no idea," Domenic said.

Hajek stiffened and resisted saying I know more about loss than you think. "I'm reviewing the facts of the case in hopes of finding something new."

"It's been years," Domenic said.

"Please tell me what you remember about finding your wife."

"Is this really necessary—what's the point?"

"Someone killed a young woman in Manhattan. There are similarities with Maura's murder. Many killers repeat their patterns," Hajek said.

"Check with the Bethel police. They'll tell you what you need to know."

"I've spoken with them by phone and plan to go to the police station. From what I reviewed online in our database there may be gaps in their reports."

"That's hard to believe."

"Please tell me what you remember."

95

Hajek heard a sigh. "It was October 3rd. I came home from work around 6:00. I parked in the driveway because we were going out to dinner."

"You came in the front door?"

"Yes."

"Any evidence of a break-in?"

"No. The door was locked. When I walked into the kitchen…" Domenic stopped. "Maura laid on the floor… a rope around her neck.. I untied it. I tried to revive her. It was hopeless… Her body felt cold. I called 911 and kept doing CPR. I wanted to save her."

Hajek barely heard the last sentence. It sounded like Domenic stifled a sob. "Take your time." Hajek rubbed his forehead and waited.

"Next, I heard sirens."

"Tell me about the layout of your house."

"We had a three bedroom ranch with a back porch. Our property backed to a wooded area."

"Was the porch off the kitchen?"

"Yes."

"Is it screened?"

"In the summer but we had already put in the storm windows."

"How do you think your wife came into the house?"

"From the garage into the kitchen."

"Was the porch door locked?"

"Yes."

"Any windows broken on the porch?"

"No."

"How would someone get in?"

"I really don't know," Domenic said.

"Did anyone else have a key to the house?"

"Just Maura's parents."

"Tell me about the wooded area behind your house."

"There's a buffer of trees between the houses on White Birch Drive, our street, and houses on Shady Glen Drive, the street behind ours."

"Could someone easily walk from Shady Glen to the back of your house?"

"I guess so. There's shrubbery but not so dense that it's impassable."

"How long did you live on White Birch?"

"Three years."

"Did you get along with your neighbors?"

"Yes."

"Just a couple more questions about Maura. What happened when the EMTs and police arrived?"

"The technicians said that Maura was dead. A police officer found Foxy on the back porch."

"Foxy?"

"Our dog."

Hajek made a note to find out more about the dog. "Was there urine present?"

"Yes. The police figured it was Maura's and said that happens all the time."

Hajek scribbled in his notepad to recheck the police report. He did not recall any mention of urine at the scene.

"Do you know if the police took samples and confirmed it was Maura's?"

"No. I don't remember anything about police testing urine. It seemed obvious. You think that matters?" Domenic sounded annoyed.

"It could. Tell me what else you remember."

"I most remember the nightmare of the police questioning me. They asked about our marriage and where I was all day. They should've moved faster to find the murderer and not think I killed my wife."

Hajek understood that the police believed they knew who did the killing. "Did the police talk with any of your neighbors about that day?"

"At some point they did. I don't know exactly when. No one noticed an unfamiliar vehicle. Only a couple of people were home at the time."

"What have you been doing since?"

Domenic reviewed the events in his life over the past couple of years. He had decided to leave Connecticut soon after Maura's death. Most nights he did not return to the home he shared with his wife. He often stayed with his parents in New Canaan and sometimes with a single buddy. Five months after his wife died, Domenic put the house up for sale and it sold quickly.

"Houston was not on my list of favorite places to visit never mind live, but it offered work and a new start," Dominic said.

"What's your work?"

"I'm a chemist with EPH Petroleum. I test crude oil samples for sulfur content."

"Do you like it?" Hajek asked.

"Developing new products at Clairol in Stamford interested me more. This job's routine and boring."

"How do you like Houston?"

"The climate's stifling hot most of the year. I miss the varied scenery and weather of the northeast. But I do like living and working with people who know nothing about Maura's murder."

"That makes sense."

"I miss Maura every day. Here I don't endure the pitying looks of co-workers. That was excruciating. Maura's family is great but they remind me too much of her. Living in Texas works for me."

"Bethel Police first thought the killer was someone who knew Maura. Can you think of anyone that would want to hurt her?"

"No. She was sweet. People liked her. I can't think of anyone. I have to stop."

"Thank you, Domenic. This information's helpful. Take care." Hajek closed his phone.

After he finished the call, Hajek thought about how close he came to sharing his own difficulty with sympathetic, well-intended comments about Francine's death. Unlike Domenic, he stayed in the home he shared with Francine and returned to the same job. He took the picture of Francine from his desk. With tears in his eyes he gazed at it.

"I will get this killer."

Chapter 19

Friday morning Hajek found the unmarked police car he had signed out for the day in the police garage. He placed his iPod, laptop, and GPS on the passenger seat. He entered his destination, 49 Plumtrees Road, Bethel Connecticut, into his portable GPS. As expected, his sixty-five mile ride would take him north along the Hudson on Route 9 a short distance before cutting east and north again. Before this case, he never heard of the rural town of Bethel and his infrequent jaunts to Connecticut had not included most of this morning's drive.

At the first traffic light, he turned on his iPod. The blasts of "*Round Midnight*" from Miles Davis' trumpet obliterated the traffic noise. He might actually enjoy this drive.

In an hour, he turned onto Route 84 east and after another 20 miles, he took Exit 8. The big box stores surprised him. A little further on he turned on Payne Road and saw the expected scenery of pastures, stonewalls, and brooks.

At the Bethel Police Station, he parked in a nearly empty lot. He walked up to the entrance of the simply constructed one-story building. With laptop in hand, he greeted the uniformed officer at the front desk. "I'm Peter Hajek with the NYPD and I have an appointment with Chief Hubbell."

"I'll let the chief know you're here."

While waiting, Hajek looked at the wall of photos depicting earlier days in Bethel and Danbury. One shot caught the various hues of huge pumpkins in a massive display. Another photo depicted yoked oxen in front of a cart loaded with boulders. A farmer dressed in what looked like his Sunday clothes complete with a wide brimmed felt hat posed next to his animals.

A uniformed man with short dark hair approached. "The Danbury Agricultural Fair was a big event in my childhood. Welcome to Bethel. I'm Police Chief Hubbell."

Hajek extended his hand. "Glad to meet you, Chief. I'm Peter Hajek."

Hajek glanced back at the pictures. "Do you still have the fair?"

"No. Today the Danbury Fair Mall sits on the old fairgrounds."

"That's the name of the mall?"

"Yes. Shopping, not farming, is celebrated now. Are you a city boy?"

"Yeah, grew up in Queens and still live there. The only animals we saw were cats, dogs, pigeons, and rats." Both men laughed.

"Brookfield—just north of here is my home town. Let's go to my office."

"Chief Hubbell, I appreciate you meeting with me."

"Your Captain told me there's a possible connection with a Manhattan murder and one in Bethel."

Hajek followed Hubbell down a hallway. "That's right. I'd like to find out for sure."

The back-corner office had a comfortable high back chair, a glass jar of peppermints and a cluster of three chairs in front of the desk. Two large windows looked out on trees and shrubs. The chief's brag wall included a couple of framed newspaper articles with photos of Hubbell, diplomas from the University of New Haven for a Bachelor's degree and a Master's in forensic science. Hajek pointed to a picture on a shelf, "Is that you and the famous forensic scientist Dr. Lee?"

Hubbell beamed. "Yes. He's been an inspiration to me. It's impressive what he has done with tiny clues."

"I'm an admirer of his skills."

"Please sit down, Detective." After Hajek took a seat, Hubbell sat in the chair across from him. "I understand from Wilcox you want to look at our file on the Maura Santori case," the chief began.

"Yes, I'm investigating a recent murder and I'm struck by some similarities with the Santori murder."

"Such as?"

Hajek summarized his thoughts on the killer's methodical technique for gaining entry, strangling the victim, and his theory that he targeted both women specifically. He did not mention his uneasiness with the Bethel police work.

"I welcome fresh eyes. I'll help you any way I can. Let me give you a place to work." Hubbell picked up a file and a video tape and directed Hajek to a small windowless room near the front of the building.

He placed the file on the table and said, "The usual rules apply. You can look at this file but don't remove anything—notes are okay. If you need a photo copy of anything let me know." He put the tape in the video player. "When you're ready hit play. Coffee's at the end of the hall and so is the john. Let me or anyone here know if you need anything. When you're done, I'd like to review your findings before you leave."

"Thanks."

Hajek flipped to the report section of the file to read the medical examiner's autopsy report. It confirmed the presence of a seven-week embryo, mentioned involuntary urination, and concluded strangulation caused her death. Hajek looked for testing information on the urine. He found none.

Fingerprints lifted from the home had no hits from the police database. Most belonged to the victim and her family. The bullet that killed the dog had no markings linking it with previous crimes.

Hajek carefully examined the photos of the crime scene showing the victim on the kitchen floor. One close-up indicated bruising on her neck at an angle consistent with a rope pulled from behind. The autopsy note of a bruise under her chin from blunt force caused Hajek to think the killer was face to face with Maura as he crushed the life out of her. Hajek knew this was not a quick process. Did the murderer enjoy torturing Maura, he wondered?

Next, he read the police notes in chronological order. It was clear that the police suspected Domenic at the start. Hajek read the transcripts of all the interviews. In addition to Domenic, they questioned the victim's parents, Teresa and Vincent Jenkins, and two days later her sister Kaitlin. They interviewed several neighbors and employees at Clairol where Domenic worked. Coworkers verified that he had participated in a marketing meeting that lasted from noon until the end of the day. At no time did Domenic leave the building. With this airtight alibi, the police shifted their thinking to Maura's death being the unfortunate result of a random robbery gone bad.

He played the video. From the time and date, he realized it was taken the day after the murder. It gave him an overview of the house. Without the body, it did not offer much help in showing the details of the crime scene. He looked at the crime scene photos again.

Hajek got up, used the restroom and helped himself to a cup of hot water. He took teabags from his jacket pocket and immersed them to brew. Back in his temporary workplace, he sipped his drink and flipped again through the file. Deciding that he had learned all he could here, Hajek returned everything to the file and walked to the front desk. He had some questions for the chief.

He approached the reception area and asked the police officer on the desk for Chief Hubbell. The officer called Hubbell and announced, "Detective Hajek would like to speak with you, Sir. Right. I'll tell him." He put the phone down. "The chief will meet you in his office."

Before walking away he asked the man, "How long have you been a police officer?"

"Eleven years."

"All in Bethel?"

"No, just the last two here." The officer smiled.

"Where before that?"

"Bridgeport. World of difference. My wife's happier. My blood pressure is lower. How can you work in New York City?"

Hajek shrugged. "It's all I know."

The chief sat at his desk and when Hajek walked in, he got up and moved to where they had sat earlier.

"So what'd you find?" Hubbell shifted sideways and rested an elbow on the chair arm.

"A puzzle I'd like to solve. May I look at the physical evidence you have from the crime scene?"

"Sure. It's in a locker downstairs. Give me a moment." The chief leaned across the desk, picked up his phone, and tapped in three numbers. He requested the items related to the Santori murder be brought to his office.

Hajek ran his fingers through his hair. "Thanks. I'd also like to talk with any of the police officers who had worked on the Santori case."

"No one from the investigation is still here."

"Where'd they go or rather why would they leave the police force?"

"To answer your first question, the lead guy moved out of state—last I heard he joined a force in Idaho. The others…I'm not sure any are still doing police work," Hubbell said.

"That's surprising."

"A good thing from my point of view. Like many small towns, Bethel had an old boy network that included the police. Suffice it to say that at the time of the Santori case the department lacked professionalism. They were over their heads and I'm sure they made mistakes. The days of putting on a uniform, practicing a few rounds at the firing range and believing you're a qualified law enforcement professional are over."

"I'm glad to hear of the changes."

"So what's your thinking, Hajek?"

"Usually when a dog is shot the bullet goes right through the animal. This bullet stayed in the dog," Hajek said.

Hubbell shook his head. "A silencer would lower the bullet's velocity. It may have helped if someone on the scene noticed that detail."

"And realized the killer planned this attack."

"Right."

"I understand the police concluded that Maura interrupted a burglary," Hajek said.

"Yes. That's what's in the file."

"Tell me about other house break-ins around that time."

"Nothing stands out. We don't have many. Most typically, a neighborhood teen takes small electronics and jewelry. Usually we catch him."

"How about neighboring towns?"

"Danbury has more crime but nothing like the violence we're talking about in this case."

"The murder of Maura Santori was not a robbery and it was not random." Hajek leaned forward. "It was personal."

A uniformed police woman appeared in the doorway holding a standard-sized file box. Hubbell stood. "That was fast. Thanks, Doris." He turned to Hajek. "Let's go back to the conference room."

When the chief opened the box, Hajek noted the lack of special care to preserve this evidence. He saw Maura's clothing on top in a plastic bag and he wondered about the usefulness of DNA testing with the lack of refrigeration. At the bottom of the box was a rope. Hajek looked at thick braided twine with knotted frayed ends.

"Chief, this is the same kind of rope used in my Manhattan murder. It's the same perpetrator. We need to secure it. And we should test the clothing for DNA."

Chapter 20

In his car, he entered a Fairfield address. The GPS indicated it was a forty-seven minute drive to Teresa Jenkins' home. He called. "Mrs. Jenkins, this is Detective Hajek."

"Glad I answered. Usually I ignore unknown on my caller ID."

"I know this is short notice but I'd like to stop by. I'm about 50 minutes from you."

"Sure. I'll be home."

Hajek drove south on Route 58 passing Putnam State Park, a Revolutionary War Memorial and New England homes that looked like movie sets. The road wound alongside a reservoir. The memory of the thick-braided rope with frayed ends prevented his enjoying the country scenery.

Teresa opened the door as he approached. "You have news?"

"No, Sorry I should have realized you'd have your hopes up."

She stepped back. "Come in."

"Just a few questions."

"Anything I can do I'm glad to. Coffee?"

"Tea, please."

They walked into the kitchen where the aroma of coffee and the smell of spices from muffins cooling on a rack on the counter greeted him.

"I transformed my applesauce cake into muffins for a change. I hope you'll try 'em." Teresa slid the muffins onto a plate.

"I never had applesauce cake or muffins…they smell delicious." Hajek sat at the table and picked up a book with a city skyline on the cover. "*Five Star Fraud* any good?"

107

"I'm only on page thirteen. I'll let you know. My book club is reading it this month." Teresa fixed his tea, poured her coffee, and placed the mugs, cream, plates, silverware and muffins on the table. She sat down. "What's on your mind?"

"I keep trying to find a link between you and Angela Hanson. It strikes me as strange that two friends have daughters murdered on their mothers' birthdays."

Teresa gasped. "I never made that connection… Courtney died on Angela's birthday. We stopped remembering each other's birthdays after college."

"Who else did you and Angela Hanson hang out with in high school?"

"You think the date is significant?"

"I don't know. Who else did you and Angela Hanson hang out with in high school?" Hajek repeated.

"Roberta Barlow and Marsha Flynn. We were a foursome."

"Do you have a yearbook?"

"I hate my high school picture but I'll show you the book. Promise not to laugh." Teresa retrieved her copy of Witness from a shelf in the den and handed it to Hajek.

"Witness?" he traced the gold letters of the cover.

"Named by nuns I'm sure." Teresa brushed a strand of hair from her face.

Hajek flipped through class photos, sporting events, and pictures of staff, stopping at the page with Teresa's senior picture. He read out loud, "Good voice, likes music, drawing and field hockey. Field Hockey?"

"One of the few sports available to women when I was in high school."

"Doesn't fit my image of the turbulent 60's. Too wholesome." Hajek scanned the other photos on the page.

Teresa stirred her coffee. "The first half of the sixties differed from the second half. You're too young to know that."

108

"The Vietnam War heated up in 1965." Hajek looked up.

"That may be true but it didn't affect my world. During my high school years, I was very removed from national turmoil. Think about it. The popular movies were 'My Fair Lady' and 'Sound of Music'. That's what we saw in the theaters."

"Not my image of the sixties."

"Right."

"How about civil rights?" Hajek sipped his tea.

"There were sit-ins and protests reported on the evening news but they weren't in Stamford, Connecticut. For me the chaos and violence started in 1967, two years after I graduated. I was insulated during my high school years. Unbelievable as this sounds, no black students were in my class."

"When my wife's parents reminisced about the sixties they talked about marches they attended and protest speeches."

"They must have been more politically aware than I was. And your parents?" Teresa asked.

"They also opposed the war. My father's luck gained him a high number and he never served. My mother worried that he would have fled to Canada to avoid the draft."

"Are they still alive?"

"My father died seven years ago. My mother is in a facility in New York. She has Alzheimer's."

"That's tough. I'm sorry. Does she know you?"

"I tell myself she does. When I visit, I see flickers of recognition. Most of the time she talks to me as if I'm my father. She was a smart, fun woman and I miss having real conversations with her." His blunt revelation surprised him.

"Tell me about your wife."

Hajek took a sip of his tea, amazed that he mentioned his wife to this total stranger.

"She died of breast cancer."

"I'm so sorry."

He focused on the yearbook in his hand and turned to the page with Angela Hanson, read the entry and moved on to Roberta and Marsha. In silence, he continued glancing at students in the class of 1965 unsure of what he hoped to find.

"Have you stayed in touch with Roberta and Marsha?"

"No. We were in different states for college and later their families moved. We didn't see each other during school breaks. I don't think they were at our wedding. I can't remember."

"It happens."

"Is Vincent in this class?"

Teresa smiled. "Oh, yes. Mr. Personality."

Hajek found the page with Vincent Jenkins. "He writes a nice note to you here—'To the sweetest gal in the senior class, may we always be friends. I forgive you for seeing Mickey Mantle without me.' What's this about Mantle?"

"He liked to tease me that I was cruel not to invite him to the Yankees game. My father took me many years before I met Vincent. I was probably seven when I first saw Mickey Mantle play."

"That must have been a thrill."

"It was. Vincent regrets never seeing the slugger play."

"Did you marry right after college?"

"No. We started dating in our senior year of high school, but broke up during my senior year of college. Vincent disagreed with Americans fighting in

Vietnam. He switched his major several times to stay in school and avoid the draft."

"Why not grad school?"

"Those grad deferments ended in 1967, two years after high school. He didn't have connections to get into the National Guard."

"That saved a select few."

"My brother Douglas didn't go to college. He ended up in the army." Teresa paused and blinked. "He was killed in '68."

"I'm sorry."

"My parents and I were devastated. We hated the protesters. Vincent insisted that my brother's death was senseless. I could not accept that. It was of course, but my parents and I believed otherwise then. I stopped going out with Vincent."

"Did your father serve in World War II?"

"Yes."

"Holding onto an image of a hero is certainly more palatable than thinking any soldier's death is pointless. World War Two vets didn't realize that Vietnam was a different war."

"My father was proud of his military service. He did well after the war. As a veteran, he bought a new house in Stamford for ten thousand dollars with a government-backed mortgage. He earned four thousand a year in 1947 working at Olin Matheson. He didn't go to college. His salary provided a comfortable living for my family."

"He expected your brother to do the same."

"Right." Teresa nodded.

"Stamford must have been very different then."

"It was a small town. No big corporate headquarters. Manufacturing jobs a family could live on."

"When did you and Vincent get back together?"

"Many years later at our fifteenth year class reunion. We started dating then but we didn't marry until three years later."

"Really? Second marriage?"

"No. We both skipped the early marriage of our peers. I pursued a few different paths and Vincent studied at UCONN for years, worked as a teaching assistant, and got a PhD."

"Is he a college professor?"

"No he worked for different corporations. At the reunion I enjoyed hearing about his different jobs. He made physics interesting."

"What were you doing?"

"After college, I spent five years in the Peace Corps in Chile."

"Five years. Don't most volunteers serve two?"

"Yes. When my two years were up, I extended my stay. I loved the experience. I first worked on a water sanitation project. The people were beautiful. The last three years I worked with teachers to develop and implement an environmental curriculum for elementary schools."

"Did you teach when you returned?"

"No. I didn't have the credentials and to be honest I wasn't interested. When I got back home, I had a hard time. Trust me, culture shock is real. I felt so out of place. Dealing with people was difficult. Eventually I took a job doing routine office tasks at Xerox in Stamford. It worked for me."

"Sounds like you and Vincent were meant to be together."

"Funny you say that. At the reunion if felt like no time had passed. He was interested in my experiences and I liked his enthusiasm for a new product he invented, a smaller and more efficient diode."

"What's that?"

"An electronic component needed in cell phones and a zillion other things we can't live without."

Hajek laughed. "Good for him."

"Vincent would like to make more efficient batteries. He loves to talk about the Yankee ingenuity of 100 years ago."

"Does he still have a sense of humor?" Hajek asked.

"Oh yes, but he's much more somber since Maura's death."

"Are there any old boyfriends of yours in this class that may still be jealous?"

"Decades later. I don't think so. Besides, I didn't date much before Vincent."

Teresa picked up the yearbook and scanned several pages. "Most of these guys I wouldn't be able to name if it weren't printed under their picture. It was a long time ago."

Hajek resisted saying anything about his hunch that the murders of Maura and Courtney were the result of an old grudge. He needed to know more.

"Which guy did every girl want to date?"

"Frank Campanelli," Teresa answered without hesitation. "Hard to believe we were ever that young." She showed Frank's photo to Hajek. "A nice guy. Everyone loved Frank."

"The star football player?"

"No. We didn't emphasize sports in my high school."

"Let me have another look," Hajek said.

113

Teresa handed him the yearbook opened to the photo of Frank.

"In today's world he'd make plenty as a model." Hajek turned more pages. He stopped. "What's this?" Hajek pointed to five young men dressed in black slacks and identical red pullover sweaters. They held extra-long megaphones.

"The Bishop banned girl cheerleaders."

"Really."

"He objected to the short skirts. He had the final word."

"Imagine what he'd think about the vuvuzelas that fans blow at soccer matches today."

Teresa laughed. "Those noisy horns would be forbidden for sure."

Turning back to the yearbook, Hajek said, "Without being a jock, Frank won all the girls' hearts. That's great. And who did the girls run from when they saw him approaching at a dance?"

"I forget names but there were a couple of those." She flipped some pages. "Here's one, Keith Farley. We were not nice to him." She looked at a few more pages, smiled, and set the yearbook down.

"May I borrow this?"

"You think there's a connection with Maura and my high school?"

"I don't know. I like to research everything."

"I want it back. And promise not to show my photo to anyone."

Chapter 21

Hajek returned to the city just after six. On his desk, he found a note from Nick Kostas—*call me when you're back.* He placed the green, leather-bound yearbook on his desk. Research could wait. He called Kostas.

"You're at the precinct?"

"Just got here." Hajek turned on his computer.

"I'll be right over. Stay put."

Hajek knew Kostas wasn't looking for assistance with his police work. He was checking on how his friend was coping. Hajek rated himself a two on a scale of ten and guessed his struggle to maintain normalcy would be obvious.

He stared at his desktop screen thinking about how to learn more about the people in Teresa and Angela's high school class. Hajek hoped that his search would reveal something plausible to pursue. He could not shake his belief of a connection with the mothers' high school days.

Kostas appeared at his desk. "I'm not taking no from you tonight. Get your jacket. We're going for dinner."

"It's Friday night. Go home to your wife."

"It's Camille's idea. She told me not to ask-- just show up. Her friend Angela's visiting from San Francisco. I don't think she wants me around."

Hajek laughed and put the yearbook in his briefcase.

They walked out of the station and took a cab to their favorite Astoria restaurant, the Bohemian Beer Garden, known for great food and Czech beer. They chose an inside table. Even with patio heaters the outside temperature was cool.

An older woman with Helga on her name tag spoke with a German accent. "Good evening, gentlemen. What can I get for you?" She placed a menu in front of each man.

"Whatever beer you recommend, Peter," Nick said.

"A pitcher of Staropramen."

The waitress smiled. "Good choice. I'll be right back."

Without opening the menu Hajek said, "The sausage sampler and potato pancakes are outstanding."

"Sounds good. I'm hungry." Kostas relaxed into his seat.

"Nick, thanks for getting me here. I love this place. I may have told you that my paternal grandparents were born in the Czech Republic when it had a different name. That little country got trampled on and taken over several times. My father grew up with stories of Prague."

"Your father was born in the States, right?"

"Yes. My grandfather came to America when he was nineteen and kept up with the news of the old country. The story I most remember my father telling me, and probably anyone here that would listen, was about Reinhardt Heydrich who worked directly for Hitler. Czech and English agents assassinated him. My father believed that marked a turning point in bringing down Hitler. Anyhow he never tired of coming to this place. I can't believe he's been gone for six years."

The waitress set down chilled glasses and a full pitcher of lager. "Have you decided?"

Hajek ordered while Kostas poured the beer. Then Hajek raised his glass and with a nod made a silent toast.

Kostas put his glass down. "So if I hadn't rescued you, how late would you have stayed at your desk?"

"No telling."

116

"Hard to go home?"

"Yes." Peter looked down.

Kostas winced. "I can't imagine."

For another minute the two men sat in silence.

Hajek took a sip of his beer. "It helps to be back at work. Even though I'm nowhere with the Stover case, the guy that died at the Columbia University event."

"The one with the autopsy results that worried the medical examiner?"

"Yeah. Earlier this week I met with Mrs. Stover. She kept her three kids home from school, insisting they had colds and the school would send them home."

Kostas fingered the beer coaster. "Maybe she didn't want to be home alone."

"I'm perplexed. I expected to find an upset woman and I didn't."

"She could be in shock. When did her husband die?"

"Three weeks ago." Hajek watched musicians walk by carrying a trumpet, a trombone and a tuba to a stage.

Kostas poured more beer into their glasses. "Some people function on auto pilot for a while. And if she has children that may work for her."

"Yeah, you're probably right. She doesn't know me. Could be a private person." Hajek heard himself talking about Joan Stover and realized he behaved the same way.

Kostas nodded. "Sounds like she's managing."

Hajek made the connection that he and Joan Stover had similar methods for handling grief. He brought the conversation back to work. "I'm trying to find a link with a Connecticut murder from seven years ago and the woman murdered on the upper Eastside." He told Kostas his theory of an old grudge. With oompah-pah

117

music playing in the background, they traded work stories and discussed news events, the upcoming Five Boro Bike Ride they planned to ride in, and Nick and Camille's plans for a trip to New Mexico in June.

Around nine-thirty they headed to their homes with a promise to do this again soon.

Chapter 22

It was already light when Hajek woke, turned on the radio at his nightstand, and recognized the Saturday weekend edition program on public radio. He wondered how he would get through the day. In the past he had enjoyed a leisurely breakfast with Francine and made plans for that evening or a future day. There always seemed to be a concert, a play, a museum exhibit or a new restaurant. Now weekends presented hours of endurance. He brewed tea, toasted bread and opened a jar of peanut butter. *I'll never get over this* repeated in his mind as he ate his breakfast.

He opened Teresa's yearbook. Looking through it, he saw that most girls in the class wrote by their photo. Both Angela, Roberta and Marsha signed their lengthy notes *friends forever*. Fewer than ten boys had messages by their photos. Reading those entries, Hajek, noted '*to a sweet girl*' from Keith Farley, '*I'll never forget you*' from Harold Griffin, '*When I think of you, I'll always see the four of you in field hockey uniforms*' from Eugene Thompson, '*wishing you all the best*' from Stanley Crane, '*may every success be yours*' from Roger Bradley, and '*thanks for your help in English class*' from Brian Towle.

Maybe I'll feel less miserable if I get to work. Might as well start with what I have. Some research could be done at home. After pouring a second cup of tea, he turned on his computer and started to Google members of the Stamford Catholic High Class of 1965. He found teachers, lawyers, doctors, business owners, executives in healthcare and nonprofits, social workers, electricians, a politician and accountants.

Some names had a link to a newspaper. A *Stamford Advocate* 1979 newspaper article reported that Albert Gerber spent seven years in Canada to avoid the Vietnam War and returned after President Carter granted unconditional pardon.

He started a program to find housing and jobs for veterans in Fairfield County. The *Hartford Courant* recognized Janice Borden for her work with Habitat for Humanity. The Bridgeport Post had an article on Teresa and Vincent Jenkin's support of Catholic Charities programs in Bridgeport.

After looking for all 225 students, Hajek listed fifty-nine class members with no information; twenty-three of them were male. These men might lead him nowhere but he could not ignore them.

At the school website, Hajek found references to Stamford Catholic and two other high schools that the Diocese had consolidated into Trinity Catholic in 1991. He jotted the Director of Alumni's name and the school number in his notebook to call on Monday morning.

Pain in his shoulders caused him to look at the time, 1:37P.M. He stood and stretched. Smiling, he remembered Francine kneading his aching muscles at moments like this. Then she would talk him through a few moves she learned in yoga class. Tears welled as he found himself crossing his left arm under his right at the elbows and slowly lifting and shifting first to the left and then to the right. He repeated this with the opposite arm. *Thanks Francine. You're still taking care of me. Wish we could go to lunch together.*

Wanting a change of scenery and something more than peanut butter, he left his apartment to find lunch. He deliberately walked in the opposite direction they usually took searching for a new lunch spot. When he saw the sign for Anthony's Sports Arena he stopped.

He crossed the threshold and heard cheering on the television. Normally the noise would have sent him out the door. Not today. He sat on a bar stool. The bartender handed him a menu and took his order for a beer. Pretending to care about the game, he sat with his eyes focused on the TV screen.

The bartender placed a full beer glass in front of Hajek. "The Blue and White are hot today. Who you rooting for?"

"Neither. I mean either." He tried to see the name of the other team. "Sorry. It's not a good day."

When his sandwich arrived, the bartender made no attempt at conversation. Hajek ate, paid in cash and left.

Back on the street he walked aimlessly for forty minutes delaying his return home. When he got back to his apartment, he looked through his World War II DVD collection and pulled out *The Best Years of Our Life*. At difficult times he found solace in watching war movies. Terrible things inflicted on good people put his pain in perspective.

***

Sunday morning he woke at 7:40. The same segment of a dream had interrupted his sleep several times---he sat on a bus looking at the hooks that served as his hands. In the movie he had watched last night, a soldier faced a hard adjustment returning home. It did not matter that Peter had his health and a job he liked. Without his wife, life was lonely.

Usually he attended mass with Francine at St. Clemens's Catholic Church. Last week he could not face the people in the parish. The sad looks, kind, well-meaning greetings tore at his heart. Today he wanted to immerse himself in the comforting ritual. While having tea he decided to find a church near his mother's facility and have a meal before visiting her. A quick search gave him the address for St. Francis Catholic Church and several nearby restaurants. Two had excellent reviews. He bookmarked Evelyn's Diner. Relieved to have a plan to fill a few hours, he dressed.

Once outside the brisk air and blue sky brightened his mood. On his short cab ride he sensed the calmness of Sunday morning with quieter traffic and fewer pedestrians.

At St. Francis an usher handed him a parish bulletin. He made his way to a seat midway down the left aisle behind a family of four. Once seated, he glanced around. An elderly man sat three pews down to his left. Couples of all ages were scattered around the church. Two altar servers were lighting candles. A couple with an infant resting on the Dad's shoulder was on the far right. A girl, about three, sat cross-legged on the seat in front of him clutching a cloth kitten. Her brother, a couple years older, sat on the floor pushing a small truck along the kneeler. Being anonymous but not alone felt good.

The parish choir sang at the late morning mass. Hearing the first notes on the organ of "Be Not Afraid", he felt his body relax. The slow pace and comforting lyrics calmed him this morning as it had at other times. Participating in the traditional responses to prayers soothed his nerves. The singing of "Eagles' Wings" concluded the mass and lifted his spirits. He was smiling as he approached the priest at the front of the church who greeted parishioners as they filed by him.

Hajek walked the six blocks to the diner. The aroma of bacon and fresh baked bread greeted him. The waitress seated him by the window. As usual he began with tea. He was in no hurry. Passersby on the street and families gathered around tables provided welcome distractions. Several items on the extensive menu tempted him. He ordered pancakes, bacon and fruit.

Enjoying his food he thought about his mother. She never asked him about Francine and he did not tell her that she had died. When Francine became too ill to accompany him on visits, he worried about what to tell his mother. At first it hurt him that she never asked.

Waiting to pay the cashier, he picked up a few peppermint candies from a bowl. His mother always had them in her purse. Then he remembered she could no longer have them. Like with a small child, they posed a choking hazard for her. He dropped the mints back into the bowl. "I'd like a chocolate éclair to go," he said.

The woman smiled. "They're my favorite. You know we make them here." She handed him a bag and his change.

Believing it mattered to spend time with his mother, he felt better making his way to the Forest Hills Nursing Home. She would never remember the visit and probably no longer knew him but his presence brought her smiles and in fleeting moments she may recognize him.

Just inside the facility door, the bulletin board listed Bingo as an afternoon activity. He found his mother sitting in her wheel chair looking out her room window. He bent and kissed her. "Hi Mom." She smiled. Pointing outside, he said, "There will be flowers in bloom soon." She stared. The courtyard had a wall of ivy on a lattice structure at one end. Large containers held tulips about to burst. Hydrangea bushes and other shrubs he did not know the names of were scattered throughout the area.

Hajek opened the bag for her to peek into. She did not. Then he tore the bag showing the éclair. She gazed expressionless. Hajek broke off a piece and put it to her lips. "You'll like this."

His mother's face brightened and made a sound he convinced himself was yummmm. He waited for her to finish and then gave her another small portion. Hajek sat on the edge of her bed while his mother enjoyed her éclair bit by bit. "Mom, the choir sang beautifully this morning."

When she finished the pastry, Hajek wiped her hands and mouth and suggested they go to Bingo. Not expecting a response, he released the locks on her chair and moved it so he could walk behind. In the large activity room, three women and two men sat with cards in front of them. At the end of the table were stacks of cards, a box of red chips and a wire globe for spinning the numbers. A middle aged woman placed a handful of chips near each player. "Please take a card and come join us. We'll start in a few minutes."

Hajek selected two cards and sat next to his mother. The other five players concentrated, scanned their cards quickly and covered the called numbers all the while seeing how they fared with the competition. Hajek handed a chip to his mother and pointed to G9 for her to cover. She closed her fingers over the chip. He took another from the pile and put it in place. As the game continued his mother seemed to enjoy watching the others. She could not participate. Even when she won, she showed no reaction.

One man shook his head. "We're playing without help."

Hajek cleared the chips for the next game. "She has a lucky card today."

One woman muttered to the person next to her.

The behavior on this unit is similar to kindergarten Hajek thought. Fortunately he liked children.

After fifteen minutes, the leader announced a special game with a handmade pillow for a prize. His mother had the first Bingo again. The female resident furthest from them pointed at Hajek and yelled, "That's not fair. He helps her."

Not wanting to agitate anyone, Hajek stood. Reading the staff person's name tag he said, "Thank you, Mrs. Lawrence. My mother would prefer you give the pillow to whoever gets the next Bingo."

Chapter 23

At his desk Monday morning, Hajek looked over his research on the class of 1965. He focused on the twenty-three men with no current information. He had wanted to speak with Roberta and Marsha, Teresa's other two high school friends but did not know where they lived. Using the police database, he found arrest information on several 1965 graduates including four of the missing men. He paid particular attention to assault charges, restraining orders, and disorderly conduct. He added the criminal facts to his master list. He might get lucky and find a suspect in this group. He would give more thought about how to proceed. The list of males with no information shrunk to eleven. Then he called Brad Oster.

A pleasant female voice answered, "Trinity Catholic, how may I help you?"

Hajek hesitated and then remembered the school had changed its name. "Alumni office, please."

"One moment."

"Brad Oster."

"Mr. Oster, I'm Detective Peter Hajek with NYPD. I'm hoping you can help me with some information on individuals in the class of 1965."

"What information?"

"Addresses and phone numbers."

"Our former students' personal information is confidential. I definitely can't give you anything over the phone. I'm sure you understand I have no way of verifying that you are a police officer. Send a request on your letterhead and I'll see what I can do."

"Time is critical. I'm trying to solve a crime before the perpetrator strikes again."

"Detective, let me speak with the principal. Can you hold the line?"

"Sure."

Hajek waited. He understood today's school security issues. He heard a click and then "Detective, Principal Miller is on the phone with us."

"This is Barbara Miller. I understand from Brad that you think alumni are in danger and our information may help prevent a crime."

"That's right."

"Is there a potential threat to our current students? Do we need to take any precautionary action?"

"None of my information indicates a risk for current students."

"We'll do what we can to help. Give me your number and I'll get back to you."

"Thank you Ms. Miller. Here's the phone number for the precinct, Ask for me, Lt. Hajek in Homicide."

He continued his research. Wilcox appeared at his desk. "Peter, I have a report from CSI."

"Did they figure out the cap?"

"Yes. The letters are NRA. Nothing useful."

Hajek scowled. "I had hoped for something distinctive. Those caps are so common."

"Right. Bad break. I'll be out of the office most of today and I'll check in with you later." Wilcox left.

When Hajek's phone rang he saw it came from Connecticut.

"Detective, I'm Officer Sal Simmons with the Stamford Police Department. I review security policies and procedures at Trinity Catholic. I'd like to meet with you in person before we go any further with your request. Can you come to Stamford?"

Hajek took a deep breath. He could hardly say no. "I could be there by one this afternoon. Give me an address."

"Our department is at 805 Bedford Street in Stamford. You take Exit 8, Atlantic Street from Route 95. Atlantic becomes Bedford and we're on the right. Take my direct number."

"Thanks. See you in a few hours." Hajek gathered Teresa's yearbook, a file of papers and his laptop.

In Stamford he parked in the garage across from the Municipal Center, a six-story glass structure that included the police station. After clearing the security checkpoint, he walked over to the desk sergeant. "I'm Peter Hajek and I have an appointment with Officer Simmons."

The Sergeant called Simmons and continued scanning computer screens on his desk.

Hajek stepped aside and watched people enter the building, keeping an eye on the doorway that led to the inner chambers.

A uniformed officer who looked about forty entered the lobby. He had a medium build, about 5'10" with a clean shaven head. "Detective Hajek?"

Hajek extended his hand and showed his badge. "Thank you for giving me some time on such short notice."

"Glad to. Hope I can help." Simmons led the way from the lobby. "Are you a Yankee fan?"

"Yes." Hajek swallowed unable to say more.

"This season I plan on seeing a couple of games. I need to check out that new stadium. Have you been?"

"I like the old one better but everyone raves about the food and comfortable seats. My father took me as a kid and I have nice memories of the original. That's me. I'm sure you'll like the new one." Hajek repressed mentioning that he had season box seats because Francine had worked for the Yankees.

At Simmons' work area he pointed to a chair next to his desk for Hajek and then he sat. "What's the story?"

"Early April, I was assigned a murder case in Manhattan. During my investigation I found similarities with a Bethel murder of seven years ago. The mothers of both victims were in the class of 1965. They were friends."

Hajek handed Simmons the yearbook. Using the tabs stuck on pages he opened to the pictures of Teresa and Angela. "Both of them had a daughter murdered?"

"Yes."

"What do you want from the alumni office?"

"Up-to-date information on members of the class of 1965."

"You think that may help capture a killer."

"It's worth a try."

"Let me call the school and tell Brad Oster to expect us."

When they arrived in the Alumni office, Simmons handled the introductions.

Oster positioned his computer screen at an angle. "I have the 1965 class list in front of me. What do you need?"

From his folder Hajek pulled a spreadsheet and placed it on the desk. "I have gathered what I can on the students in this class. I'm most interested in these eleven males. Pointing at his spreadsheet he asked, "Can you tell me what you know about these men?"

Oster looked at the names and checked his data. "Two are deceased."

"Are the dates noted on your list?"

"Yes."

"It would help me to have this information. Can I have a copy?"

Oster looked at Simmons who nodded.

"Give me your email address, Detective."

Hajek handed Oster his card with his email address. "Please tell me what you have on the others."

"It looks like many never responded to requests for updates. Mailings to the last known residence were returned with no forwarding address or never answered," Oster said.

"Any idea who might have information about the students we have nothing on?" Hajek leaned back and stretched his shoulders.

"Sister Dolores Healy might. She taught them math when they were freshmen. It was her first year teaching. In the yearbook her name is Sister Herman Gregory but for decades now she uses her birth name, Dolores Healy."

"She'd be old," Hajek said. "I was thinking more of a class member. You know someone in the class who keeps up with everyone. In my high school class it's Leslie Garden."

"Sister is very sharp. Students and parents both liked Sister Dolores and still keep in touch. She lives in a convent in Westchester."

"Do you have her address and phone number?" Hajek asked.

Oster switched screens. "Here it is."

Hajek wrote down the address and added Sister Dolores to his list of people to interview. "Brad, I really appreciate your help."

"I want to hear your take on Sister Dolores. Please call me after you meet her."

"Deal."

Chapter 24

Driving back to his precinct, Hajek reflected on Simmons' encouraging comments. He accepted the possibility that the killer sought to settle an old score. Hajek planned to speak with Teresa's two friends and probe their memories. Oster's information included an address and number for Roberta Barlow Cronin. Phoning her might lead him to Marsha Flynn. Maybe one of them could remember an incident with a boy in their class.

Back at his desk, he consolidated his data with Oster's into one spreadsheet. He noted the time, 2:20. He should stop for lunch but raring to push on, he called Roberta Cronin, identified himself as a NYC detective, and explained that he was talking with graduates of Stamford Catholic High class of 1965 about a couple of his cases.

"I've been in Illinois for decades. Why would you think I could help? It's been years since I've been in New York."

"I'm following up on the possibility of a connection with someone in your class. I recently spoke with Teresa Jenkins and understand you two were friends."

"Yes, we were. I'm sorry I lost touch with Teresa."

"Can I ask you some questions about classmates?"

"Okay."

"I have a list of nine men I'd like to know more about. Please tell me if you know anything about any of them."

"Go ahead."

To each name, Roberta replied, "No, I don't know anything."

"Thanks."

"Sorry, Detective. High school was a long time ago. I only kept up with a few girlfriends."

"Please tell me about your family."

"I met my husband, Eric, in college and we've lived in the Chicago area since we married."

"What's his work?"

"He's a manufacturing rep for a restaurant supplier."

"Do you have children?"

Hajek heard what sounded like Roberta gulping air.

"I have two sons and a daughter. I had two daughters. One died."

Hajek tensed. "I have to ask how."

"Olivia was murdered last year."

Roberta's words were barely audible. She cried quietly.

"This is difficult, but can you tell was she shot?"

Roberta's almost imperceptible *she was strangled* chilled him.

"I'm sorry to cause you pain. What was the date of her death?"

"July 8," Roberta sobbed.

"Was that your birthday?"

"Yes but how did you know that?"

"It seems to be a pattern. Where did Olivia live?"

"About twenty miles from here. She had an apartment in Western Springs."

"Is that where she was killed?"

"Yes."

"Anyone apprehended?"

"No."

"Have you stayed in contact with Marsha Flynn?"

131

"We did for many years but not recently. The last time I called, a message said her number was disconnected. Figured I'd hear from her eventually but I haven't."

"When was that?"

"Maybe three years ago. I'm not sure."

"Do you have an address?"

"Yes. Just a minute."

Roberta returned to the phone. "Marsha lived at 5 West Ferry Street in Buffalo, New York."

Hajek wrote in his notepad. "Any idea how long she lived in Buffalo?"

"Years. When she was first married she lived in Pennsylvania. That marriage didn't last long. Then she married Philip and they moved to Buffalo for his job. He taught and coached at a high school there. Still does as far as I know. Both their children stayed in the area. At least that was true the last I knew."

"Do you know the name of her first husband?"

"Stephen Dodson."

"What's Marsha's last name now?"

"Rubino."

"Do you know the names and ages of her children?"

"Tabitha would be about forty and Phillip Jr. three or four years younger."

"And as far as you know Marsha's still married?"

"No. She and Phillip divorced many years ago. I can't remember exactly."

"I won't take any more of your time. Thank you for speaking with me."

Hajek stood and stretched still thinking about his phone call with Roberta. He probably should have told her about Teresa's daughter. The similarities in

Olivia's death in Illinois told him that murder must be linked to the ones in Connecticut and New York City. Hajek called Wilcox.

"What's up, Peter?"

"I just spoke with Roberta Cronin in Illinois. She was a classmate of Angela Hanson. Her daughter was strangled in her apartment last year. The killer has not been apprehended."

"You think it's the same guy?"

"I do."

"I'll alert the Bureau."

"Thanks."

First he needed food. He made his way to the street and walked several blocks to Lenny's. The cool air felt refreshing and he quickened his pace. As Hajek entered the deli, the aromas of tomato sauce and baked bread let him know he waited too long to eat. After glancing at the overhead menu board, he ordered the daily special to go. In less than five minutes he was back on the street retracing his steps to the precinct.

At his desk he removed the cover from an aluminum container, put a spoon in a paper cup of soup, and tossed packets of oyster crackers on his desk,

An officer walked by. "Lunch or dinner?"

"Late lunch."

"Enjoy."

His brief walk outside failed to dispel the anxiety his call with Roberta caused. Learning of another unsolved murder alarmed him and required time-consuming investigation. As he ate his soup and moussaka, he thought about the fourth friend in Buffalo. He needed to know more.

Hajek searched the Internet for Marsha Rubino. He found her obituary in a Buffalo paper, December two years ago. Scanning for cause of death, he read 'after a brief illness'. Survivors included a former husband and a son Philip Jr. Then he read *predeceased by a daughter, Tabitha*.

The next hit brought him to a Buffalo news article stating that Tabitha Rubino was found dead in her home. No details, a usual statement about police investigating. In her obituary he saw that her survivors included both parents and a brother. Hajek weighed the merits of which one to call first, the son or the father. Uncertain, he postponed his decision and took another bite of his now lukewarm eggplant dish. Looking back at Marsha's obituary he saw that her birthday matched the date of Tabitha's murder.

***

Hajek concluded he should first learn what he could from the Buffalo Police. He called, identified himself, and asked to speak with the Buffalo detective assigned to the Rubino murder. After some searching, the desk sergeant identified Detective Bill Pike as the lead and connected Hajek with him.

Pike believed some 'john' got rough with her and she ended up dead. Without evidence of a break-in, he assumed that Tabitha knew her killer. Pike had no comparable cases and no leads. More than once the Buffalo officer made a derogatory comment about her neighborhood and implied that Tabitha was a prostitute.

"I'm not surprised anymore at who works the streets," Pike said. "The area where she lived is notorious. If I remember correctly there was no forced entry to her apartment."

In response to Hajek asking what he learned from neighbors, Pike barely concealed a snicker. "The people in her building aren't the most reliable witnesses. No one knew anything."

"Do you know if she had a job?" Hajek asked.

"No. But I doubt it. I'd have to check the file."

Hajek guessed that the police made no effort to find out if she worked. "Was Tabitha strangled with a rope?"

"Could've been. A rope, a scarf, electric cord…I don't remember. I don't have the details in front of me," Pike said.

"I'll need to know if the killer used a rope."

"Tell me what connection you think this murder has with New York City." Pike sounded more interested.

Hajek struggled to contain his anger. "Three mothers have murdered daughters. All in different cities. All three were friends with Tabitha's mother at one time. Learning someone killed her daughter is too much of a coincidence to discard."

"From what you say we may need to take another look at Tabitha's murder."

"Please fax me a copy of the autopsy report and photos of the crime scene and photos of the physical evidence, especially a rope," Hajek asked.

"Will do. And send me your stuff."

They exchanged phone numbers, email addresses, and concluded the call.

When Hajek slammed the receiver down, he yelled "BASTARD!"

He located a phone number for Philip Rubino Jr. He called, listened to the start of a message, and hung up. Deciding to wait until evening to call Rubino, Hajek picked up his file on Stover.

Maybe the medical examiner overreacted to the autopsy results and sounded an unwarranted alarm. Possibly the Stover case was not a crime. Food poisoning can cause accidental death. He searched news reports of food poisoning, toxins, and common ways to contaminate food. For the next few hours his scattered approach yielded no new information.

At 7:20 P.M., he called Rubino in Buffalo.

135

"Hello," a man's voice barked, TV blaring in the background.

"Are you Philip Rubino?"

"Yes."

"I'm Peter Hajek, a New York City detective. Do you have a few moments to speak with me?"

"About what?"

"I'm investigating a New York City murder that I thought your mother might have some relevant information about. In looking for her, I'm sorry to find that she died."

The noise stopped. "What would my mother know about a New York City murder? She hadn't been there in decades."

"A former classmate of hers is the victim's mother. Your mother hung out in high school with Angela, Roberta and Teresa, right?"

"I remember Mom mentioning a Roberta. The other two aren't familiar," Philip said.

"Someone, and I'm now thinking it's the same person, murdered Roberta's daughter less than a year after Tabitha."

"My mother's friend Roberta had a daughter murdered?"

"Yes. I think I'm dealing with the same killer. Tell me about your sister."

"I still can't believe someone murdered Tabitha. She was a sweet person."

"I've contacted the Buffalo police and asked for information."

"They're useless."

"How so?"

"The police never did look for her killer." Hajek heard the disgust in Philip's voice. "At first I showed up at the police station every few days for updates on their progress. Once I realized they really weren't investigating, I

136

stopped. My sister lived in a tough part of town. That's how you're treated when you're poor."

"Tell me what you know. Start with how you learned of Tabitha's death."

"My sister and I planned to meet at my mother's place and have birthday cake. When Tabitha didn't show up at our mother's or answer her phone, I went to her place." Slowly Philip summarized finding his sister dead in her home, calling police, their insisting that she knew her attacker, and the days of frustration that followed.

Hajek scribbled some notes. "Your mother's death three months after your sister's murder had to be hard."

"Yeah."

"Your mother's obituary mentioned a brief illness. What was it?"

"Alcoholism."

Hajek winced. "I'm sorry."

"After my sister died, my mother never had a sober day. I can't remember how many trips she made to the ER in her last two months." Philip paused. "Six days after my sister's funeral, my mother broke her right arm. Three weeks later, she shattered her knee, requiring surgery. She drank too much for years but..." He didn't finish the sentence.

"I'm sorry."

"I hope you get the bastard."

"Did your sister have a job?"

"Yes, at Target."

"Did she ever mention anyone bothering her?"

"No."

"Can you think of anyone who would want to harm her?"

"No. I assumed she surprised a burglar."

137

"Do you know how she was killed?"

"Some monster strangled her."

"With what?"

"Probably his hands. I don't know."

"I'd like to speak with your father."

"Why?"

"Talking with relatives may help me fill in the gaps. You never know."

"I'll give you his work number. That's the best place to reach him. His home's chaotic."

"Do you think he'll speak with me?"

"Yeah, especially if he thinks you might help find my sister's killer. They were close. My father feels bad about what happened to our family…the divorce and all…He tried to get treatment for my mother but she refused. I don't blame him for walking away after we were grown."

Hajek wrote down the number for Philip, Sr. "Philip, I'll get back to you if I learn anything more. Can I call you at work?"

"No, I can't talk on the job. This number in the evening is best," Philip said.

"What do you do?"

"I work at Milkbone.

"Like dog biscuits?"

"Yes. I operate a forklift and move pallets stacked with dog food from warehouse to the shipping dock."

"Philip, thanks for speaking with me. When I have more information, I'll get back to you. Here's my number if you think of anything else."

Chapter 25

The next morning while Captain Henry Wilcox enjoyed a coffee and donut, Hajek walked into his office to bring him up to date.

"Captain, I found another murder similar to the Hanson murder. This one was in Buffalo two years ago. I spoke with the victim's brother last evening."

"Strangled by rope and the victim's mother was a high school friend of the other three mothers?"

"Right. Four victims in three states and they are all daughters of women who were friends in high school. All killed on their mother's birthdays."

Wilcox stopped eating. "You're sure the mothers of both these new victims were friends?"

"Yes. And friends of Angela Hanson and Teresa Jenkins."

"What next?"

"I've requested the records from the Buffalo and Illinois cases. Something in those records might provide a lead that will help with the Hanson case."

Wilcox sipped his coffee. "I'll update the Commissioner. The mayor calls him each day about the Courtney Hanson murder asking when we'll apprehend this guy. I've informed the FBI about the Illinois murder and they told me they've assigned agents to check out the possibility of other murders. They will investigate all female students in the classes of 1964-1966 to see if other women had daughters murdered."

***

Later that afternoon a phone call from police computer specialist, Russ Gibbs, interrupted Hajek going through his notes. "We got into Stover's files, accessed his emails for the last six months. We can go back further if necessary."

"That's great," Hajek said. "Anything financial?"

"Oh yeah, investment accounts, checking and credit cards. What you *really* need to see is the porn."

"I'm on my way."

Hajek grabbed a cab outside his precinct. As he rode south along the Hudson on the West Side Highway to the NYPD headquarters in lower Manhattan, he hoped this new information might point to someone with a motive to kill Stover.

At City Hall he showed his badge at the front desk, and asked for Russ Gibbs. It had been a while since he visited this location for assistance with an investigation.

The stairs to the second floor led to a maze of desks. He stopped at the first one and asked for Gibbs.

"Over here, Detective." A tall, slender man dressed in black pants and a black shirt waved from across the room.

"Gibbs, I'm Peter Hajek. Thanks for your call."

"You figure Stover was murdered?"

"Not sure if someone killed him or if he died from bad food. So far, I've got no leads. I hope you'll help."

Gibbs pointed to a chair. "This guy's a sicko. Take a look."

Hajek sat next to Russ in front of multiple monitors and scanned the list of Stover emails on one. "My father's air traffic control station looked simpler than this setup."

"Stover's computer had multiple layers of security and a separate password protecting these files." Gibbs opened another file. Photos of young girls, no more than ten years old, many closer to five, engaged in various sexual acts flashed on the screen.

After a few moments, Hajek said, "He has three daughters."

"That's not good." Gibbs closed the photo page. "I figured him for a loner, someone socially inept."

"Married, nice family, big job. Can you trace the source of these?" Hajek ran his finger through his hair.

"Sure. Probably an overseas site," Gibbs said.

"It's a crime to download them. Not that anyone can arrest him. See if he forwarded them."

"Will do. I downloaded a copy of Stover's files on this desktop. You can browse 'em. I'll use another computer across the room." Gibbs walked away.

Hajek searched for clues of personal threats, financial troubles and recent changes in Stover's mental status. He read emails to Stover's pastor and other committee members about a church project. A few messages to classmates from Columbia were business related. No one showed up as a close friend. He did not make golf dates, exchange day-to-day events or share ideas on politics with anyone. Stover's recent searches related to college basketball and old Disney artwork. At eBay, the day before he died, he bid on an early animation drawing of Snow White and the Seven Dwarfs. He used several aliases when he chatted online at known pedophile sites.

Computer activity ended the evening before Stover's death. Hajek detected no difference in frequency or tone of messages in the days leading up to his death. No one threatened to blackmail him.

The financial information proved Stover did not have money problems. He owned his house. There was no evidence that he gambled or dealt with loan sharks. His investment accounts showed balances totaling 1.7 million dollars. Gibbs had accessed Stover's credit card records. Nothing in the statements caused

Hajek to think Stover had a mistress on the side. He did have multiple payments to AX Dreams for hundreds of photographs.

Gibbs returned. "The website appears to be in Cambodia."

"Your department can follow up with that. Stover isn't the only person paying for this porn."

"I've added the site to our database," Gibbs said.

"Can you list each time someone accessed this computer for the last month?"

"Sure."

"I'd like the timeline for computer use and credit card information and emails on a flashdrive."

"Okay but you'll need to sign for that."

Gibbs downloaded Hajek's requests and obtained his signature.

"Impressive work Gibbs. You guys are the best. If I think of anything else I need, I'll let you know."

"Fine. Happy to help out." Gibbs handed Hajek a flashdrive.

He pocketed it. "Thanks, Gibbs."

Chapter 26

On the street outside City Hall, exhaust fumes burned the inside of Hajek's nostrils. Maneuvering away from the wind's direct path, he regretted pinning his hope on Stover's computer files. The unexpected findings gave no leads. When Wilcox handed him this case he referred to it as a simple case. Stover's death baffled Hajek.

After walking ten minutes, he made High Line Park his destination, and continued north on Sixth Avenue for several more city blocks before turning west. At Gansevoort Street, he climbed the stairs to the former elevated railroad that had served lower Westside businesses for decades. Above the traffic, a paved railroad bed created a walkway that wound between grassland and wildflowers. The height offered views of the Hudson River. After a few blocks he stopped at the Taco Truck kiosk and ordered a water and a braised beef taco with guacamole. Sitting on a bench, he ate his lunch. In this oasis, Hajek contemplated how to tell Joan Stover about the child pornography on her husband's computer. He did not look forward to raising the question of possible molestation of her daughters.

At west 20th street, he exited the park, hailed a cab, and returned to the precinct. Walking to his desk, he acknowledged officers with a passing wave or nod. Remembering Stover's young girls, Hajek kept thinking about the sickening porn. He pulled a photo of Francine from a drawer. This is one of those cases you would not want to know about.

The front desk sergeant rang Hajek's extension. "Good, you're in. A lawyer with the DOJ is on the line for you."

Hajek frowned. "Put it through."

143

"Detective Hajek, I'm Attorney Alex Dawson with the Department of Justice. I need to meet with you about the Grant Tomb case. Can I come by tomorrow morning at ten?"

"I'll be here." Hajek put his wife's photo back in his desk.

"Your testimony will help convict this guy. He makes a great example. So far we have at least thirty-one charges against him including attempting an act of terrorism, using a weapon of mass destruction, transporting an explosive device, using and carrying a destructive device, attempting to kill and maim people, and attempting to damage a building, vehicles and other property. Several carry potential lifetime incarceration. Forensics is still examining all the evidence."

"Sounds extreme to me. He's no Bin Laden." Hajek drummed his fingers on his desk.

"We pursue all terrorists."

An overzealous descendent of a Confederate general deserved punishment for setting off an explosive at a national monument but not three dozen federal charges. Dawson had skewed priorities.

"See you at ten tomorrow." Hajek ended the call and sat at his desk thinking that the feds had plenty of dangerous criminals to pursue. Hajek walked to Captain Wilcox's office to relay the news of the DOJ visit.

"Please tell me that you got the Hanson killer?" Wilcox asked when Hajek appeared at his door.

"I wish. It's about General Grant."

Wilcox sighed. "Oh. I hope you're not looking into his death."

Hajek laughed. "A DOJ lawyer Dawson will be here tomorrow about the Grant Tomb incident."

"What time?"

"Ten."

"I'll be available. We'll use my office."

"He mentioned thirty-one charges," Hajek snorted. "He sounded as proud as a new father."

"We want to cooperate. It's good to remind the feds of the fine work you did in this major case. Makes the whole department look good." Wilcox smiled.

***

The next day, wearing a dark suit, white shirt and striped tie, Dawson greeted Hajek exactly at ten. "Pleased to meet you, Detective. Congratulations on bringing in Gordon."

"Thanks." Taken aback by how young the lawyer appeared, Hajek asked, "How long have you been with the Department of Justice?"

"Eleven months."

"Where did you practice law before?"

"First job since I graduated from Harvard Law. Lucky break."

"Yeah." Hajek resisted saying anything about the value of experience in the real world. "We'll meet in Captain Wilcox's office." Hajek led the way.

Wilcox stood and greeted Dawson. "Pleased to assist any way we can. How about some coffee?"

"No thanks. I'm good. I'd like to start by reviewing the facts of the case." Still standing Dawson removed a file from his attaché case and handed Wilcox and Hajek each seven pages listing potential charges against John B. Gordon. "This is what we've compiled. There may be more. We're ready to indict him on these soon and the grand jury may add more."

Hajek set the typed pages on his lap. "You know this fella is not with al-Qaida, right?"

Dawson sat down. "We do not tolerate terrorists."

145

Hajek clenched his jaw. "No one got hurt. Gordon made a large firecracker and set it off in the early morning with no one near the monument. He didn't try to injure anyone."

Wilcox gave Hajek a 'keep a lid on' look.

"An attempt to blow up a federal monument is a serious crime," Dawson said. "He may be part of a larger conspiracy."

"He acted alone. He used a primitive device. He had no other explosives. He didn't even have a gun."

Wilcox looked sternly at Hajek. "We don't know his intentions."

"Exactly. Or what other targets he intended to hit," Dawson said.

Hajek waved the list of charges. "I believe in justice but this is over the top. A misuse of resources."

"The worse he's portrayed the better all of us in law enforcement look." Dawson straightened in his chair.

"That's a valid point," Wilcox said.

"We're counting on your testimony, Detective Hajek."

"You can count on me to tell the truth on the stand." Hajek's annoyance with Dawson increased. "A reasonable sentence is a couple of years in jail. Let DOJ focus on real terrorists."

"Gordon broke federal laws. I'll review our meeting with my supervisor and get back to you about your testimony, Detective Hajek."

Wilcox stood and extended his hand. "Please keep me posted on the progress of this case. Thanks for stopping by."

Dawson exited and Hajek stood to leave.

"Peter, wait." Wilcox closed the door and turned to Hajek. "What are you doing arguing with this guy? Let DOJ do whatever they want with Gordon. I need you to stay focused on the Hanson case."

146

"Dawson's inflating his ego. More than a two-year sentence for Gordon is excessive."

"This is good for the department. I can't have you taking personal offense with Dawson."

"DOJ is wasting time and money. It infuriates me. Didn't they learn anything from the Martha Stewart debacle? No one went to jail for the bank fraud that caused the great recession."

"Where are you with the Hanson case?"

"I'm working a lead. And there may be a break in the Stover case." Hajek told Wilcox about Stover's computer and his hope that his next interview with Joan Stover might lead to identifying a suspect with a motive to kill Stover.

Chapter 27

At eleven, Hajek left for his afternoon appointment in Westchester. Happy to be out of the office, he joined men in suits and well-dressed women wearing sneakers on the street. In snippets of conversation he heard about a Wynton Marsalis concert at Lincoln Center and a Dancing with the Stars participant whose name meant nothing to him. Enjoying his eavesdropping, Hajek continued another ten blocks before descending into a subway station. The train's deafening sound shut out all conversation.

At Grand Central Terminal, the aroma of fresh baked bread drew him to Zaro's. Standing in line he watched the overhead board and noted the train to New Rochelle would leave in ten minutes from Gate Eighteen. With tuna salad on a croissant and a bottle of water Hajek made his way to the Metro North platform. He easily found a seat in a half-empty car.

On the thirty-minute train ride to New Rochelle, Hajek thought about the nine men in the class of 1965 that eluded him. He knew nothing about their occupations, marital status or residences. Being anonymous did not make one a criminal but he could not shake his belief that a man on this short list killed the young women.

From the train station, Hajek walked to The Convent of Holy Faith on Locust Avenue and rang the bell. An elderly woman opened the heavy wooden door. She wore sturdy black shoes that added two inches to her five-foot stature. A large silver cross hung from a thick chain at the neck of her dark print dress.

"I'm Peter Hajek. I have an appointment with Sister Dolores Healy."

"Please come in. I'll let Sister Dolores know you're here."

"Thank you." Hajek closed the door behind him.

The nun shuffled more than walked, leading him to what would have been a parlor of an earlier era. "Please wait here, Mr. Hajek, while I find Sister Dolores."

He sat in an upholstered wingback chair. Across the room a couch with a curved-back looked scratchy and lumpy. Other furnishings included a ladder back chair, antique lamps on heavy wooden tables and a well-worn rug. The ornate mirror hanging over the fireplace mantle looked like it had been there for decades. At one time it probably reflected grand gatherings. Today, with the uncomfortable furniture and heavy velvet drapes, he doubted the room saw much activity. Hajek wondered how many lived in this former single family residence.

A woman with short gray hair wearing black slacks and a royal blue sweater entered. The energy in her step hinted at someone much younger. Her skin could advertise a beauty product for aging without wrinkles.

Hajek stood. "Good afternoon, Sister Dolores. Thank you for agreeing to meet with me."

The nun scrutinized his face. "You didn't go to Stamford Catholic High, did you?"

"No, I grew up in New York City."

"If you don't mind, I'd like to meet in our kitchen and have some tea. Or coffee if you prefer."

Hajek smiled. "I'd love some tea."

They walked to the back of the house. A kettle simmered on the stove. Cups, saucers, spoons, a strainer, small plates and a basket of scones sat on a tray next to the stove. A round table in front of a large window caught the afternoon sun.

"Have a seat, Detective."

"May I move the tray for you?"

"Yes, thank you. I'll fix the tea. Black okay?"

"My favorite." He placed the items from the tray onto the table and returned it to the counter.

Sister Dolores spooned loose tea into a pot and poured boiling water over it. She placed it on a trivet in the middle of the table. "It will be a few minutes. When you called to make an appointment, you surprised me. I had no idea how I could help a detective but I'll certainly try."

"As I said, a case I'm working on may have a connection to graduates of Stamford Catholic High. Brad Oster suggested you might have information useful to me."

"Brad's a nice man. His class was the last one I taught." Sister Dolores sighed.

"Tell me about your time at Stamford Catholic High."

She informed Hajek that the diocese built the high school and many other schools during a population explosion in Fairfield County in the late 1950s and early 1960s. Stamford Catholic High was her first and only teaching assignment. She stayed more than thirty years.

"I loved my job." Her face brightened.

"Brad tells me you hear from many former students. I'd like to ask about some in the class of 1965."

She laughed. "That will test my memory."

"Do you remember Teresa Collins?"

"No, can't say I remember any Teresa."

"How about Vincent Jenkins?"

"Maybe. I remember a Vincent from my early years. He wasn't a serious student. I didn't think he was very smart. At graduation he caused a big fuss, landing several scholarships to good universities and some national awards in science."

"That's him."

"What happened to him?" Sister asked.

"He invented a better diode."

She chuckled. "Whatever that is. I think this is ready." She placed a strainer over Hajek's cup and poured.

"Looks good and smells delicious."

"Have a scone."

"Blueberry is too tempting to resist." Hajek put one on his plate.

"So Vincent had a brain. I'm happy to hear he made use of it." Sister poured cream into her tea.

"Did you know that someone murdered Teresa and Vincent's daughter in Bethel, Connecticut seven years ago?"

"Goodness no. How awful. I read the in memoriam notices in the alumni news. Usually it lists parents of alumni. It saddens me to learn a former student's child died. No, I don't recall that girl's death."

"My current case is the murder of a young woman in Manhattan. Her mother Angela Hanson—Jurczyk was her maiden name—graduated in 1965," Hajek said.

"That's terrible. And you think they're connected?"

"Yes."

Hajek asked about former students, Roberta Barlow and Marsha Flynn, but Sister Dolores did not remember either. "Did something happen to them?"

"Their daughters were also murdered."

Her hand shook as she returned her cup to the saucer. "Detective, you must find the killer."

151

I'm tracking down all in the class. "Do you remember anything about these students?" Hajek handed her an index card with nine names.

"Eugene Thompson and Harold Griffin…for sure…the others…I'm sorry I can't recall." Sister Dolores continued to look at the list.

Tell me about Thompson and Griffin."

"Both their mothers were friends of the convent. We relied on Ursula and Louise. They drove us to medical appointments, brought us baked goods and flowers from their gardens, and sometimes treated us to a movie. When their sons went to Vietnam they were sick with worry. That I clearly remember. All of us in the convent prayed for those boys."

"And did the mothers stay in touch with you after the war?"

"Oh yes. Ursula Griffin and I became great friends. She often stopped at school in the afternoon to see me. Sometimes she called the convent to chat. After I moved here, Ursula visited several times. Louise Thompson moved to Maryland and dropped me a note from time to time."

"Did they keep you up to date on their sons?"

"Yes. When Eugene Thompson came home from Vietnam, his heavy drinking upset his mother. Not too long after he returned, his father took a job in Maryland and the family left Connecticut."

"How's Eugene today?"

"He's back in Connecticut. I think he's doing all right."

"Stamford?"

"No, Norwalk. Louise told me she really likes the woman Eugene married. I can't remember her first name. But I know her last name was Larsen. I have relatives with that name so it stuck with me. The Larsen girl's father had a roofing business and I believe Eugene manages it."

"Amazing memory, Sister. I'm impressed."

152

"Louise is back in Connecticut. She returned when her husband died. Her health is not too good. I still get a Christmas card from her. Most likely someone in her family sends it for her."

"And Harold Griffin?" Hajek asked.

"Ursula always said her son was never the same after the war."

"Did he have a drug or alcohol problem?"

"I don't think so. He just never seemed to find his way. His father had a good job and provided well for his wife and son. Unfortunately he died young…a heart attack. I think Harold was only nineteen. He continued to live at home with his mother and without his father's income they struggled."

"Where was home?" Hajek asked.

"In Stamford…Faucett Street, number 9, I think. The neighborhood has changed in recent years. I remember Ursula complaining about condos. It had been a street of single family homes built in the 1930's."

"What work did Harold do?"

"He operated a machine at one of the Stamford area manufacturers for years…Electrolux or Pitney Bowes… I'm not sure which. Both closed a while back. Then he had different jobs…nothing special."

"When did you last speak with Mrs. Griffin?"

"It's been years. Ursula died five years ago, maybe six. She was very sick for the last three years of her life."

"I've taken enough of your time. Thanks for the kind hospitality."

As they walked to the front door, she said, "I don't like hearing that a graduate of Stamford Catholic High may be involved in a serious crime. I'll pray for the Lord to assist you with your work."

153

Chapter 28

On his return ride to Manhattan, he wrote all he recalled of his conversation with Sister Dolores. Remembering her comment on evil he wondered what she thought of all the clergy that had abused children or stole from their parishes. Most people found that behavior inconceivable. Entering the underground section of Grand Central, he put his notebook in his pocket. When the train doors squealed open, Hajek stepped onto the platform and coughed as gusts of stifling hot air swirled. He picked up his pace to get beyond the stink of rotting garbage, rodents, and musty air emanating from the lower depths of the terminal. With foul odor still in his nostrils, he exited onto 42nd Street.

Hajek walked west to Times Square and caught the redline subway north. Back at his desk, he scanned his notes and turned on his computer. He looked up roofing companies in Fairfield County, Connecticut and found the address for Larsen's roofing on Water Street in South Norwalk. He tried unsuccessfully to find a home address for Eugene Thompson. His next search, a phone listing for Ursula or Harold Griffin in Stamford, generated nothing.

Hajek thought about how to best approach these men. He had no grounds to question them. Captain Wilcox would balk at involving Stamford and Norwalk police. These individuals were two men that Hajek wanted to meet to satisfy his curiosity and eliminate them as possible suspects. They lived in towns near Joan Stover's Westport home. He needed to interview her again and could combine those interviews in Norwalk and Stamford.

Preferring to stay with the Hanson case, he called Teresa Jenkins to schedule a time to return her yearbook and to elicit any new information about the men that remained on his 'persons of interest' list. They agreed on eleven the next morning.

Driving to Connecticut, he reflected on Thompson and Griffin's yearbook messages to Teresa. Penned so long ago how could those words have any significance today? Still he pondered *foursome… never forget you* …and kept trying to interpret. Today's task took him out on a limb. His captain would not approve of his interviewing two men outside NYPD's jurisdiction.

At Teresa's home, Hajek asked her to look again at pictures of the nine boys who had written notes in her yearbook. She could not recall anything.

"You really think a high school classmate of mine killed Maura?" Teresa looked up from the yearbook.

"It's a possibility."

"If I angered a boy in my high school class…" She shook her head. "Fifty years is a long time…Seems to me he'd have tried to harm me years ago."

"Resentment can fester. Some people never get over mistreatment, real or perceived."

Accepting that Teresa had nothing to add, Hajek asked about her husband and daughter.

"In our last conversation Kaitlin said work is overrated and she doubts she can do fifty plus hours a week for the next thirty years." Teresa laughed.

"The pain of realizing college is over." Hajek pushed his chair back.

"I miss her being close enough to go to our Berkshire home with Vincent and me."

"Berkshire?"

"The mountains in western Massachusetts. Have you never been?"

"No. My family camped in the Adirondack Mountains."

"It's rural and lovely. The area is most known for Tanglewood, the summer home of the Boston Symphony Orchestra. We picnic on the lawn...the setting is beautiful. We usually go to the James Taylor concert in July."

"My mother liked him, but she loved Carole King." Hajek smiled remembering how often his mother played the *Tapestry* album.

"How is your mother?"

"Same. I tell myself she knows me when I visit. She doesn't say much, just smiles. I do all the talking. It's hard but comforting that she appears content. Do you go to your mountain home often?"

"We're going next week. Vincent's most relaxed there. One of our favorite things to do is to hike segments of the Appalachian Trail. I haven't given up asking him to meet you."

"Don't pressure him. I understand his reluctance."

"Can I fix you lunch?" Teresa asked.

Hajek hesitated. Teresa's inquiry about his mother engendered a fondness for her and reminded him how much he missed simple meals and real conversation with his mother. Teresa seemed to understand the enormity of his losses-- Francine's death and his mother's dementia. Hajek was relieved that Teresa did not ask how he was coping without his wife. About his mother's age, Teresa was easy to be with and he wanted to stay. He paused before saying, "No thank you, I have more appointments. I need to go." Her thoughtfulness and lack of bitterness impressed him. He left promising to keep her updated.

As they walked to the front door, Teresa picked up *Five Star Fraud*. "My group meets next week. I'm looking forward to our discussion. We can all relate to inept federal regulators and corporations beating up little guys. You're probably not a fiction reader, Detective, but I bet you'd enjoy this story."

"What city's on the cover?"

"Charlotte. I suggested the book to Kaitlin. The story takes place in North Carolina and Connecticut."

Chapter 29

After driving six miles south on I95 to Exit 15 for South Norwalk, Hajek made his way to Water Street. Before walking into Larsen Roofing, he strolled along the edge of the parking lot and took in the pleasant scene of sun sparkling on the water amidst moored boats and a nearby oyster processing plant. He inhaled the fishy smell.

Wondering how Thompson would respond to his unannounced visit, he opened the door.

A woman looked up from a desk next to the office entrance. "Can I help you?"

"I'd like to speak with Eugene Thompson."

"May I tell him who's calling?"

"Peter Hajek, NYPD."

"I'll tell him." She kept her eyes down, her face expressionless as she called her boss and told him he had a visitor.

"He'll be right out." She resumed working.

A man with wisps of gray hair on his head opened a door to the left of the receptionist. He wore a denim shirt with the company logo on a pocket.

"Mr. Thompson, I'm Peter Hajek with NYPD." He showed his badge.

"We can talk in my office." He led Hajek through shelves of supplies into a glass walled office. One corner of a green blotter stuck out beneath piles of papers and stacked folders. Thompson sat on a wooden chair and rolled up to his desk. Hajek took the white molded resin chair just inside the door.

"I had a hard time finding you, Mr. Thompson. I would have contacted you at home." Hajek placed his hands on his knees.

"When you own a business in this suit-happy world you protect your assets. Everything's in my wife's name…house, cars, everything. How can I help you?"

"I'm speaking with members of your high school class hoping to find a lead in a Manhattan murder."

"Really. My high school class?"

Hajek, looking for any flicker of uneasiness, thought he saw Thompson pull back in his chair.

"Yes, someone killed a classmate's daughter two weeks ago."

"Who?"

"Courtney Hanson, daughter of Angela Jurczyk Hanson. Someone murdered Courtney in her Manhattan apartment."

"I don't remember any Angela. Not sure I can help."

"This is the fourth victim I know about, all daughters of women in your class."

"That doesn't sound right." Thompson picked up a pencil and tapped it on the desk. "All in New York City?"

"No. Do you remember Teresa Collins?" Hajek asked.

"Can't say that I do."

Hajek removed a folded paper from his pocket and placed the copy of a yearbook page in front of Thompson. He pointed to Teresa's photo. "Does this help?"

Thompson looked at the paper. "Sorry, she could be anyone."

He handed Thompson another yearbook page. "How about this?"

"I know that guy. Good looking isn't he?" Thompson laughed.

"Read the note."

"To a sweet girl."

159

"You wrote that to Teresa."

"And probably any other girl that asked me to write in her yearbook." Thompson shook his head. "Her daughter's the victim?"

"The first one. Seven years ago."

"With all due respect, Detective, 1965 is probably not where to look for the killer."

Thompson's dismissive comment annoyed Hajek. He asked Thompson to look at photos of Angela, Roberta, and Marsha. Thompson remembered Marsha as someone who lived in his neighborhood and that Roberta sat next to him in an American History class. He did not recall anything specific about Angela.

"There were over one hundred guys in my class. Why are you asking me questions?" Thompson moved forward in his seat as if to get up and then sat down again.

"I'm checking out everyone. From the entry I thought you knew Teresa better."

"The sixties are years to forget. Two years after high school I shipped out to Vietnam. I'm lucky I'm alive and luckier that I'm not in the gutter."

"What do you mean?"

"My parents saved me. I started drinking in Vietnam. Most guys drank or did drugs to block the horrors. For three years after I came home I rarely had a sober moment. Constant flashbacks…just awful…My parents checked me into a facility in Baltimore, Maryland and it saved my life. I was lucky. Many more soldiers never recovered from their stint in the jungle."

"I'm sorry to resurrect such unpleasant memories. Please look at this list." Hajek handed Thompson the index card with the nine names. "Can you tell me anything about these men?"

Thompson glanced at it.

"Keith Farley went to Canada to avoid the draft. Good move for him. His parents helped him. Keith went to college in Toronto, got married, and as far as I know he's still there. Lawrence Sullivan…that's a sad one…we were good friends. He killed himself years ago."

"Where?"

"Patterson, New Jersey." Thompson's tone lowered, husky with emotion.

After a moment, he looked again at the names. "I hung out with Victor Ferris in school. I have no idea what happened to him. Probably drafted…

"Is this your family?" Hajek pointed to a photo taped on his computer monitor.

"Yes." Thompson smiled and turned the monitor for Hajek to see the picture of him with a woman and three children.

"Nice looking," Hajek said.

"I'm very fortunate."

"Are you still friends with anyone from high school?"

Thompson shook his head. "Detective I don't look back…it's too painful…I've moved on."

Hajek stood, retrieved the index card and yearbook pages, thanked Thompson for his time, and gave him his card. "Please call if you think of anything that might help."

Hajek navigated his way through the narrow South Norwalk streets to the highway. Then he drove south nine miles on the Connecticut Turnpike to Stamford. Following his GPS guide, he turned onto Faucett Street and pulled into the driveway of a yellow house that needed a coat of paint. He parked behind an Oldsmobile. The small lawn showed little evidence of grass, mostly patches of brown. Drape-covered windows made it difficult to determine if anyone was home. Hajek knocked on the front door. Silence. He knocked again. Footsteps

161

approached and a deadbolt turned. An unshaven man holding a cigarette in his hand cracked open the door

Hajek showed his badge. "I'm Peter Hajek with NYPD. Are you Harold Griffin?"

"Yes, Officer." Griffin said.

"I'd like to talk with you." Hajek waited for Griffin to invite him inside.

After an awkward silence, Griffin said, "My house is a mess. You can't come in. I'm sorry."

Hajek glimpsed piles of papers and bags covering most of the floor behind Griffin. "I'm speaking with members of your high school class hoping to find a lead in a case I'm working on."

"I doubt I can help."

"Do you remember Teresa Collins?" Hajek pulled the yearbook page from his pocket.

"No."

Hajek unfolded the paper to show him Teresa's photo. "Does this help?"

"A girl in my high school class I suppose." Griffin shrugged. "No one special."

"You don't remember Teresa?" Hajek asked again.

"No."

"Look what you wrote."

Hajek showed Griffin the page with his photo and pointed to the sentence 'Teresa, I'll never forget you'.

Griffin shook his head. "Teenage nonsense."

Hajek then showed Griffin the photos of Angela, Marsha and Roberta. In each case, Griffin responded 'don't remember'.

"What did you do after high school?"

162

"Vietnam. Served my country as asked. Fought to stop the spread of communism. I paid a high price. The draft dodgers got ahead. Most of them are pretty comfortable today."

Griffin seemed willing to talk about his time in the army. Hajek listened to him describe the silliness of his training that included boot camp drills, uniform inspections, and saluting. Hajek stayed with the Vietnam topic more out of his own curiosity than expecting it would help the case.

"Surviving jungle heat, seeing soldiers ambushed and slaughtered." Griffin stopped. "That was horrible. Much worse was returning home to chants of 'baby killer'.

"I heard about the lousy reception from the public. No Vietnam veteran deserved that treatment."

Griffin looked surprised at Hajek's empathy. "I wish I could help you, Officer. Any other questions?" He took a drag on his cigarette, turned his head and blew the smoke inside the house.

"Yes. Please take a look at this list." He showed Griffin the index card with names of classmates. "Do you know any of these men?"

Griffin scanned it. "No, sorry."

Hajek handed him his card. "If there is anything you remember that might help, give me a call. Take care."

Griffin closed the door.

Chapter 30

Hajek sat in his vehicle looking at the Griffin residence. A couple simple Cape Cod style houses looked out of place with the condo building and newly remodeled multifamily homes. Griffin's was an eyesore. Shrubbery blocked a quarter of the front windows. Several roof shingles protruded from an overgrown rhododendron. Hajek saw a woman looking at him through the window of the house next door.

He moved his car out of sight of Griffin's home and walked back to the neighbor's house. This person might offer a useful perspective on Harold Griffin. When he knocked on the door, an elderly woman opened it a crack.

"Police." Hajek showed his badge. "May I speak with you?"

She hesitated.

"We've had some complaints about your neighbor's yard."

"I didn't call. I don't want any trouble."

Hajek smiled. "You'll get none from me. May I come in?"

She opened the door and he walked into a living room furnished circa 1970. Fireplace tools hung on a wrought iron stand on a brick hearth and bellows leaned against the wall. Sunlight streamed through windows framed with heavy drapes. A worn wool rug covered most of the wood floor.

"I'm Peter Hajek."

"Agnes Holland."

"I won't take much of your time, Mrs. Holland. Has the Griffin property been a problem for a long time?"

She pursed her lips. "Since Ursula died. Harold's parents would be mortified if they saw what's become of their home. They were good decent

164

people. Harold was their only child. Ursula babied him. Mr. Griffin died… he was young…only forty-three…it was hard for Ursula and Harold after that."

"Did he get along with the other kids in the neighborhood?"

"Funny you ask. He mostly kept to himself. I don't know how he ever survived a stint in the service."

"What do you mean?"

"Ursula complained that he never was the same. Couldn't seem to settle down. She always hoped he would find a nice girl and get married."

"Might have made a difference. I need to be going. Thanks for your time."

Driving back to New York took an hour longer than Hajek expected. While traffic crept toward the accident site, he mulled over the day. He had hoped to find evidence that the killer was a classmate of the victims' mothers. Eugene Thompson appeared as the more capable of the two men. He spoke calmly and showed no fear of a detective questioning him at work. Remembering his comment that looking at high school relationships was off track, Hajek wondered if Thompson calculated that statement to shift the investigation's focus. Griffin, on the other hand came across as a pitiful soul, struggling to get through the day and probably rarely leaving his home.

He returned the car to the police garage and walked into the precinct around 7P.M. Three people waited to speak with the desk sergeant. He heard bits of phone conversations. When he neared the stairs, the desk sergeant looked up and waved him over. "Wilcox wants to talk with you."

Hajek acknowledged the message with a nod. He continued to his desk and left his laptop before proceeding to the captain's office.

Wilcox got up and closed his office door. "You visited John Gordon at the Metropolitan Correction Center."

165

"Yes."

"You shouldn't be doing that. Why did you do it?"

"I wanted to understand his mind set."

"Our role is over. It's up to the DOJ to deal with him. Don't do it again."

Hajek did not respond.

"Starting tomorrow you're working with Snyder. The Hanson case is your number one priority. You need to stay focused on the Hanson case. That's all." Wilcox looked down at a paper on his desk.

Chapter 31

The next morning Hajek woke to a steady, cold rain with darkness more like November than late April. He arrived at the precinct at 6:30. After moving his case files to his new desk, he organized the paperwork in chronological order, anticipating Snyder's take on his work and his suggestions for proceeding. Hajek didn't wait long.

"Good morning. How are you, Peter?" Snyder set a white paper bag on the desk. "Still like cinnamon raisin bagels with cream cheese?"

"Absolutely." Hajek grinned and looked up at Snyder, a forty-seven year old man who resembled a young Sean Connery from his Bond days. The former Army M.P. wore a dark blazer, gray slacks and blue shirt with a striped tie. His dark hair was cropped short.

Hajek stood and shook his hand. "Nice to see you, Otto."

Snyder took two cups from the bag. "Large black tea, cream on the side." He placed them in front of Hajek. A smaller cup landed on his desk. The bagel wrapped in wax paper went next to the tea.

Snyder took a sip of his coffee. "Wilcox is pretty stressed and wants the Hanson case finished. He reassigned all my cases."

"I know what he wants, a confession from the killer and no loose ends. I'm frustrated that I don't have a suspect. What we have is an unknown serial killer. The Bureau is on the case now."

"Before you tell me what you have on the female victim, how are you doing?"

"So-so. Solitary meals are the worst." Hajek's voice trailed off. He blinked. "It helps to be back at work. How's your family?"

"We're fine. My wife and I cannot believe Abby is finishing her first year at NYU. Next month we'll go to Jessica's graduation from the University of Texas in Austin."

"May is coming fast. Good for Jessica, finishing college. Hajek shifted back to work. "Another case I have is a thirty year old advertising executive who died after ingesting food borne toxins. He dropped dead at an event at Columbia University."

"Why are we involved?"

"The medical examiner thinks someone may have poisoned the advertising executive because he had never seen this combination of lethal toxins in an autopsy before."

"Doesn't sound like a matter for homicide. Let's hold off on that for now. Tell me about Courtney Hanson."

"Here's the file." Hajek slid it to Snyder's desk.

"Give me an hour and we'll talk."

Hajek took the bagel and tea to his old desk to finish packing. Snyder's quick dismissal of the Stover case surprised him. Wilcox prioritized the Hanson murder but Snyder understood the significance of a referral based on autopsy results. Thinking about the Stover loose ends, he ate his bagel. He needed to check Stover's phone records and question some people in Westport including Joan Stover and the pastor. The movie *Good Girl* popped in his head. A character in that movie died after eating unwashed, contaminated berries. After seeing *Good Girl*, when he and Francine ate berries, one or the other would laugh and ask 'any extra flavoring on those berries?'

Hajek opened a desk drawer. He took out a framed photo of Francine and him on bikes in southern France. He sighed. Her smile told the story of how she felt, delighted to be on two wheels in a gorgeous setting. He stared at it, blinked

168

and put it face down in the empty computer paper box. His desk had minimal items: a few favorite pens in a Yankee mug, small spiral notebooks that fit in a shirt pocket and three sizes of Post-it pads. The stuff he packed covered the bottom of the box.

Before unplugging his laptop, he opened the spreadsheet for the class of 1965 at Stamford Catholic High. Hajek entered the information he learned from Eugene Thompson. Keith Farley moved to Toronto and Lawrence Sullivan killed himself years ago. This shortened his person-of-interest list to seven including Thompson and Griffin. After saving the file, he shut the computer down.

Chapter 32

"What do you think?" Hajek set his box on the desk across from Snyder's.

"I want to know more about the residents in Courtney Hanson's apartment building and her friends. Are you sure she doesn't have a boyfriend? DNA and chemical tests on urine show the killer was a guy."

"According to parents and coworkers there was no one special in her life."

"We need to talk with everyone in the building again. Maybe we'll find someone helping a relative with a place to stay. It's also possible someone noticed a different person hanging around and they didn't think to say anything. We need to spend some time questioning and try to dig up some useful information."

"You're right." Hajek took the cover off the box, removed the Yankee mug, filled it with pens, and placed it on his new desk. He put the photo in a drawer.

"Tell me more about your thinking. Start with these yearbook pages." Snyder flipped his thumb over a stack of copy paper.

"I believe we're looking for a serial killer whose photo is in your hands and his motive goes back to high school." Hajek shifted in his chair sensing Snyder's skepticism.

Snyder set the file down. "Walk me through how you came to that."

Hajek reviewed his first contact with Courtney's parents. They told him that a young woman murdered years ago in Bethel, Connecticut was the daughter of a longtime friend. The common denominator of mothers that were friends since high school alerted him to think there was a possible link. With further investigation, Hajek speculated that the killer in each case first gained access to the woman's home and then attacked. With both Maura Santori and Courtney Hanson, the killer surprised the woman when she returned home. He then attacked and possibly tortured the victim by tightening and loosening a rope before strangling her. The rope left in the Manhattan apartment and the one found in the Bethel, Connecticut home were comparable. In both cases the killer did not take anything. Without robbery as motive, Hajek assumed something personal compelled these crimes.

"That makes sense. I see Wilcox contacted the FBI. Where are they with this?" Snyder tossed his empty coffee cup into a trash basket.

"I don't know. According to Wilcox, the FBI are not convinced the current case is connected with the Connecticut one. I don't think the FBI and I are on the same page, or even reading the same book," Hajek said. "FBI wants all our info but won't give us any of theirs."

"You may have annoyed them with the Grant case but we need to keep open communication," Snyder said.

"For sure. Unfortunately the Connecticut testing results done at my request showed nothing conclusive. Urinalysis at the time of the murder may have helped but it didn't happen. I have no doubt that the rope I saw in the evidence box in Bethel is the same kind as the one used to murder Hanson. I'm waiting for forensics to reach the same conclusion."

"I see in the file that you interviewed the Connecticut mother," Snyder interrupted.

"Yes, I met Teresa Jenkins, the first known victim's mother, at her home. She and the three others, whose daughters were killed, were close friends during their high school years. I asked to take her yearbook."

171

Snyder's eyes widened. "And proceeded to check out an entire class. Maybe there's a connection with Stamford Catholic High but how can you be sure it's '65 and not '66 or '64?"

"According to Teresa, she and her friends socialized primarily with other members of their class and did not have a wide circle. We're talking pre-Facebook days. You think I should get those yearbooks, too?" Hajek laughed.

Snyder shook his head. "Not at this time. I'm sorry I mentioned it. Peter, it's good to be back with you. I've missed your hunches and jumps in logic. Continue."

"The yearbook hunt brought me to two other murder victims."

Snyder nodded. "Their mothers were the rest of the foursome."

"Exactly."

Hajek's desk phone rang. When he picked up, he recognized Teresa's voice. She sounded upset.

"Four FBI agents came to our home last night unannounced. Two talked with me and the other two questioned Vincent. Is there something new we don't know about?"

"No. We're pursuing various leads. The FBI's involved because we're looking for someone who killed in more than one state. This is good. They have great resources and they're taking the case seriously."

"Okay. If you say so. Please keep me updated."

"Teresa, I will."

"Teresa, the mother of the first victim, called asking you about the FBI?" Snyder asked.

"Yes. She's wondering why agents questioned her and her husband last night."

"So the FBI really aren't telling us anything."

172

"No surprise."

"Tell me about the other victims." Snyder said.

Hajek told Snyder about his phone calls with Angela Hanson's classmates. "When Roberta in Illinois revealed that her daughter was strangled, I felt these murders have a connection. Then I spoke with the fourth friend's son and learned his sister met a similar end in Buffalo."

Snyder looked pensive. "Can't be a coincidence. Did you travel to Western Springs, Illinois and Buffalo?"

"I didn't think Wilcox would go for it."

"Daughters of friends. Hard to make any sense out of this," Snyder said.

"I spoke with both the Western Springs, Illinois detective and the one in Buffalo. Without leads, they each moved these cases after a few weeks to inactive status and made the assumption that the crimes were random."

"Illinois and Buffalo couldn't have known that the mothers were friends," Snyder said.

"That's right. I got the records from both. When I reviewed the Illinois file, I found an interesting piece of this puzzle from its urinalysis."

Snyder sifted through the file to the section on Olivia Cronin, the victim in Western Springs, Illinois and pulled a copy of a lab report.

"Male, over 55 years old with early Type 2 diabetes. That's not our victim's urine," Hajek said as Snyder looked at the lab results.

"You think this killer peed on her after killing her."

"Yes."

"Anything helpful in the Manhattan crime lab information?" Snyder asked.

"No hit with fingerprints but the urinalysis tells me the same man who killed Olivia Cronin in Illinois killed Courtney Hanson."

173

Hajek pulled a lab sheet from the section on Hanson and pointed to 'male over 60 with Type 2 diabetes'. The DNA matches with the sample from Illinois.

"The mothers of these girls must have done something terrible to piss this guy off."

"Pun intended?"

Snyder stretched his arms to the side and rolled his shoulders. "Who are you focused on?"

"I narrowed the list to seven and questioned two of them in Connecticut yesterday. Their messages to Teresa in the yearbook raised my curiosity."

Snyder frowned. "Does Wilcox know?"

Hajek shook his head.

"Peter, you're expected to follow protocol. You can't go off interrogating people outside our jurisdiction."

"I had a nagging feeling about them and I had another appointment in Connecticut."

"Wilcox will be furious if he finds out you kept the local police in the dark. Are your notes here?" Snyder pointed to the file.

"Not yet."

"Did either strike you as a possible suspect?"

"I haven't made up my mind. Eugene Thompson runs his own business and Harold Griffin seems pathetic."

"What else did you discover about them?" Snyder asked.

"Both served in Vietnam. Thompson in the Army. Griffin was a Marine."

"I don't suppose you got a urine sample from either," Snyder joked.

"I wish. Do you have any military contacts?"

"Where are you going with this?"

174

"Soldiers stay tight don't they? Maybe others in the unit with Thompson and Griffin could help us understand them. Some of the others on my persons-of-interest may have been in the military."

Snyder laughed. "Sure, I'll break into the Department of Defense database. What are you considering?"

"It's a long shot but one way to learn more about these guys' younger years is to look into their military record. That might shed some light on connections with today."

"I'll think about it. For now we need to interview the residents in the Hanson apartment building."

"I'll give the building manager a courtesy call."

"Good idea." Snyder put on his jacket.

Snyder drove an unmarked police car to the Eastside apartment building. They systematically knocked on apartment doors, showed the two surveillance photos of a workman with a toolbox and a back view of a man wearing a jacket with elbow patches. At six that evening, they met at the elevator on the fifth floor.

"I know you want to be back here tomorrow, Peter, but I have plans tonight and all weekend. We'll continue Monday."

Back in Queens, Hajek stopped for Chinese takeout on his way home. After eating, he printed his person-of-interest list. Grabbing a pad and pen he wrote the seven names on separate sheets of paper and taped them to his kitchen counter.

He searched population statistics and found that 61,000 people lived in Stamford during the 1940's. Logging on to a genealogy website, he brought up the last available United States census, 1940 and entered Bradley and Stamford, Connecticut in the search boxes. Three Bradley families turned up. Hajek set up a spreadsheet and listed the male names for each Bradley, their ages, and street

175

addresses. Continuing with the last name for each person-of-interest he generated possible connections, added them to his spreadsheet and then printed it. He transferred to individual pages the first name of any male old enough to have a son born in 1947 or 1948.

Noting the time was eight thirty he called the Stamford library. The automated response gave Monday through Friday hours as nine to nine and Saturday hours as ten to five. He listened to the extension options and entered 321 for reference.

"Reference, may I help you?"

"I'm interested in reading *Stamford Advocate* obituaries."

"What time period?"

"The 1980's to now."

"We have them."

"Any chance of accessing them online?"

"Only the last five years. But our microfilm is user-friendly and our staff will certainly help you."

"I'm coming from New York City. Is the library far from the train station?"

"A twenty minute walk, I'd guess." She gave him the address and he put it and the number in his phone.

Then he logged onto the Social Security Death Index and entered possible fathers of the men he wanted to locate. The index would tell him the date and place of death. If the man died somewhere other than Stamford, Connecticut, he hoped the family would still put the obituary in the local Stamford paper and list all the children and where they lived. For each realistic hit, he added the death date to his spreadsheet. When he finished with all the names he had sixteen obituaries to pursue.

176

At 11:30 Saturday morning, he arrived at the Ferguson Library in Stamford with his laptop. The obituaries proved worthwhile. In all but one, he found the survivors included the sons he wanted to locate and their siblings. Reading the senior Leonard Emerson's death notice, he learned Leonard Junior had predeceased his father and removed him from the list. For those remaining, he added the known relatives next to the person-of-interest. Using search engines he hunted for addresses and phone numbers. With each successful hit, he added the data to his spreadsheet. After an hour he had someone to call for each man he wanted to know more about. Victor Ferris' brother Andrew lived on Roxbury Road in Stamford. He collected his papers, stepped outside the library, and called Andrew Ferris.

"Hello."

Hajek heard a television in the background. "Andrew Ferris?"

"That's me."

Hajek delivered his pretext for wanting to speak with Victor. "Sister Dolores, one of the nuns that taught at Catholic High is celebrating sixty years as a Sister of Mercy. We're asking former students to send a card or message to mark this occasion."

"Is she still alive? I also had her in class."

"Yes and in good health. Please consider sending a card. The Alumni Director, Brad Oster, is accepting the cards and will present them to her. His address is at Catholic High."

"Okay, I'll tell my wife, she's better at that stuff. I can also tell Victor."

"That would be fine but if you don't mind I'd still like his address and number to update the alumni information."

"Victor lives at 12 Tuttle Street in Stamford."

"Thanks." Hajek jotted down the address.

"Tell Sister Dolores Congratulations. Thanks for calling."

Hajek returned inside and sat at a table. Using MapQuest he found that Tuttle Street was two miles from the library. Next he called a taxi service. "I'm at Ferguson Library and want to go to 12 Tuttle Street."

The dispatcher said, "A cab will be there in less than ten minutes. Wait outside at Broad and Bedford."

"I'll be there. Thanks."

Back on the street, Hajek noticed clouds replaced the bright blue sky of the morning. Hearing a piercing scream, he turned in its direction and laughed when he saw the source, three teen age girls in conversation a half block from the library.

When a yellow cab pulled to the curb, a woman about forty, rolled down the window and looked at Hajek, "You the guy that wants Tuttle Street?"

"Yes." Hajek opened the back door and got in. "I'll only be there a few minutes and then I need to get to the train station. Can you wait?"

"I have to run the meter."

"That's fine."

They passed Stamford Hospital and turned left. He spotted a pickup basketball game in a park. The neighborhood had many older multifamily homes and a couple of small markets.

At Tuttle Street, the cab pulled into the parking lot of the condo complex on the left.

"I'll be back." Hajek knocked on Victor's door.

"Come in. It's open."

Startled, Hajek turned the door knob and entered. A thin man looking much older than mid-sixties moved like someone who had a stroke. As he dragged his left leg the short distance to greet Hajek, it was obvious that he was too short and too thin to be the suspect.

The simply furnished room had a recliner with a three shelf bookcase right next to it. A glass of water and a folded magazine on the top shelf were an easy reach from the chair. The off white walls had no photos or artwork. A small rocking chair sat in the far corner near the television cart.

"I'm sorry to bother you. My name's Peter Hajek. I'm a friend of Sister Dolores' nephew and I'm helping the family contact her former students at Stamford Catholic High."

Victor laughed. "That takes me back."

"Do you remember her?"

"Absolutely. She was one of the few smart teachers I had in high school. I enjoyed her history class. Everyone liked Sister Dolores. Is she okay?"

"Yes, she's fine. I really am sorry to barge in on you. I couldn't find your phone number and tracked down your brother, Andrew. When I spoke with him a half hour ago, I realized I was so close that I decided to come by."

"That's fine. I have an unlisted number. Too many telemarketing calls. They drive me crazy. Want a soda?"

"No thanks."

"Have a seat." Victor motioned to the rocking chair.

"I've a cab waiting. I just wanted to tell you that Sister Dolores is celebrating sixty years as a Sister of Mercy this year. Her family is planning a celebration and asking former students to send cards."

"That's nice. She deserves it. I'll write a note and tell her what history related books I've been reading."

"She'll like that. You can send the message to Brad Oster, the Alumni Director, at the high school. I better head back to New York. Take care." Hajek shook his hand, thanked him, and left.

Returning to the cab, Hajek reflected on Victor living alone and coping so well with serious disability.

**

After the train ride back to New York, Hajek stopped and picked up lamb stew and a Greek salad. Still thinking about Victor, he reminded himself that many people were worse off than he. Such thoughts did not make eating alone any easier or lessen the pain of life without Francine. He set his meal on the kitchen counter, turned on his laptop, and filled a glass with water. As he ate, he reviewed his contact list. With the last bite, he felt excited that he might be closer to finding the killer.

Knowing Saturday and Sunday were good times to find people at home he called the number for Craig Epps sister. "Mrs. Walsh, I'm hoping you can help me connect with your brother Craig. I'm on a committee planning a celebration for one of the nuns that taught at Catholic High. Sister Dolores is celebrating sixty years as a Sister of Mercy. We'd love to have former students send cards to mark this special occasion."

"Does the furthest one get a prize? My brother lives in Singapore. He's been there for more than twelve years."

"Does he ever visit the United States?"

"Rarely. I think the last time was three years ago."

"What's his work?"

"International banking."

"Does he have a family?"

"Yes. He met his wife there and they have two children."

180

"I'm sure Sister Dolores would love hearing from him." Hajek gave her Brad Oster's name, the high school address, and quickly ended the call. *That eliminates Craig Epps.*

Calling Leo Hodges' brother, Hajek got an answering machine. Noting the Brooklyn address, he decided that it would be easy to get there and a personal visit might reveal more. He hung up without leaving a message.

Next he called Brian Towle's brother in Virginia and got his voicemail. He left his number for Michael Towle to call him back.

Roger Bradley's sister lived in New Jersey. He started calling her number, when M. Towle flashed on his phone screen. He took the call.

"You just called me. Do I know you?"

"No but thanks for returning my call." Hajek repeated his story.

"I'm surprised you found me and not Brian. He's in New York. That's where you are, right?"

"Yes."

"I think he's attended some reunions over the years. He'll probably be glad to respond to your request. Let me give you his number."

Hajek jotted it down and ended the call.

Before continuing with Bradley's sister he did a reverse lookup with Brian's phone number and found a Tarrytown, New York address not far from his partner's home. Instead of calling, he decided to ask Snyder to stop by and get a firsthand impression.

He gave Bradley's sister, Ashley Inch the same spiel about Sister Dolores' celebration. In their conversation he learned that her brother Roger had multiple sclerosis and lived in a rehabilitation facility near her. She promised to give him the message. Hajek marked him off the list.

His next call was to Fred Crane, Stanley's brother. His wife answered. Hajek asked for Fred and she offered to take a message. Hajek explained that he wanted to speak with Stanley and hoped Fred could help him.

"I'm glad I got this call. It would upset to have someone ask about his brother. No one in the family has heard from Stanley in years. We're so worried about him."

"I'm sorry to hear that. Do you know where he last lived?"

"New Haven, Connecticut, I think. That was more than twenty years ago. He was on the streets…homeless…we lost contact."

"The family tried to help but he resented them and eventually disappeared from our lives."

"Mrs. Crane, I'm really sorry to have troubled you with this call. Please forgive me."

***

Sunday, Hajek arrived at the last possible moment for the eight o'clock Mass in his parish. He selected an empty pew on the left side of the church. Not wanting to make eye contact with anyone, he kept his head down. When the organist began the final hymn, he exited and made his way to Brooklyn. On Seventh Avenue he stopped at a café for breakfast and enjoyed the anonymity.

It was after eleven when he finished eating. He walked a couple blocks on Seventh Avenue and turned north onto Garfield Place. A short man with a trim beard and mustache answered the door. Hajek identified himself and asked about Leo Hodges.

The man laughed. "Who's that? You can't mean my brother. He stopped using Leo years ago. He goes by Conrad these days, his middle name."

"Is he in New York?"

"Only every couple of years. I usually visit him. He lives in Sante Fe."

182

"Can you give me his number?"

"Sure. Ready?"

Hajek opened his phone and entered the number that Hodges recited. "Thanks."

"Don't call before next week. He's spending two weeks in Hawaii with his wife. I think they're back next Wednesday."

"Nice."

He walked toward Prospect Park considering the best way to get to his mother's place for his weekly visit. A cab would be fastest and he was already later than usual. Laughing to himself he acknowledged that time meant nothing to her. He continued to the subway station at Grand Army Plaza. Thirty five minutes later he stood in the doorway of his mother's empty room.

"There's music in the dayroom at the end of the hall. We took every one there." A staff member responded to his confused look.

"Thank you."

Patients sat at tables or in wheel chairs. Hajek observed his mother tapping her fingers. She appeared focused on the musicians. A woman played piano and three others sang "When the World was Young".

Hajek approached a staff member. "How long will the program be?"

"They just started. I expect they'll sing about an hour, less if they lose their audience."

"Not much chance of that. I haven't seen my mother interested in anything for a long time."

He stood and watched. When he heard the beginning lyrics of "Fly me to the Moon", he did not want to break the spell of the music by interacting with his mother. He went to speak with the shift manager at the nurses' station. The charge nurse had nothing out of the ordinary to report about his mother's week.

He made his way back to the dayroom, sat in a chair by the door, and listened to "Try to Remember". A few patients clearly recognized this selection from the Broadway musical *The Fantasticks*. The popular "Over the Rainbow" elicited participation from a few members of the audience. Although his mother did not join the sing-along, she swayed a little in her seat.

When the music stopped and staff began returning patients to their rooms, Hajek thanked the musicians. "Great program. My mother loved it. Sinatra was a favorite of hers." As he wheeled his mother back to her room, he felt more light-hearted.

Returning to his apartment he reflected on his day and realized he had not told Brad Oster about his conversations. He left him a voicemail message, "Expect some cards for Sister Dolores' in your mail."

Happy to have upbeat news for Roland about their mother he would call later. They frequently talked around seven o'clock Seattle time on a Sunday evening. His mother's enjoyment of the musical program would please Roland.

Chapter 33

Hajek filled his partner in on his weekend research including the ruse involving the Director of Alumni at Catholic High. "It would help if we found soldiers that served in the military with Eugene Thompson and Harold Griffin."

Snyder ignored the reference to the military. "Did you do anything fun this weekend?"

"Besides a train ride to Stamford, Connecticut?"

Snyder shook his head. "Today job one is our questioning residents in the Eastside apartment building, remember?"

Hajek nodded. "I'm with you. One more thing from the weekend."

Snyder sighed.

"Brian Towle lives in Tarrytown. Maybe you could pay him a visit …a little detour on your way home."

"Why not call?"

"You'll get more from a personal visit."

"You're right. I'll do it next week. For now, back to the apartment interviews."

***

On Wednesday afternoon Hajek and Snyder finished canvassing Courtney Hanson's apartment building. They returned to the precinct.

They had knocked on every door in Hanson's apartment building and showed residents the two views of the man in the surveillance tape hoping for something that would point to a suspect.

With meticulous questioning, they had identified regular visitors and a few individuals who had briefly stayed with a friend or relative. Mr. Howe, the building manager, verified that no one had moved out after the murder.

Hajek shared his partner's frustration. They were at the building early Monday, Tuesday and Wednesday. They stayed into the evening and spoke with eighty-two tenants. Three units were empty during the time of the murder.

One lead surfaced when two residents in separate conversations mentioned seeing a man in the building who they believed was not a resident. Both responded to the photos saying 'could be him'. Both were sure his stay coincided with the time of the murder. Asking the doorman about this individual led them to Unit 10C, Eleanor O'Donnell. This woman, easily in her eighties, confirmed that her great-nephew stayed with her a couple of days while on leave from the service. She showed them a photo of a man in a Navy officer's uniform. The serviceman's build did not match the man Hajek had observed on the surveillance tape.

"I forget the date," she apologized. "About a week ago maybe. His aircraft carrier left New York for Hawaii. It's on my calendar."

Hajek looked at a calendar hanging on a bulletin board in the kitchen. He noted Timothy written across three days confirming the young man visited before the Hanson murder.

The detectives had followed up with the construction company's Bronx office and spoke with the owner about all the subcontractors who worked on that job. Many were easily disregarded for not being a good physical match, wrong color skin or too short or too tall.

At their desks Hajek and Snyder pondered the lack of credible information. "After all this time talking with the residents of the apartment building, I can't believe we have nothing." Snyder shook his head and reached for his water.

"Wilcox will have to release the photos and see if the public can help."

Snyder grimaced. He drained his water bottle. "I dread dealing with the hundreds of false leads and crank calls. I'll ask the Bureau for more help with the photos. More information on the man's height and weight would help."

"NYPD's technical staff would do the job well.. possibly faster. I understand you want a cooperative relationship. Better you than I asking for their expertise." Hajek rolled his shoulders, stood and stretched his arms behind his back. "I'm going to the corner deli for a snack. Want anything?"

Snyder looked up. "Yeah. Surprise me."

Back in their work area, Hajek tossed a bag of Nabisco's Double Stuff Oreos on Snyder's desk.

Snyder opened his cookies. "These are the best. I have loved them since they were first introduced."

"When was that?" Hajek asked.

"Forty years ago. Wish I had a glass of milk." Snyder started on a second Oreo.

Hajek ate a cookie. "Back to the case. Any progress with the photos?"

"I called my FBI contact Larry. He's out of the office for a few days. I spoke with the head of photo analysis and explained that it would help if they pinpointed height and weight for us and maybe even age within a few years.

Hajek took a sip of water. "Our techs are also on it. We'll probably have something tomorrow."

Otto leaned back in his chair. "Let's postpone asking Wilcox to release the photos and give the FBI seventy-two hours."

"I'd like to get back to Joan Stover and see if we could wrap that case up." Hajek said.

"We'd better get our paperwork in order on the Hanson case first. With the FBI involvement, Wilcox will want our notes up to date."

187

"You're right. I'll finish our report on the canvassing. I am interested in your take on Joan Stover. I'll see if we can meet with her late morning tomorrow."

"Okay. I'm out of here. See you in the morning."

Chapter 34

The next morning walking from the subway to the precinct, Hajek noted more green patches scattered between asphalt and concrete. Bright yellow daffodils in planters on apartment building steps diverted his eye from a storefront's peeling paint and soot-covered windows. Without the burden of overcoats, pedestrians bounced more than walked to their offices and classes. Some brave souls signaled warmer days approaching with their short sleeves and lightweight fabrics. This April day defied the poet's description of cruel. If it were not for the task at hand, he would look forward to his drive out of the city.

"Nice day for a road trip." Snyder said when Hajek arrived at his desk. On the way to Connecticut, Hajek reviewed his previous encounter with the victim's wife and his surprise that the children were home during the visit. He shared his nagging feeling that Joan exaggerated their illness to keep them from school.

"It does seem odd that all three were home," Snyder said.

"Her reserved manner baffles me. It's not easy to get a read on her," Hajek confessed. "Managing three children alone would challenge most women. Joan seems to take it in stride. It's hard to know how to interpret—a Jackie Kennedy emulation of strength."

"Peter, I wouldn't ignore your intuition. Do you think Mrs. Stover knows anything about her husband's interest in kiddie porn?"

"I doubt it. Our technical experts saw a pattern of computer access on evenings and weekends. This agrees with Joan's statement that Nathan didn't let anyone use his office computer."

"Peter, I think it's best that you tell Joan Stover about the experts' findings. Maybe her reaction will help us determine what else she knows."

189

Arriving at the Stover home in Westport, Snyder commented, "Imagine coming home to this place every night. I'm not sure I could sleep without the sirens and traffic sounds."

"Not my scene but it's beautiful for sure."

"My grandmother had a dogwood tree like that." Snyder pointed to branches of delicate pink blossoms. "She lived in Duchess County." Snyder stood a moment taking in the landscape before walking to the front door.

Hajek rang the bell. The men waited in silence.

"Good morning, Detective."

"Mrs. Stover, this is Detective Otto Snyder."

"Please call me Joan." She wore a light blue turtleneck and jeans.

"We can meet in the kitchen." She turned and led the way.

When they walked from the front door through the dining room, Hajek stopped and looked at note cards scattered on the table.

"I'm late sending some thank yous," Joan explained.

"Staten Island Ferry, nice drawing." Hajek bent over and looked more closely at the artist's rendering.

Joan smiled. "I met the artist at South Street Seaport. I love how she reflects light in her work."

"Staten Island is frequently overlooked. I think its history is interesting.

"I grew up there," Joan said.

"Really." Hajek said.

"Tea or coffee?"

"I'd love some coffee," Snyder said. "I guess you know my friend here is a tea drinker."

"Yes, black tea with cream. I remember." Joan started toward the kitchen.

"May I see your husband's office first?" Snyder asked.

"Of course." Joan led the detectives from the dining area, through the living room to Stover's office and opened the door. "I'll be in the kitchen when you're finished."

Hajek raised the pleated blind and looked at the apple tree while Snyder pulled open the desk drawers. Finding only pens and pencils he said, "Guess you've taken anything worth examining."

Hajek lowered the blind. "Only the hard drive. Nothing was in the desk."

Snyder moved closer and looked at a large framed poster. Isn't this a strange choice for a man's office?"

"I thought so."

Snyder stood in front of framed pencil sketches. "What do you make of these?"

"Stover wanted to be a cartoonist. He collected Disney drawings. Those are originals for animation. Pre-computer days."

Snyder glanced around the room again. "I'm done."

Hajek closed the office door and followed Snyder to the living room.

Snyder walked over to the aquarium. "This is saltwater."

"Is that unusual?" Hajek stood next to his partner.

"More challenging… especially when you include coral. Look at the color on the Angel fish. Very clean…healthy…I like the live plants."

Joan appeared in the doorway. "Are you fish lovers?"

"Admirers." Snyder smiled and walked toward Joan.

"My girls love to sit and watch the fish. It's very soothing."

All three continued to the kitchen.

On a tray at one end of the granite-top island sat a bright yellow creamer and sugar bowl. Cups, saucers and plates marked places for three.

191

"Is this okay, gentlemen or do you prefer the table?" Joan looked toward a round table in the kitchen corner.

"This is fine," Hajek said. Snyder nodded in agreement. The men sat down while Joan poured coffee and tea.

"Are your girls at school?"

"Yes."

"How are they doing?"

"Good. Thank you." Joan pulled out a bar stool and climbed on it.

While they each fixed their drink, Joan chatted about her daughters' soccer and softball teams, music lessons and school events. She assured the detectives that they were happy to be back in their routine.

Hajek cleared his throat. "Mrs. Stover pursuing every avenue in an investigation sometimes brings us down strange paths. Our computer experts examined your husband's computer. We found some troubling material on it." He looked for a reaction. Joan looked straight at him waiting for him to continue. "I don't know when or if I'll be able to return the hard drive. Nathan had pornographic photos of children."

Joan's shoulders sagged. From her came a sound like a balloon deflating. She bent forward. Her elbows supported her from sliding off the stool. Hajek recognized the look of someone given a terminal diagnosis.

"Do you know anything about this interest of his?" Hajek spoke in a calm tone.

She managed a weak, "No."

"We wonder if this activity connected him with someone who might want to kill him. Can you tell us about any conflicts your husband had with anyone."

Hajek saw her hesitation. He took a sip of tea. She pressed her fingertips to her forehead and glanced down. He waited.

192

Snyder placed his cup in the saucer. "Anything that may not have seemed important at the time may help us, Mrs. Stover."

"There was an incident on Cape Cod last summer."

"What happened?" Snyder asked.

"The father of my daughter's friend came to the cottage we rented. He was very agitated and told my husband he should be in jail but he wouldn't put his daughter through a court process."

"Did you know this man?"

"Yes. He's a year-round resident in Chatham. He lives with his wife and three children, two sons and a daughter."

"What did Nathan say?"

"Calm down. Or something like that. Nathan stayed composed. I don't know how because this guy called him a pervert and kept yelling. I think Nathan also said 'you're mistaken'."

"What exactly did he accuse Nathan of doing?"

Joan sobbed. Between gasps for breath, she managed to say that his daughter told her mother, 'Emily's father touched me.'

With difficulty, Joan informed the detectives that the man's daughter, Hannah, and her middle daughter, Emily, were friends. They had met the previous summer on the beach and played together while the Stovers vacationed in Chatham. They reconnected last summer and spent a lot of time together.

On the evening before the confrontation, Hannah had stayed overnight at the Stover cottage. Her husband denied any contact with Hannah. The girl's father insisted that even though he did not plan to involve the police he wanted to stop Nathan from scaring little girls.

"We'll need his name, Mrs. Stover."

"Donald Jaffe."

"Do you know what he does in Chatham?"

"He works for the town."

"What did you think? Your husband acted inappropriately?"

"The thought sickened me. I wondered if the child made it up."

"But you didn't think so."

"I don't know."

"Anything like this ever happen before?" Snyder asked.

Joan looked away. Hajek sensed fear and a reluctance to answer. He followed her gaze to a squirrel scrambling along the top rail of a wooden fence in the backyard. A woodpecker's tapping punctuated the silence.

"I don't know of anyone else accusing him of mistreating a child." Joan's voice cracked. She pressed her face into her hands.

"How did Mr. Jaffe leave things?" Hajek asked.

He said, "Find another place to vacation. You better not return to Chatham. And Hannah will not have anything to do with Emily." Then he left.

"Did your husband respond?"

"No. The visit upset Nathan but he dismissed it …said Jaffe's lost his mind and I should ignore him."

"What did you tell Emily?" Snyder asked.

"Not much. The girls were asleep when Jaffe came to our place. We left a couple of days later. Emily cried because she did not get to say goodbye to Hannah. I couldn't tell her the truth." Joan got up and took several tissues from a box near the sink.

When she returned to her seat, Hajek asked, "Did your daughters ever indicate their father acted inappropriately with them?"

Joan burst into tears again.

194

Chapter 35

The detectives walked from the Stover home in silence and got into their vehicle. As he drove to the turnpike Snyder said, "I wasn't expecting that. Do you think Stover abused one of his daughters?"

"That's how I read the look on her face." Hajek said.

"The Medical Examiner's instincts may be right about Stover's death—no accident. We may have a homicide case after all." Snyder waited on the entrance ramp for a break in the traffic.

"It's difficult to see how a guy on Cape Cod would have access to Stover. First let's find out if he missed any days at work that gave him time to travel to Connecticut or New York City. Joan said he worked for the town of Chatham. It'll be easy to get Jaffe's schedule for the last two months." Hajek pulled his phone from his pocket.

"I wouldn't blame the guy for wanting to kill Stover. If he messed with my daughter…." Snyder's sentence hung unfinished.

"I shouldn't be surprised but I am. Your notes indicated Stover's co-workers described a decent guy…remembering the receptionist's name and that he got along with other employees. He even volunteered for his church. I don't get it," Snyder tightened his grip on the wheel.

"There's no one profile of a pedophile. I'll call Wilcox and see if he'll authorize our going to Chatham." Hajek hit talk.

Snyder crossed the Connecticut state line and into New York.

When Hajek told Wilcox that he and Otto would like to question a possible suspect in the Stover case on Cape Cod, he objected. Hajek summarized their reasoning and persuaded the captain to acquiesce by saying this interview could wrap up the case and they would devote all their time to the Hanson case.

Wilcox agreed to contact Chatham police and ask for an appointment for his detectives the following day.

"Good job, Peter. It's even true that we could solve the Stover case tomorrow."

"Any idea how far Chatham is?" Hajek asked.

"Never been to Cape Cod." Snyder switched lanes to pass a UPS tandem truck.

Hajek checked directions. "It's at least a five hour drive. What time do you want to start?" Hajek put his phone back in his pocket.

"Seven works. Earlier than that is inhumane." Snyder laughed. "If Jaffe's our man most likely he did the deed over a weekend."

"Stover died on a Wednesday and the medical examiner believes he ingested what killed him that day."

Hajek's phone rang, Chatham police flashed on his screen.

"I just spoke with Captain Wilcox. Someone, most likely Chief Farrell, will be available tomorrow to meet with you. Tell me what you want with Jaffe."

Hajek summarized important details of what they knew about their case, including the toxins in the victim's system, the child porn on his computer and that Jaffee and Stover had a verbal confrontation last summer. Speaking with Jaffe, Hajek hoped would shed some light on other people that had problems with Stover.

***

The next morning Snyder arrived at the precinct armed with bagels, water, coffee, and tea. The detectives walked to the garage.

"Another nice day. Want me to start?" Hajek asked.

"No, I want you to drive home so I can nap."

196

"Deal." Hajek settled in the passenger seat and placed their cups of hot drinks in holders.

The detectives drove out of Manhattan for Massachusetts chatting intermittently about lame portrayals of police officers on television, current events, Yankees and Red Sox. A good part of the way they drove in silence taking in views of Connecticut marshland with egrets, roadside wildflowers and dilapidated apartment buildings in Norwalk, Bridgeport, and New London.

Crossing the canal onto Cape Cod, Snyder announced that he wanted decent seafood for lunch. Barely had he made his wish known, when a sign for Captain Jack's appeared. "This will do." He pulled into the unpretentious place with picnic tables outside. Snyder ordered fried clams, coleslaw and fries. Hajek chose a lobster roll with coleslaw.

"In honor of the land of bogs I'm having cranberry juice," Hajek took a bottle from the drink cooler in the cafe.

"Good idea."

"Gentlemen have a seat and I'll bring your food out when it's ready." The waitress said.

Early for lunch and weeks before the tourist season, they found the outside area had only one other table occupied. A young couple sat facing each other and their infant in a seat on the table.

Hajek inhaled deeply. "We're not in New York anymore, Otto. No exhaust smell."

"City boy, you'd get tired of all this clean air. What do you expect from Jaffe?" Snyder asked.

"A tough guy. From what Joan Stover told us, Jaffe directly confronted Stover."

"You're right. He went to Stover's rental cottage and called him out."

197

"It's likely Stover bothered other little girls. Maybe Jaffe will know. We'll ask."

The woman placed their lunch in front of them.

"Smells wonderful. Thank you." Hajek unwrapped the plasticware.

"Let's first have the Chatham police introduce us to Jaffe's boss. He should be able to tell us if Jaffe took any days off earlier this month. Then we'll talk directly with Jaffe."

Hajek nodded. "You take the lead, Otto."

Forty more miles on Route 6 brought them into the village of Chatham. The narrow streets, gray shingled houses with window boxes overflowing with colorful flowers, and trimmed hedges revealed the accuracy of Cape Cod postcards.

Snyder slowed as they passed the marina dotted with fishing boats. "It's been quite a while since I've done any fishing. I think I could enjoy some time here."

Hajek looked at the GPS screen. "The police station is up on the left."

When they pulled in front of a two story clapboard building, a uniformed police officer who looked about fifty came out and greeted the detectives. "I'm Chief Kieran Farrell, pleased to meet you."

After introductions, Farrell made it clear that he hoped they were wrong about his town having any connection with a murder. "The officer you spoke with informed me of your concerns about Jaffe. I understand Jaffe had a verbal confrontation last summer with Nathan Stover about inappropriate contact with his daughter."

"That's right. After speaking with Mrs. Stover we thought Jaffe might have a motive. At the very least, Jaffe might shed some light on other people that had problems with Stover.

198

"Jaffe's supervisor expects us. His office is a couple miles away. Let's go."

They got back in their car and followed Farrell's cruiser to a gravel parking lot with town trucks in a row, mowing equipment, bags of mulch, and storage sheds. A large pile of sand sat at the edge of the property. To the right they spotted a small trailer that served as an office.

As they walked toward it, Snyder said, "Before we meet Mr. Jaffe, we'd like to see his attendance for March and April."

Once inside, Farrell introduced Hajek and Snyder to Carl Warren and asked him to provide Jaffe's work record for the last two months."

Warren sat at his desk and pulled out a ledger and opened to Jaffe's page. "We have all this on our computer for payroll but it's faster for me to look at the log." He turned the book for Snyder and Hajek to review.

Donald Jaffe worked every week day in March and so far in April.

Warren shifted in his chair. "Jaffe's a good man, a hard working family man."

"We'd like to speak with Mr. Jaffe," Snyder said.

"Sure. I'll call him. He's not far." Warren punched in a few numbers and asked Jaffe to come to his office.

"Can we use your office?" Farrell asked Warren.

"Sure." The manager put the ledger back in his desk drawer, got up and stood by the doorway watching for Jaffe.

When he arrived, Jaffe gave Farrell a surprised expression. Jaffe wore jeans and a Patriots sweatshirt. He had a runner's build, tall and thin and looked about 35. Warren introduced Snyder and Hajek. Jaffe remained silent. Farrell explained that the detectives had a few questions for him. Then Warren exited.

"Thank you for coming in," Snyder began and pointed to an empty canvas director's chair.

"What's this all about?"

"Your name came up in an investigation and we have some questions."

Jaffe sat down in a chair and pushed it back against a windowless wall. He glanced briefly around the room and then focused on the New York officers.

"How long have you lived in Chatham?" Snyder asked.

"All my life."

"This is our first visit to your neck of the woods. It looks nice." Snyder smiled.

"Lots of New Yorkers visit our town. We like their money but their attitude can be hard to take. No offense but they act as if they're better than us. Off season is the best here."

"Tell us what you know about Nathan Stover."

"That pervert. I hope you arrested him."

"Why do you say that?" Snyder asked.

Jaffe proceeded to repeat what they had learned from Joan Stover about the incident with his daughter Hannah. "The man had no shame. I hope you put him away."

"Someone already has. We're investigating his death."

Jaffe moved forward in his chair, mouth open. "Dead? I'm glad the bastard is dead." A hint of a smile flickered on his face.

"When were you last in New York City or Connecticut?" Snyder asked.

"Are you accusing me? I'm glad he's dead but I'm no murderer."

Snyder continued, "I have two daughters. If I knew someone harmed either of them-- honestly I don't know what I'd do. So please tell us the last time you visited New York City so we can eliminate you."

"Eight, no nine years ago my wife and I went in December. We did the Christmas stuff, Radio City Show, tree in Rockefeller Center, Fifth Avenue windows, usual tourist things. We never went again. Too expensive, not us."

"You haven't been there this year?"

"No."

For another ten minutes the men talked. Nothing in Jaffe's answers struck the detectives as responses of a guilty man. They needed more than anger with Nathan Stover to charge him. Snyder continued his questioning to determine if Jaffe had the ability to carry out this murder. Jaffe did not come across as a self-taught scientist or someone with the skills to pull off a complicated poisoning scheme.

Snyder dismissed Jaffe and the three remained in Warren's office. "Thanks for your hospitality, Chief Farrell. Jaffe's not our man."

"I'm sure glad about that. There was a bad case of food poisoning in Chatham last summer…at the 4th of July Congregational Church picnic. It's an annual fundraiser. Stover may have gone to it. It's popular with visitors and locals."

"Unlikely it would kill him months later." Hajek said.

"Maybe weakened his system and made him more susceptible to bad food," Farrell suggested.

"Anyone die?" Hajek asked.

"No, but a lot of people were real sick for a few days, some a week. It was terrible."

"Did they determine a cause?" Snyder asked.

"I heard it was the mayo on the potato salad."

Chapter 36

As promised, Hajek got in the driver seat.

Snyder fastened his seat belt. "Poor guy I feel for him. Amazing he didn't beat Stover with a baseball bat."

"His little girl… so sad…" Hajek thought about the long term consequences.

"Jaffe was our best and only prospect. He has the motive but not the means or opportunity to put toxins in Nathan Stover's food from a distance of 300 miles. We're back at square one."

"Afraid so."

"We can't spend any more time on this case right now," Snyder said.

"Maybe Stover's death was accidental." Hajek put on sunglasses and lowered his window. They drove on in silence. As Snyder dozed, Hajek replayed the medical examiner's words. Dr. Perkins suspected foul play. If not Jaffe, who? Maybe Stover bothered other little girls closer to his home. If that were true, those parents would have most likely contacted authorities. Maybe they took action on their own. We have no real suspects.

***

The sun set as they crossed into Connecticut. Near New Haven, cars backed up in all directions close to where Route 95 met 91. Snyder opened his eyes when Hajek hit the brakes hard to avoid hitting a car darting into his lane.

"Sorry about that."

Snyder sat up. "I could take over if you want. That nap revived me."

"Sounds good. I'll stop at the next rest area."

"Good I need one." Snyder slipped his shoes on.

When Snyder took over driving, Hajek asked, "Mind some music?"

"Can we first get the news headlines?"

"Sure." Hajek put on all-news New York radio station 88.

After a few stories, Snyder said, "Nothing catastrophic happened in our absence. That's good."

Hajek switched to a jazz station.

Snyder parked behind the precinct. "First thing Monday I'll call the FBI for an update on the Hanson case. I'm afraid we'll have to release the surveillance photos of our man who never read *Gentleman's Quarterly*."

"Wilcox will want to release it at a press conference." Hajek gathered his stuff.

Snyder shrugged. "Unless the Police Commissioner objects."

Chapter 37

Monday morning Snyder and Hajek updated Wilcox on the Hansen case. Wilcox agreed the public's assistance might be needed. "I'll call the Commissioner."

Snyder learned from the FBI more about the naval officer who had visited his aunt in the eastside apartment building. On April 7, days before the murder, he sailed out of New York Harbor on an aircraft carrier bound for Hawaii and its mission in the Pacific. The agent offered nothing new on the man in the surveillance photo.

"The FBI agent sounded smug and pleased that NYPD asked about the wrong suspect." Snyder relayed to Hajek.

"I'm glad you're dealing with the arrogant SOBs."

"I've been thinking about what you said about looking into military records. You convinced me not to dismiss the long shots," Snyder said.

"Great."

"I found a website, Vetfriendship. More than a million former servicemen use it. Soldiers post messages for buddies they served with and many have reconnected after all these years."

"Any connections with Thompson or Griffin?"

"Yes for both."

"Really. What's the chances of that?"

Snyder shrugged. "Pretty good when you pose as them."

"Otto, you impersonated soldiers on this site?"

"Got a message out and a couple responses came in fast. I'm hoping for more."

"Anything on Brian Towle?"

"Not yet."

Snyder's desk phone rang. The call was brief.

"Peter, that was Wilcox. The photos will be on the news this afternoon."

***

At two that afternoon Mayor Lockhardt, with Commissioner Sullivan and Captain Wilcox at his side, held a press conference. Sullivan asked the public's help in identifying the man who killed Courtney Hanson and released two photos. The first showed a front view of a man with a cap covering his face, carrying a toolbox and the second gave a back view of a man wearing a jacket with patched elbows. Minutes after the photos aired on the Monday evening news, callers inundated the tip line.

The following day, Wilcox assigned more staff to deal with the calls and assist the detectives. Hajek and Snyder prioritized those that merited a personal visit. They assigned officers to follow up on twenty-six tips.

People called asking about a reward. Some seemed interested in settling a vendetta. Others thought the photo resembled a former boyfriend, a co-worker or boss. Snyder moved many calls to the low priority category and a few he classified as moderate.

"Detective Snyder," a woman officer called out. "You'll want to listen to this one."

Snyder and Hajek listened to a caller around 4P.M. report that he was one hundred percent certain he knew the man in the photo. They wrote down the name and address the caller provided and decided this was a good excuse to get out of the station.

"Please replay that." Hajek pulled his small recorder from his pocket and taped the tip.

When they arrived at the address on Amsterdam Avenue, a ten year old boy answered the door. The odor of hamburgers filled the small apartment.

"We're with the New York Police Department and would like to speak with your father." A woman appeared in the kitchen doorway. Snyder showed his badge.

"You're welcome to come in and wait. My husband will be home from work soon."

Before she could ask the purpose of their visit, Kenny Farmer walked through the front door, his backpack swinging from his right arm.

"I'm Detective Snyder and this is Detective Hajek," Snyder explained to the surprised Kenny.

This man with thick dark hair and glasses lacked any resemblance to the man in the surveillance video. Hajek explained that they were following up on calls to a hotline in hopes of identifying a person of interest in a recent crime.

"May we speak with you alone?"

"Kenny Jr. Come in the kitchen." Kenny's wife directed their son.

"What do you do for work?" Hajek asked.

"I teach at R.O. Academy across town."

"Where were you about 4P.M. on April 11?"

"I'd still be at school then, at a meeting or with a student."

"And later that evening about 9P.M.?"

"By then I'd be home."

Snyder showed Kenny a glossy of the photo. "This is who we're looking for. Do you know this person?"

"No. He's not familiar. Those photos have been on the news, right?"

"Yes."

"I saw them on my computer before I left school yesterday and again on the late news."

"A tip someone called in brought us here," Snyder said.

"You think it's me?"

"Please listen to this call." Hajek played the call that triggered their visit. He noted Kenny's eyes widen.

"Do you recognize this voice?" Snyder asked.

"I'm afraid I recognize the lisp. A student in my Algebra II class struggles to pronounce words with the letter L in them. I'm sure it's him."

"Why would he do this?"

"He's failing Algebra and blames me."

"Mr. Farmer, we'll need his name and address."

"Seth Judd. I'm not sure of the exact address it's the apartment building on the south side of The Dakota. His father is a doctor. I've spoken with him many times about his son."

"Thanks for your cooperation. Sorry to bother you."

Back on the street, Snyder said, "We're paying a visit to this math flunkie."

The detectives drove to Central Park West and parked on 72nd Street. They walked into the large apartment building next to The Dakota, identified themselves to the doorman, and asked for Dr. Judd.

The doorman paged the Judd residence. "Sir, Detectives are in the lobby and would like to speak with you."

Through the intercom the detectives heard. "I'll be right down."

After quick introductions, Snyder explained that they were following up on leads called in to the police hotline. "We need to speak with your son."

207

Dr. Judd started to ask a question and stopped. He led them to his apartment, offered them seats in the living room and went to get his son. When father and son returned, Snyder said, "We'd like you to listen to this."

The son sat with his chin touching his chest. Dr. Judd glared as the recording played.

Hajek produced the photo for Dr. Judd.

"This looks nothing like Mr. Farmer. You're in big trouble, young man. I'm sorry you wasted time on this, detectives. Last quarter Mr. Farmer told him he needed to improve his grades to pass. He even offered to help him. I assure you I'll take care of this."

Hajek looked at Snyder and both nodded.

In the elevator Snyder pushed the lobby button. "Whatever Dr. Judd says or does will be more effective than our arresting the kid."

Chapter 38

First thing Wednesday Snyder reported on his Tarrytown visit with Brian Towle. "He's bigger than New Jersey's Governor Christi."

"Not our guy. Thanks Otto."

Snyder picked up the box of donuts on his desk. "Let's see what the tip line delivered."

Four officers looked up from a table in a conference room. They smiled when Snyder opened the box. "Any good news?"

"Cinnamon crullers. My favorite. Thanks." The officer took a bite.

"Here's our list." A Tom Hanks look alike turned his laptop for Snyder and Hajek to review.

They scrolled through and noted six calls were flagged as promising. "What's the follow up on the potentials?" Hajek asked.

The officer finished his donut. "Nothing viable. Three did not resemble the man in the photo at all. Two were someone twenty years younger and the last one has been in jail in Jersey for the last six months."

Wilcox marched into the room. "Tell me we're close to identifying the man in the photo."

Hajek repeated the update. Wilcox frowned.

"Thanks guys. Let us know if anything breaks." Wilcox turned to leave. Snyder and Hajek followed.

Back at their desks, Snyder said. "Let's go over what we have from the earlier murders and see if we can learn anything new." The detectives reviewed the crime scene photos and reread the reports.

At 11:30 Snyder said, "I'm ready for lunch."

Hajek stood. "Not even noon and it feels like 6P.M. Let's get out of here."

Once seated with their food Snyder said, "Tell me again about the two men you questioned in Connecticut."

Hajek recounted his interview with Thompson at his office and the strange encounter with Griffin through a half-opened door. "I'm sure there is a high school link between the killer and our victims' mothers. I'm surprised no one has recognized this guy as their co-worker or neighbor or brother."

"Most calls to the tip line have been from New York City. The photos are on all the Connecticut stations as well as national news. Wonder why we haven't had much response from Connecticut?"

Hajek shrugged. "Maybe we should ask the technical staff to project today's look of several males from their yearbook photos…you know…show how they aged."

"I don't know. It is such a long shot." Snyder picked up his pickle.

"We need to crack it soon. I'm worried the killer might strike again. Days like this are so annoying. I don't think I can reread those reports anymore."

Back at the precinct they tossed around possible next steps. Nothing grabbed them. Snyder stood. "I'm going to talk with the officers on the tip line again."

"Good luck." Hajek's mind drifted back to Chatham. Jaffe did not know of any other incidents of Stover molesting a child. That did not mean Stover had not.

If Stover bothered another summer visitor rather than a resident, that person could live in the New York City area. Having the opportunity to tamper with Stover's food still posed a unique challenge.

Hajek remembered Snyder saying it was a lucky break that Stover's father and wife weren't convinced that anyone killed Nathan Stover. They believed his death was accidental. Even without family breathing down their necks to find a killer, Hajek was not totally comfortable relegating it to inactive status.

***

Snyder cleared his desk and turned off his computer. "Peter, just to remind you, my wife and I leave tomorrow for a week."

Hajek looked up from his computer. "It's already May? How did that happen? Graduation, right?"

"Yes. Jessica's college graduation is this weekend."

"You and Sadie must be so proud. I've heard Austin is a nice place. Are you staying right in the city?"

"We are. We've done the tourist stuff on other trips…capital, LBJ Library, and the O'Henry sites. I was hoping this would be the last trip but my daughter is looking for work there. With my luck she'll marry the current boyfriend and stay there."

"Is he a musician?" Hajek asked.

"How'd you know?"

"The city is famous for its music."

"I doubt he earns enough to support a family. We'll be meeting his parents while we're there. They live in some little town called Cranfills Gap, Texas with a couple hundred other people. How can my daughter go from New York to some hamlet with more pastures than people? I don't get it."

Hajek laughed. "Maybe she likes the contrast."

"She wanted a horse when she was six. I thought she outgrew that dream."

"No harm in experiencing a different life for a while. No guarantee she'll be there forever." Hajek felt badly that Jessica staying in Texas disappointed Snyder.

211

Returning to business, "I hope we get a break with Hanson soon. I'm sorry about abandoning you now."

"Family comes first. I'll be fine."

"Maybe you can take care of phoning Stover's wife while I'm gone. She needs to know we spoke with Jaffe and that we do not consider him a suspect."

"I'll let her know."

"For now we can put that case on the back burner."

Chapter 39

On Thursday calls continued to the hotline, although at a slower pace than on the first two days. Hajek let Wilcox's extra staff chase down tips that rated moderate or high in probability. Hajek had no faith in these calls. He believed they would get a hit quickly or not at all.

He focused again on the Stover case. His partner wanted him to report to Joan Stover on the Cape trip findings. A nagging feeling that he missed something prevented him from picking up the phone and informing Mrs. Stover that he and Snyder did not consider Jaffe a suspect. Instead he decided to learn more about Joan.

Hajek googled Stover wedding, May. He regretted not asking for her maiden name. When he added Rodney and Isabella, Nathan's parents' names, he found the marriage announcement for Nathan Stover and Joan Palmer in *The Greenwich Times*. It interested him that they married in Nathan's church and not hers.

Using various databases and search engines he located Palmer family information. Joan, her parents, and one sister had resided at 65 Montgomery Avenue on Staten Island. Her father Fred worked as a self-employed carpenter. Joan and Colette attended Curtis High School.

The school website included links to yearbooks. Scanning Joan's class, he found photos of her in a science lab with other members of the science club. Comments under her individual photo included *destined to be the next Marie Curie.* The local newspaper from that year reported Joan Palmer received a high score on a national science exam.

His phone rang, Sloane registered as the caller, time 11:40AM.

"Hi Darren."

"Peter, do you know a Department of Justice Attorney, Alex Dawson?"

"That asshole. Why?"

"I have an appointment at two this afternoon to give a statement regarding our friend John Gordon."

"He wants your help putting the guy away for life."

"He didn't give me any details. Has Gordon done other crimes?" Sloane asked.

"No. Dawson has no experience. He thinks Gordon's an international terrorist."

"The FBI agrees with him."

"If they put Gordon away for an act of terrorism, Dawson figures he'll impress his boss. It's not right."

"Not much we can do. Want to meet for coffee when I'm finished?"

"How about I show you Grant's tomb?"

Sloane laughed. "I'd love it. I've never been there."

"Call me."

Hajek smiled as he put his phone down. Taking Sloane to Grant's tomb presented a diversion from being nowhere with either the Hanson or Stover cases. Maybe with Sloane's help they could offset Gordon's bad luck in having a zealous attorney handling his case.

After a moment, he looked again at the article on Joan's science achievement. He saved the data in his file on Joan and closed it. He remembered that Joan met Nathan in college and married before she graduated. When he first discussed her husband's autopsy, Joan gave the impression that she had no knowledge or interest in scientific terms. This withholding of information about her talent could be more than the disappointment of a dream deferred.

214

Next, Hajek found articles about the food poisoning at the church picnic in Chatham. Both *The Cape Cod Chronicle* and *The Cape Cod Times* reported that sixty-four people went to the hospital, hundreds more were sickened, but no one died.

His curiosity drove him to research more about salt water aquariums. The one in the Stover home had impressed Snyder. Hajek struggled to remember the names of the fish Joan mentioned when Snyder asked. He looked up information on maintaining a saltwater aquarium. The meticulous care required would deter most from having one in their home. For one with scientific skill, however, this offered a unique hobby. Tending to the rigorous testing of pH balance and oxygen and salt levels provided regular experiments for a frustrated scientist. The fish environment also had ample contaminants to cultivate.

Wanting to say more to Joan Stover than 'we concluded Jaffe did not poison Nathan, Hajek considered it necessary to see her in person. Her reaction would confirm his hunch. He called and asked to see her the next morning. Joan did not ask anything about Donald Jaffe. She did ask if Detective Snyder would be with him.

***

When Sloane called at 2:40, Hajek agreed to meet him at the front of the monument. Happy to leave the precinct, he secured his files, reserved a vehicle for his Connecticut trip the next day, and left to meet Sloane.

His less than a mile walk to the monument took only ten minutes. Knowing Sloane's trip could easily be forty-five minutes he went inside and picked up a few brochures. It had been years ago since he spent any time looking at the exhibits. When he told Francine about the place, she would say, "You'll have to show me sometime." They never got there. One of many things he thought they would do in the future. He went back outside and sat on a bench.

215

"It's larger than I thought." Sloane walked toward Hajek.

He stood and shook Sloane's hand. "Hi Darren, You're a welcome break. Thanks for calling."

"You look tired, my friend. What are you working on now?"

"Two murder cases. One's a serial killer and I'm worried he'll hit again."

"If anyone can get him, you will."

Hajek handed Sloane a brochure. "Let me show you the scene of the terrorist crime."

"Even with your preparation, Dawson surprised me."

"Cute, isn't he?" Hajek led the way to the front door.

"He really wants Gordon to get life."

"Ridiculous."

"I mentioned you and told him how impressed I am with your detective work," Sloane said.

"Bet he didn't like that."

"He did give me a strange look, but didn't comment."

"This area was covered with soot." Hajek outlined an area to the right of the door.

Sloane looked closely. "I see some hints of a darkened area. No real damage, just like you said."

"Gordon did this when no one was around. He never intended to harm anyone."

"I agree. What's inside?"

"A museum. It's open for another forty minutes. Let's walk through. The brochure tells the story of how the monument came to be built. I'll show you the highlights."

As they looked at the tapestries, flags and photos of the construction process, Hajek explained his wish that the Department of Justice would quickly wrap up Gordon's case and get on with more serious matters. "I told Dawson I might testify for the defense."

"You actually said that?"

"Yes, hoping to motivate him to see it my way."

"A jail sentence of a couple of years would make the point," Sloane said.

"Dawson is trying to inflate his pompous self at Gordon's expense. Ironically Gordon's store in Petersburg, Virginia is doing record business."

"How do you know?" Sloane asked.

"I visited Gordon in jail and he told me his local paper made him out to be a hero and mentioned the store in the article. People are coming from a distance to shop and show solidarity with Gordon."

The men walked outside. Sloane looked at the towering monument. "Now I know the answer if someone asks who's buried in Grant's tomb, Ulysses and his wife."

"Darren, I'm glad you got to see the scene of the crime and that there is no damage."

"I wish you luck with Dawson. My statement reinforces your point. I emphasized that your skills led to Gordon's arrest and told him Gordon never acted violently. He cooperated with my officers."

"Thanks. We'll see."

"Peter, I'm very grateful I got to work with you. I've made collaboration with other police departments a priority. So when a patrol officer spotted the truck in your bulletin he acted."

Hajek nodded. "Excellent teamwork."

"I get calls from other Police Captains to talk with officers about interdepartmental police work. You've made me a bit of a celebrity."

***

Friday morning Hajek arrived at the Stover residence ten minutes early. He saw Joan looking out the living room window. She opened the door as he walked up the steps. Her hair fell softly around her face, a dramatic contrast to her usual style, pulled back with a clip or barrette. She wore ivory dress slacks, a pale green top with a ruffled scoop neck, and strapped sandals.

Joan extended her hand. "Nice to see you again, Detective Hajek."

"Good morning, Mrs. Stover. I won't take much of your time."

"You'll have some tea I hope."

"Sure." He detected a scent of perfume and dismissed it as flowers in the house.

In her kitchen, the table set for two had a cluster of wildflowers in a cut-glass vase.

"I didn't mean for you to fuss," Hajek said.

"Oh, I felt like baking and thought you'd like something with your tea. Have a seat."

Hajek stood behind a chair, taking in the scene. Joan placed a two-tiered, ceramic server of mini muffins, nut breads, and spiral pastries filled with jam on the table. He heard a hint of soft piano music. Nothing prepared him for this equivalent of high tea with a hostess clearly working hard to impress him.

Joan placed a silver teapot next to Hajek's cup. Her own she filled with coffee.

Hajek started with his usual question. "How are your daughters?"

"They're fine. Emily will be a fairy in the school play. She loves her costume and dances around here all the time. Rebecca won a poetry contest. Her teacher expects it will be published. And Tanya mimics everything her sisters do."

"Do they mind that?"

"No, they're good with her."

"I'm glad they're okay. They impressed me as sweet girls. It's hard to lose a parent. I'm thankful they have a mother that's crazy about them." Hajek enjoyed listening to Joan's updates on her daughters. Details and anecdotes about their activities interested him. If Joan talked longer about them it would not have bored Hajek.

When Joan smiled her eyes sparkled. Hajek realized he had not thought of her as pretty. His mind returned to thinking about her daughters and their good fortune in having Joan for a mother. Her calm, loving, mothering style as well as her enthusiasm about everything they did provided a healthy environment for children. He refused to consider the alternative, life without their mother.

"We followed up on Donald Jaffe. He did not poison Nathan." He picked up his teacup and put it down without taking a sip. Looking directly at Joan he asked, "Did you know about the food poisoning at an event in Chatham last summer?"

"Vaguely. I heard there were problems with food." She pushed the pastries closer toward him.

"High levels of E.coli in the potato salad."

"Whatever that is."

"I'm really surprised you don't know about E.coli?"

"Surprised. Why?" Joan's lips parted into a smile.

"You were quite the science student at Curtis High."

Her smile disappeared.

219

"I expect you know quite a lot about various microorganisms." Hajek spoke in a firm even tone. "Your fish tank could be the perfect environment to culture toxins."

Joan's hand holding her cup trembled. She placed the cup in the saucer and stared at her hands on the table.

Hajek continued. "Someone with your scientific knowledge knows that type E botulism has been traced to contaminated fish. I believe you have the skill to grow this poison, disguise its odor, and mix into your husband's sandwich without him suspecting anything."

She looked up but said nothing. Fear replaced the sparkle in her eyes.

"Although this type of poisoning is rare, the mortality rate is high." He let his words sink in.

Joan sat in silence.

I have no other leads to pursue. Until we get something new, your husband's case will be considered inactive. We would need a confession to close this case."

Joan put her face in her hands.

Hajek stood. He left the pastry untouched and his teacup half full.

"Mrs. Stover, I know your girls need their mother. I don't expect to see you again. I'll let myself out."

Chapter 40

The slow pace of heavy traffic on the Connecticut Turnpike let him process what just happened. The meeting with Joan matched no other in his career. Lacking solid evidence, it would be hard to prove his conclusions on this case. A good lawyer would shred his circumstantial pieces of information. He encountered abused children on the beat and the thought of their futures haunted him. The worse were sexually abused by relatives. An image of the three Stover girls drawing pictures came to mind. Had their father molested nine-year old Rebecca? Joan's sobs when he asked about Nathan's possible abuse of their daughters convinced him the girls were much better off with their mother. Arresting Joan served no good purpose. He moved to the far right lane. As he passed a Stamford exit, his phone rang. He hit the speaker button.

"Where are you, Peter?" Nick Kostas asked.

"In Connecticut driving south on 95. About six miles from the New York border."

"A break in the case?"

If he only knew…"More dead ends."

"Camille and I are looking forward to your visit tomorrow evening. After dinner a couple of our neighbors will join us for the ballgame."

"Not that Red Sox fan." Hajek worked at expressing good spirits.

"Yeah. I invited Kyle. Have to show off my new big screen."

"Sounds good. What time?"

"Six. I'll let you concentrate on driving. See you tomorrow."

With Francine, Hajek had looked forward to an evening with friends. It was silly for him to feel awkward. He knew everyone that Nick invited. He had no reason to expect an unpleasant time. For the remaining miles back to New York

City, he played scenes in his head of past social gatherings. When Nick's friend Gil started talking politics, Francine cooled the conversation by bringing up amusing baseball stories like Babe Ruth was the best because he hit 60 home runs on beer. Other times she would go on about baseball players' nicknames or do the Abbot and Costello skit--Who's on first. Remembering, he laughed and then quickly fought back tears.

Hajek parked in the police garage and slowly walked toward the precinct. A cool breeze stirred the sporadic trees along the street. His mind returned to the Stover family. What would he tell his captain? Wilcox would object to Peter ignoring an obvious lead. He passed the precinct entrance, continued to the corner deli, and placed an order for pastrami with Swiss cheese on rye. While the counter man fixed his sandwich, he took an iced tea from the cooler and sat at the table farthest from the front door. With the lunch rush over, he had time to decompress.

"All set, Detective. Extra pickle?"

"Please." Hajek paid for his lunch and carried it to the table.

He ate slowly. There was only one person he could have told that he chose the lives of three young children over carrying out the law. Francine would have approved. Although not ambivalent about his decision, he could not speak honestly with Wilcox.

When he could no longer stall, he walked back to the precinct. At his desk, he found a note from Wilcox, *see me*. Hajek first went to the men's room. Wilcox did not know that Hajek concluded Joan had poisoned her husband and he decided to disregard the evidence and relegate the case to inactive. He wished for this uneasiness to pass quickly.

The captain looked up from his phone when Hajek stood in the doorway and he motioned for him to sit down.

222

"I'll be home by six, Honey." He placed the phone down. "DOJ is willing to plea with the bomber. They're set to recommend ten to twenty with ten years' probation."

"Anything more than two is too much."

"He tried to blow up a federal building."

"Captain, he only defaced it and I believe that was his intention."

"You feel strongly that DOJ can make a point without insisting on a maximum sentence."

"I do."

Wilcox stood and paced. "It looks better for us if people think Gordon's a terrorist we brought to justice."

"He's not over his ancestor losing to a Yankee. He's pathetic but not a danger to society. I hope there will be a fair resolution."

"It's up to the DOJ to determine Gordon's charges. We did our job."

"I hope it's settled with a reasonable sentence."

Wilcox sat back down. "Now about the Hanson case. The public hasn't come through for us with an identity, have they?"

"Only wild goose chases. It's discouraging," Hajek sighed, relieved that Wilcox was not asking about the Stover case.

"I know Otto's out. Have you guys discussed a next step?"

"We're reviewing all our contacts to see if there's anything else to pursue."

"Get something."

223

Chapter 41

Saturday morning Hajek completed a twenty-five mile bike ride. Pedaling at an easy pace, he enjoyed the cool breeze on his face while he wondered about his handling of the Stover case. Those little girls needed their mother. There was no other course of action. Move the case to inactive and focus on the Hanson case. On the way back to his apartment, he stopped at a neighborhood florist where he had often bought flowers for Francine. Although it reminded him of her, he liked the owner and did not want to go somewhere new.

Nelson greeted him when he walked into the shop with his bike. "Peter, nice to see you. How was the ride?"

"Not my fastest, Nelson."

"That's better. Why rush?"

"Nelson, I'd like to bring my mother some flowers when I visit her tomorrow. Something small, she doesn't have much space."

"Sure. How's she doing?"

"The same. She always seems happy, which is easier for me, but I'm never certain she knows me."

Nelson set down his shears. "That's hard. Any particular flowers you want?"

"You're the pro. Use your judgment. Include white roses."

"How about a small arrangement in a tea cup?"

"Perfect. You're the best. I'll pick it up later this afternoon."

Hajek knew his mother would enjoy a floral display and he looked forward to visiting her the next day. Although there was no real conversation, he found spending time in her presence comforting. Soon after Francine's cancer diagnosis, Hajek explained her absence. Until a few months ago they often went to the nursing home together. Now when he dropped in to see his mother, she never asked about his wife and he had no need to tell her that Francine died.

Back at his apartment Hajek's cell phone rang. He recognized the precinct number and took the call.

"Sorry to bother you, Hajek. A woman, Teresa Jenkins, insisted I tell you that her daughter's friend was killed in Charlotte, North Carolina last night. She should be calling the police there, not you."

"Teresa Jenkins called about a murder?"

"You know her?"

"Yes."

"Well, she wants you to call her. Here's her cell number."

Hajek called.

"Detective," barely understandable followed by sobs.

"This is Vincent Jenkins. My wife is too upset to talk. Our daughter Kaitlin's friend Samantha was murdered last night. We're at LaGuardia airport waiting to board a flight to Charlotte."

"Tell me what you know."

"Samantha flew in from Nebraska to celebrate Kaitlin's birthday. They're friends from college. Kaitlin had hoped to work half a day and pick Samantha up at the airport at 2 P.M. Instead, she had to work late. Samantha took a cab to Bank of America. Kaitlin gave her a spare house key. When she got home, she found Samantha dead just inside the front door."

"Where's Kaitlin now?" Hajek spoke in an even tone.

"She's with Samantha's parents. The police called Mr. and Mrs. Neuhaus last night and. they took her to their home."

"I'm glad Kaitlin's not alone. I'll call the Charlotte police and get back to you later."

"We'll feel a lot better when the killer's caught."

Hajek sat in his living room with his mind racing about the murderer. This must be the serial killer. What did the shift to the victim's birthday mean? Did he know he killed the wrong woman? How many more children of classmates were in danger?

He found the number for the Charlotte police. When he called, he learned the lead detective was Rochelle Quintero.

"Was there urine and a piece of rope at the scene?" Hajek blurted when Quintero got on the line.

"Why do you ask?"

"I believe you're dealing with a serial killer."

"Based on what?"

Hajek got up and paced. "A young woman was murdered in New York City earlier this month. The killer let himself into the victim's apartment and then strangled her with a half-inch thick rope when she returned home. I know of three other murders with a similar pattern. We have rope from each scene."

Quintero did not respond for a few seconds. "Four young women murdered in the same manner." Her words came out like a new reader saying each word separately.

"Yes. All were daughters of four women who were high school friends. We have a DNA match for two of the four murders. The Connecticut police didn't analyze the urine found in the first murder."

"Our chief would not want us to rush into saying we're dealing with a serial killer."

Hajek sat on a stool in his kitchen. "The first victim was Kaitlin's sister. You might want to keep the victim's identity secret for another day or two."

"Too late. We've released it to the media after notifying her family."

Hajek pounded the counter. "Damn. It's already on the news."

"I'm afraid so."

"I believe he got the wrong victim. When he realizes that, he may go after Kaitlin Jenkins."

"Her residence is a crime scene. We told her she can't return there for a few days. She left the police station with the victim's family last night."

"Kaitlin's parents are on their way to North Carolina. I'm coming down also." Hajek stood and walked back to the living room.

"Take my cell number and call me when you get to town."

***

The first two airlines he checked had full planes. A 4P.M. US Airways flight had a one-way, first class ticket for $835.00. He completed the booking with his credit card.

Hajek had only forty minutes before he needed to be enroute to La Guardia. He found a car service that would pick him up. He showered, threw clothes in a backpack, and checked his camera and tape recorder batteries. He locked his weapon in the bedroom safe and made it to the street as a black Town Car pulled to the curb.

The traffic on the Grand Central Parkway crawled. *He needed to make this plane.* With an hour and a half until take-off, he arrived at the terminal.

His first class ticket made for an easy check in and a short line at security. When he reached the gate he verified that it matched his flight. He called Nick.

"You're not canceling, my friend," Kostas said before Hajek could speak. "We want you here."

"The Hanson killer struck again. This time in Charlotte, North Carolina. I'm at LaGuardia waiting for a flight." Hajek stood by the wall of windows at a

227

closed gate opposite the one for his flight. He told Kostas about the Friday night murder and his belief that the intended victim, Kaitlin Jenkins, would be next.

"Okay. I understand. Anything I can do?"

"Give my apologies to Camille. I'll call when I'm back in town."

Realizing he had not eaten since breakfast, Hajek purchased two slices of pizza and a Coke. While he ate he thought about the killer. Was he still in Charlotte? Would he attend Samantha's funeral to get near Kaitlin? Would he go to Illinois or Buffalo to kill others? Were Roberta's other daughter and son in danger? What about Marsha's son in Buffalo? Getting in this guy's head defied Hajek. He hoped the killer did not yet realize his mistake.

Hajek threw the pizza wrappings into the trash. Checking the status of his flight, he found he had thirteen minutes until boarding. He called Wilcox at home and told him what he knew about the Charlotte murder. He shared his belief that the killer targeted the Bethel victim's sister.

"You've spoken with the Charlotte police?"

"Yes. I talked with the detective in charge. They're investigating, interviewing family members, neighbors…the usual. I told her about the other murders. Detective Quintero will meet with me this evening."

"Good. You're sure the killer used the same kind of rope?" Wilcox asked.

"When I described it, I surprised the detective because no one had released that piece of information."

"Peter, your theory of an old grudge may be right on. What do you need from me?"

Hajek sank in a seat at an unused gate where he could see when his plane started boarding.

"Inform the FBI."

228

"Right. And I'll update the Commissioner. Are your notes in the computer?"

"Yes. Direct the officers on the tip line to pay attention to anyone mentioning Charlotte, North Carolina."

"I'm on it. Anything else?"

"We need to alert the families of all known victims.

Chapter 42

As the plane approached the airport for an on-time landing, Hajek saw the crown-shaped top of a building in the center of Charlotte. Hoping for a fast exit, he watched buildings, vehicles, and trees become larger. As the plane drew nearer to the ground, wind gusts bent branches and the plane bounced like it hit speed bumps. An abrupt drop completed a rough landing.

The plane taxied toward the gate and stopped several yards short. "Welcome to Charlotte. This is your captain. Thank you for flying with US Airways. The temperature is 74 degrees. There will be a brief delay before we can disembark. We're waiting for a technician to open the gate door. Thanks for your patience."

The man seated next to Hajek fidgeted. "So much for on time."

Once the door opened, passengers grabbed bags from the overhead compartments and made their way off the plane. Hajek walked with the crowd through the narrow passageway to the terminal. Then he dashed down the concourse, took the stairs two at a time down to the baggage area, and rushed out the door to the cabs lined up along the curb.

Hopping into one, he startled the driver.

"Hertz Rental," Hajek directed the man.

"Take the shuttle." The cab driver pointed to a rental car pick-up sign.

"I'm in a hurry. I'll pay you thirty dollars to take me immediately."

"Yes, sir." The driver started his vehicle and pulled away from the curb.

Hajek called Detective Quintero. "I've landed and I'm on my way to pick up a rental car."

"My boss and I are at the Center City Station," Quintero said.

"601 Trade Street, right?" Hajek asked.

"Yes. See ya soon."

The cab stopped outside the fence at the entrance to the rental car lot. "This is the best I can do. Only Hertz shuttles can drive in."

A uniformed man ran to the cab. "Move on. No walk-ins allowed."

Hajek rolled down the window. "Police officer." He flashed his badge.

The man stepped back. "Renting?"

"Yes. I just flew in from New York. I'm in a hurry."

"Okay." The attendant returned to his post.

Hajek took three tens from his wallet.

"Skip it. I don't want any trouble."

"I'm not here to harass cabbies." Hajek leaned forward and threw the cash on the seat. "Thanks for the ride." Hajek grabbed his bag and walked away. He remembered reading articles about fare abuses in several cities and that Charlotte pledged to eliminate the practice. He regretted frightening the driver who looked terrified that he would lose his job for accepting a fare 'off the meter'.

Hajek trotted the short distance to the office. The rental process was unusually painless and fast. He threw his backpack in the trunk of the red, Chevy Aveo. Before starting the car, Hajek called Teresa Jenkins' cell phone. She told him that they had a room at the Marriott Courtyard near Exit 67 on I-85 near Salisbury. He took the number and address and told her he would arrive there after his meeting with the Charlotte police.

"I'm glad you're here. I'm so afraid for Kaitlin. Call our room when you get here," Teresa insisted.

"Is Kaitlin with you?"

"Yes."

"You're in for the night, right?" Hajek hoped he did not sound as worried as he felt.

231

"Yes."

Hajek called the hotel and requested a room on the same floor as the Jenkins family. The only vacancy on that floor was a suite at the opposite end of the hallway from the Jenkins. He reserved it, then keyed the police station address into the GPS and made his way out of the rental car parking lot to Route 74 East.

For several miles on Wilkinson Boulevard he passed strip malls with empty store fronts, boarded up restaurants and run down fast food places. Tall office buildings stood in the distance. The landscape became more upscale when he turned onto South Boulevard where hotels, condos, restaurants and office buildings came into view. His electronic guide brought him through streets crowded with people out for a Saturday night. He parked at 601 East Trade Street and walked into the Charlotte Mecklenburg Police Station.

***

In the lobby a tall black man dressed in navy chinos and a starched yellow shirt approached Hajek. "I'm Wendell Ives, Chief of Detectives."

Hajek introduced himself and the men shook hands.

"Detective Quintero's waiting." Ives led the way.

At her desk, Quintero looked up from her laptop and stood as the chief introduced Hajek. She was about 5'8" with curly red hair. She wore a black suit with a powder blue top, a necklace of turquoise stones and several bracelets. Hajek could not be certain but he guessed she was close to his age.

"I appreciate you both meeting me on a Saturday night," Hajek said.

"Oh is it Saturday?" A faint smile showed on Quintero's face.

Ives started walking. "We'll use my office." Ives stopped half way down the hall, opened a door, switched on the lights and motioned to four chairs arranged around a low table. "Please have a seat."

Quintero took a seat and rested her laptop and a folder on the table. "We have a lot of questions."

"I wish I had more answers." Hajek sat in the chair next to Quintero. Ives positioned himself opposite Hajek.

"Who is this killer? How long have you been looking for him? What's the connection with this Charlotte victim?"

Taking one question at a time, Hajek told the detectives he did not know much about the killer. Three weeks ago in Manhattan someone murdered a young woman in her apartment when she returned home from work. His investigation turned up three similar strangulations of young women at their homes in Connecticut, upstate New York, and Illinois. When he said the mothers of all four were high school friends the detectives straightened in their seats.

"I'm afraid Samantha was in the wrong place at the wrong time. Kaitlin Jenkins lives in that house. Her sister was the Connecticut victim seven years ago. It looks like our killer accelerated his pace and now he's targeting additional members of these four families."

"Do you think he knows he killed the wrong woman?" Ives asked.

"We have to assume he does. The victim's name is all over the news, right?" Hajek looked for confirmation.

Ives and Quintero nodded.

"I'm very concerned for Kaitlin's safety. Samantha flew from Nebraska to North Carolina to celebrate Kaitlin's birthday. For the previous murders, the killer struck on the mothers' birthdays."

Ives clasped his hands. "We'll work with Salisbury police to provide protection."

"Thank you. Where are you with your investigation?" Hajek asked.

Quintero opened a folder. "Last evening, we questioned Kaitlin Jenkins. She's very distraught. She kept saying 'it could have been me.' We confirmed that Samantha came to Bank of America building and Kaitlin gave her an extra house key. Kaitlin planned to get home by seven. When Kaitlin arrived at 7:10, she found Samantha on the floor close to the front door. She called 911. She told the responding officers the front door was locked and she used her key to enter. Our officers saw no evidence of a break-in."

Hajek frowned. "Same pattern as the others. Locks are no obstacle for this guy. Do you have the 911 recording?"

"Yes." Quintero picked up her laptop, located the file and hit play.

A shrill female voice filled the room. *My friend...*the next words were inaudible with Kaitlin's hysterical howling. Her pain struck a chord with Hajek. He listened to the end. The dispatcher directed Kaitlin to wait outside without stating that the murderer might still be in the house.

"Thank you." Hajek swallowed hard and cleared his throat. The raw anguish reminded him of his own heartbreak.

Quintero looked down at more notes. "Last night around nine the victim's parents, Mr. and Mrs. Neuhaus, came to the station. They had spoken with their daughter around four o'clock when she called them from a cab on the way into Charlotte. They planned to see her on Sunday before she returned to Nebraska."

"What about interviews with neighbors?" Hajek asked.

Quintero scanned pages. "Officers spoke with several residents in Fourth Ward including the neighbors in the adjacent homes. No one noticed a man enter or leave the house."

"Could I see the transcripts?"

"I'll print the couple I have."

"Photos?" Hajek asked.

"Here." Quintero passed a stack to Hajek.

Hajek noted that the body lay face up. "This rope around her neck looks familiar. I'd like to see it."

"We'll make it available," Ives said.

Hajek glanced at several more photos from the crime scene and then handed them back. Quintero got up and retrieved several pages from a printer. She handed them to Hajek and sat down again.

"Captain Wilcox from my precinct notified the FBI of Samantha's murder," Hajek said.

Quintero nodded. "A local FBI agent already called. Their team will be here tomorrow afternoon. They requested we seal the crime scene and post police there. They will take the evidence and test it in the FBI lab."

"I'd like to see the crime scene," Hajek said.

"It wouldn't hurt to have another look around before the Feds arrive. You can go with us tomorrow morning," Ives said.

"Any chance of going tonight?"

Ives and Quintero looked at each other. "Sure," Ives said.

"Where's your hotel?" Quintero asked.

"Salisbury. I reserved a room where the Jenkins are staying."

"Let's continue our conversation in the car." Ives stood and moved his chair.

"Can we take the photos?" Hajek looked at the closed folder.

Quintero placed the photos in her jacket pocket. The three walked to the police garage passing two officers bringing a handcuffed man into the station. Quintero moved toward the driver's door of an unmarked Buick Regal. Hajek sat in the backseat.

Ives opened the door behind the driver. "No offense, Quintero. It's easier to talk with Hajek back here." Ives turned to Hajek. "I'm reluctant to publicize the possibility of a serial killer."

"Good. It's better the killer doesn't know we're on to him." Hajek settled into his seat.

On the way to the crime scene, Hajek asked to keep the Jenkins family's whereabouts quiet. "After they've returned to Connecticut their safety poses different problems."

Quintero stopped at a red light. "It would help if we knew whether the killer remained in this area. Do you think he'll attend the service for the victim?"

"Hard to know. We should check with clerks at hotels near the crime scene and the airport and ask if any single males from Connecticut stayed there in the last couple of days."

"That's a reach," Ives said. "What else do you know about this guy?"

"He's over fifty. I have a list of persons of interest back in New York. I'll ask my captain to email it."

"Specific names would help. We'll get on it as soon as you give them to us."

Quintero turned left on Tenth Street and left again on North Poplar.

Hajek sat up. "Victorian homes? This isn't my image of Charlotte."

Ives smiled. "Our oldest neighborhood, Fourth Ward surprises many visitors. This is where Charlotte's movers and shakers lived at the end of the 1800s and early 1900s."

"I had no idea." He continued to take in the grand, colorful homes, some with gingerbread millwork until they pulled up behind a parked CMPD patrol car.

Quintero pulled blue latex gloves from the console and tossed them to the others. "I'll grab the booties in the trunk."

The officer rolled down his window to speak with the detectives.

"Hi. Anything happening?" Ives asked.

"Pretty quiet. I've recorded out of state license numbers of cars that have driven by. Earlier, a Channel 14 news van was here. A reporter interviewed some people on the street."

"We won't be long." Quintero released the gate latch, lifted the yellow police tape and walked under it. They covered their shoes with disposable covers. Then they put on the gloves. She unlocked the front door and led the way into the house.

Tape outlined where the victim's body had been found. Looking around Hajek tried to visualize the killer's actions. Did he wait in the living room near the front hallway? Did he watch from the window until he saw a woman alone walk toward the house? When Samantha entered did she turn her back to close the door or did she meet him head-on? Most likely he stood ready with the rope and quickly wrapped it around her neck. She didn't have a chance.

"Anything taken from the victim?"

"Her purse and backpack looked undisturbed. We found them on the floor near the entrance. It appeared that she dropped them when the killer attacked."

"Can I see the photos again?" Hajek mentally matched the location of the purse and backpack with the floor of the front entranceway. They had dropped about a foot from the body. "I'd like to take a look around."

In the kitchen, Hajek searched cabinets. "At one murder site he left clothing—a disguise he wore."

"We'll make the transcripts of our search available to you. That will include anything our officers found."

Hajek opened a door to the outside. A flood light illuminated three wooden steps and a tiny enclosed yard. He walked out and noted shrubs and

237

flowers along the perimeter. Barking sounded close, but the darkness concealed the dog from sight. The wrought iron fence, at least six feet in height, would be hard to scale. He looked up and pointed to lights in the windows of a neighboring home.

"Tomorrow I'd like to speak with the residents next door."

"They'd have a good view of the backyard," Ives said. "We can get here an hour before the Feds arrive. We'll be glad to include your questions in our follow-up interviews."

"Thank you. I'll also look around the outside of the house in daylight." Hajek continued to scan the property boundary and adjacent buildings. "If you don't mind, I'll walk through the rest of the house."

"Of course." Ives held the door.

They made their way upstairs. Nothing looked out of place in the master bedroom or the other two second-floor rooms.

"I doubt he ever came up here," Hajek said.

"I agree." Ives looked at the family photo on the dresser.

Hajek pointed to Maura standing next to Kaitlin. "That's the first victim. The one on the right lives here."

Quintero stepped closer. "I recognize Kaitlin."

Ives moved toward the stairs. "We done?"

Back on the first floor, Quintero checked that the back door was locked. The detectives walked to their car. Riding back to the station, Ives mentioned that the FBI requested the medical examiner allow an agent to observe the autopsy scheduled for Monday.

"I hope that won't delay releasing the body," Hajek said.

"That shouldn't be a problem," Ives said.

Hajek made a note to ask Samantha's family for a list of people who sent flowers and for permission to copy any hand-written condolence messages. He would also review all communications in the online funeral home guest book.

Chapter 43

Driving to the hotel, Hajek reflected on his meeting with the Charlotte detectives and the crime scene. There was no doubt in his mind that whoever killed Samantha had also murdered Courtney Hanson in New York.

Shortly after nine, he checked into the Marriott and immediately called the Jenkins suite.

A man answered.

"I'm Detective Hajek. I'm in a room down the hall from you. May I stop by?"

"We're up. Please come to our room."

When Hajek knocked on the door, he held his badge in line with the peep hole.

A tall man with tired eyes and gray hair with a few dark streaks opened it. "Vincent Jenkins. Come in, Detective. I'm happy to meet you. Thank you for coming to Charlotte. My wife and Kaitlin will join us soon. Please have a seat."

Vincent pointed to the sitting area in front of a television. Hajek sat in a chair at the end of the coffee table. Jenkins sat on the couch. "My wife said you planned to speak with the Charlotte police. Is there anything new?"

"No. Not yet. I met with the lead detective and her supervisor at the station. They're conducting a thorough investigation." Hajek did not mention the crime scene.

"Tell me they're more competent than the Bethel cops."

"I think that's true. We also know more now. I have to believe we'll get him this time."

"Kaitlin's traumatized. I wanted to take her home right away. She insists on attending the service for Samantha. Isn't she in danger until the police capture the murderer?"

"Why do you think that?"

Vincent attempted a smile. "I may be stubborn and a little thick--Irish you know. I agree that Maura's murder was not random and there may be a connection with Courtney and now Samantha. When my wife told me you interviewed her after Courtney Hanson's murder, I was furious. Making her relive the horror of our daughter's death...Now I understand."

"Do you have any idea who would be this angry with Teresa and her friends?"

"Not a clue. The Bethel police had it all wrong. Maura's murder was deliberate. I want this guy behind bars. Actually I want him fried and I want to flip the switch."

The bedroom door opened. Teresa sobbed at the sight of Hajek. He stood as she walked into the room. Vincent leaped up and led his wife to the sofa. They sat with his arm around her shoulder. "You've got to get this killer." Teresa gasped and continued weeping.

Vincent asked softly, "Is Kaitlin okay?"

Teresa caught her breath. "She's taking a shower."

"Detective Hajek met with the Charlotte police." Vincent rubbed his wife's shoulder.

"The police want to apprehend this guy. They understand we're after a serial killer," Hajek said.

"Is the FBI involved?" Vincent asked.

"Yes. A team will start tomorrow at the crime scene."

"Will you work with them?" Teresa asked.

"If they allow me."

Teresa blew her nose. "Kaitlin hasn't slept in more than twenty-four hours. Friday night she was with Samantha's family at the police station. They got to the Neuhaus home very late and talked until around four this morning. We spent the day with them and checked in here about 7:00. I hope she can sleep tonight."

The bedroom door opened. Kaitlin's damp, black hair curled around her face. She wore a robe over pajamas.

"Dear, sit with us," Teresa said.

Kaitlin sank into a chair.

"This is Detective Hajek." Teresa motioned to her right. Kaitlin nodded.

"I'm sorry." Hajek knew words were lame in addressing profound loss. He wished he could offer more comfort.

Vincent got up and stood behind Kaitlin with his hand on her shoulder. "Detective, how much danger are we in?"

"That's hard to say."

"Shouldn't we go to Connecticut ASAP?"

"I think Connecticut is dangerous. You've lived there for decades. The killer knows your home address."

Teresa gasped. "Not safe in our own home!"

Kaitlin wailed, terror evident in her eyes.

"What do you recommend?" Vincent asked.

"First we need to deal with your safety here in North Carolina. Tomorrow we'll move to another hotel to rooms reserved in my name. The Charlotte police will coordinate protection with the Salisbury Police Department. How long will you be in this area?"

Vincent glanced at his wife. "We'll leave after the memorial service on Wednesday."

"What plans have Samantha's family made?"

Teresa took a deep breath. "Some of the Neuhaus family live in Kansas and can't arrive until late Monday. Visitation is set for Tuesday afternoon and the church service will be on Wednesday. I feel so sad for them." Teresa struggled to stifle tears.

"Then after the funeral, where could you go instead of home?"

"Vincent, we could go to our place in western Massachusetts," Teresa said.

Hajek nodded. "That should be safe."

"How long?" Vincent asked.

"I can't say. We'll know more in a few days."

"What about my job?" Kaitlin turned to her father.

"Like the detective said, we'll know more in a few days. We need to be cautious." Vincent gave Teresa an anxious look. "It's late. We can talk in the morning. Let's meet downstairs for breakfast at nine."

Chapter 44

Back in his room, Hajek went online and booked a suite for the Jenkins and a room next door for himself at a Hampton Inn thirteen miles away. Hoping to relax enough to sleep, he took a long, hot shower.

Stretched out in bed he felt fatigue in every limb but his mind raced. Where was this guy? Had he met him? He reviewed his two Connecticut interviews. The roofer impressed him as slick but said he did not look back. Was that true? Thompson had a successful business and a family. The Stamford guy, Griffin, came across as challenged with getting through the day. Their brief interaction in the doorway of his home revealed little. The overgrown shrubbery and peeling paint on the house showed his indifference to upkeep. From his peek inside, Hajek concluded Griffin also neglected housekeeping. Physically he looked pathetic. Wondering about those still on the person-of-interest list, Hajek knew he had to find out more. He set the alarm for seven, thinking he would be lucky to have it wake him.

How did the perp pick the front door lock of Kaitlin's home unobserved? This audacity especially alarmed Hajek. Would the killer target another victim? At some point sleep silenced his ponderings.

A siren woke him. Bleary-eyed, he read 3:20 on the clock next to his bed. It took several moments before he remembered he was in North Carolina. The piercing sound faded into the distance. He had slept less than three hours. A to-do list for the day started running in his head. Between thinking of more items that needed his attention, he told himself he needed to get back to sleep.

At seven o'clock the alarm buzzed. Once he identified the sound, he pushed the off button, stretched, and yawned. Slowly he swung his feet to the floor and sat on the side of the bed holding his pounding head. Gradually he got up.

When did he last have caffeine? He poured water into the pot next to the sink and plugged it in. From an outside pocket of his backpack, he retrieved tea bags. Coffee-tinged tea gagged him. Finding the withdrawal pain intolerable, he pulled on yesterday's clothes and went downstairs. He helped himself at the self-service counter and sat with a cup of tea in the empty sitting area in front of a fake fireplace.

With his headache easing, he flipped through the two-day-old, weekend edition of *The USA Today*. He fixed another cup of tea and returned with it to his room. More awake, he spotted on the desk, transcript pages from Detective Quintero that he forgot he had. The pile did not include the interview with the next door neighbor. Disappointed with that omission, he read five summaries that provided nothing remarkable. A woman pushing a two year old in a stroller saw two young adult males walking on Kaitlin's street. She did not think they lived in Fourth Ward. The others reported nothing specific.

He took a shower, shaved, and got dressed. Hajek needed to update his partner on the recent developments. Calling Snyder's home phone, he left a message. "Hope you enjoyed your vacation. Call me on my cell phone. I must speak with you before you go to work tomorrow. I'm in North Carolina. Another murder of a young woman that looks all too familiar."

***

In the hotel cafe Hajek sat in a booth waiting for the Jenkins.

A waitress approached. "Good morning. We have a wonderful buffet with hot and cold items. Can I get you some coffee?"

"Just tea for now. My friends will be here soon." Hajek spotted Vincent and Teresa getting off the elevator and waved.

Teresa slid into the booth opposite Hajek and Vincent sat next to her. "Kaitlin's not interested in breakfast."

245

"How's she doing?"

"She did sleep. I think we convinced her to hang out with us today. I was afraid she'd insist on going back to Salisbury." Vincent nodded when the waitress held up a coffee carafe.

"The Hampton Inn granted us an early check-in. I'd like to leave here at eleven."

Vincent poured cream into his coffee. "That's fine. We'll be ready."

"I expect to spend most of the day in Charlotte."

"Don't worry about us. We'll be okay. Kaitlin mentioned she'd like to compose something for the service. We'll help her." Teresa turned to her husband and he nodded agreement.

After breakfast they agreed to meet in the lobby at 11:00.

***

Taking a circuitous route to the next hotel, Hajek kept checking his rearview mirrors for a tail. Vincent followed driving Kaitlin's car. Satisfied that no one pursued them, Hajek pulled into the Hampton Inn. He directed Vincent to back into a space to conceal the one rear license plate. Once in their rooms on the top floor, Hajek headed out for his one o'clock appointment with Quintero.

Chapter 45

Hajek drove south on Route I-85. When his GPS directed him to take Exit 41, Sugar Creek Road, he hesitated. It seemed far from Charlotte. Then he decided not to doubt the expert. The historian in him wondered about the origins of Sugar Creek's name. After several miles, he reached North Poplar Street. Detectives Quintero and Ives stood speaking to the officer in the patrol car.

Hajek lowered his window. "Good afternoon."

"How was your night?" Ives asked.

"Okay. Where can I park?"

"There are spaces in the next block." Quintero pointed straight ahead.

Hajek pulled behind a blue sports car and returned. "Thanks for letting me look around. I know you and your staff have been over the property."

"More scrutiny can't hurt." Quintero led the way to a stone path in the yard to the right of the house. Ivy clustered along the foundation. Beds of tulips filled the space between the walkway and the property line on the right.

Hajek bent to inspect. He followed meticulously the length of the base of the house. "No evidence of trampling."

"It rained Thursday night into Friday. The ground would've been damp in the afternoon when the killer arrived," Ives said.

"I walked here just before dark Friday and didn't see any footprints." Quintero said.

They entered an area with patches of grass scattered among bunches of daffodils, a group of azaleas, a crape myrtle, and a flowering cherry.

"The back yard looks undisturbed." Hajek scanned from left to right. "

"Anyone coming in this way would leave tracks." Quintero moved closer to the back wall. "The killer had to enter from the front."

"This six foot fence with shrubbery and flowers in front prohibit easy access. There's no gate here." Hajek observed the unbroken barrier of iron and plantings that enclosed the back yard.

With the sound of a familiar bark followed by a male voice saying *Quiet, Polly*, Hajek turned to Ives and Quintero. "Let's go talk with him now."

Ives went to the property edge and called over the fence. "I'm Chief Ives with the Charlotte Mecklenburg Police. We'd like to come over and ask you some questions."

"Sure. I'll meet you out front."

Next door the detectives found a stocky man about forty-five. "Jeff Clark." He extended his hand. "This is Polly." A yellow Labrador retriever stood beside him.

"Wendell Ives." The Chief showed his badge and introduced the others.

"Like I told the other officers when they spoke with me yesterday, I wish I could be more help." Clark stroked the Lab's head.

"We're revisiting the neighbors on the chance we missed something." Ives took a small notepad from his pocket. "Mr. Clark, were you home Friday afternoon?"

"I got here around four-thirty."

"Did you notice anything unusual?"

"A cab pulled up next door. No more than ten minutes after me. A woman got out. At first I thought it was Kaitlin. When she travels for work, she sometimes takes a cab to and from the airport. But she didn't wave."

"How well do you know Kaitlin?"

"Catherine, the owner of the house, introduced us when she decided to sublet to Kaitlin while she taught in Spain. We exchanged phone numbers and I told Kaitlin to call if she needed anything."

248

"Can you describe the woman you saw?"

"I didn't really see her face. She had long hair, dark brown. She was heavier than Kaitlin but a similar height, I'd guess." Clark's dog moved closer.

"Did you think it odd that someone entered the house without Kaitlin?" Ives asked.

"I do now but at the time I didn't give it much thought."

"Did you see anyone else enter the house?"

"No. I didn't see Kaitlin come home."

"Your dog barked when we were in the backyard last night and again today."

Clark smiled. "My alarm system."

"Did she bark between four and seven on Friday?"

"For sure she made a racket when the cab stopped. I don't recall any other time until the police arrived."

"Did you walk Polly outside of your yard Friday afternoon?"

"We went around the block when I first got home. After dinner we went over to Elmwood Cemetery. She likes to run there."

"Did you see anything that looked suspicious?"

"No. Sorry, officers."

"Thank you for your time. Please call us if you think of anything that might help." Ives handed Clark his card.

"I hope you get the killer soon. My neighbors are very worried."

The detectives returned to the patrol car. The officer pointed to a vehicle parking further down North Poplar. "The Feds just drove by in that black Dodge Durango."

Watching the well-dressed agents striding towards them, Hajek regretted not packing a jacket. Ives greeted the team and introduced Quintero and Hajek.

"Agent Brandon Tatro." He identified Joshua Lutz from Raleigh and Stanley Ortiz from DC. "Thanks for the information you sent, Ives. Anything new?"

"No."

Holding up shoe booties, Tatro asked, "Did your staff wear these?"

"We're professionals, Agent Tatro."

"How about the officers who were first on the scene?" Tatro straightened up.

Ives frowned. "Probably not."

Quintero and Hajek went to her vehicle and pulled protective gear from the trunk, preparing to enter the home.

Hajek looked back as Tatro pulled a large duffle bag from the car. "Arrogant bastards. "Power crazy. Unbelievable…"

"Be nice. They're in charge."

"When I told them the murders in four different locations were connected they didn't believe me. They've done nothing to help us." Hajek's voice grew louder.

Ives came over to Quintero and Hajek. "Tatro only wants me to go inside with them. How about you follow up in the neighborhood?"

"Sure, Boss. We'll nose around. Call me when you're done." Quintero put the gloves in her pocket.

Ives walked back to the FBI team.

"They hate me."

"It's probably not personal."

"Oh yes it is."

"The Grant Tomb case?" Quintero gave him a quizzical look.

"You know about that?"

She winked. "Google's wonderful."

"It wasn't my intention to embarrass them but that's how they took it." He told Quintero about the bomber from Petersburg, his store, the lame attack, and how poorly the FBI handled the case.

Quintero laughed. "You got the guy and they didn't."

"Pretty much."

"And now they have the upper hand." Quintero spoke calmly and considerably quieter than Hajek. "Let's see what we can dig up with the time we have."

"Sorry. I can believe the feds barred me but keeping you out, the lead detective, is beyond rude."

She shrugged.

"They're pompous. I'm sure some are competent. I just haven't met them. If I wanted to know current trends in men's fashion they're the top guys, but for assistance in cracking a crime they're useless."

Quintero interrupted Hajek's rant. "They'll be a while. Before we question anyone, let me give you a quick tour of Fourth Ward."

"Good idea. I really will calm down. Thanks for putting up with me." They walked down Poplar and into Fourth Ward Park.

"This reminds me of Manhattan's pocket parks, only it's much larger." Hajek noticed a couple practicing yoga.

"Pocket parks. Never heard that term."

Hajek laughed. "In the midst of asphalt and concrete, New York City has several little oases tucked between skyscrapers. A couple have water, all have trees and flowers. People bring their lunches and escape the craziness of the city."

251

A yellow finch landed on a ceramic bird house then flew to a nearby tree. Quintero looked up at the painted artwork. "There are several scattered around. The birds like them as much as the park visitors."

"What do you know about this area's history?" Hajek asked.

"I've taken the walking tour a few times…a fun outing with visitors. I'll show you some highlights and tell you what I remember."

As they progressed, Hajek noted the ease with which someone could wander around and not draw any particular attention. His usual interest in history diminished as his mind speculated on how the killer made his way to and from 605 North Poplar Street. Quintero pointed out homes built in the late 1880s. Instead of questions about the occupants he asked, "Do you think our guy drove or walked to Kaitlin's?"

"I'd guess he didn't park right in this neighborhood. Spaces are restricted to residents. There is strict monitoring and cars need a parking permit. Seventh Street has outside lots and three or four large garages. None are very far."

"Show me."

"I haven't finished the tour."

"Later."

They made their way to Tryon Street, Charlotte's main street and turned right. Seventh Street was the next block. From the intersection, Hajek noted three outside lots and four garages. "We'll have to talk with a manager at these parking places."

"I'll add that to our list. Before this trip to North Carolina, were you any further south than Virginia?"

Hajek stopped and looked at Quintero. "You know about my time at the University of Virginia?"

"Only that you went there."

He shook his head and laughed. "No, I haven't traveled in the South."

"I have something to show you. Come on." They walked along North Tryon toward Tenth Street. Quintero stopped.

Hajek read a plaque. "The site of the last cabinet meeting of the Confederacy that Jefferson Davis attended took place in William Phifer's home at this location, April 20, 1865. I didn't know that. Thank you for pointing it out."

"Once you start on Charlotte history there's plenty of interesting trivia to uncover," Quintero said.

Hajek's thinking shifted back to the task at hand. "Maybe our killer didn't drive or fly. He may have taken the bus. How far is the bus station?"

Quintero looked west and mentally calculated the distance. "About fifteen blocks."

"The bus station may be worth checking out," Hajek said.

Quintero moved to a crosswalk. "Good idea. For now let's head back to Fourth Ward."

They made their way back to North Poplar. The FBI team were still inside.

Chapter 46

A jogger stretched her hamstrings on the corner of Poplar and Ninth. Quintero approached and introduced herself. "Do you live here?"

"No. My apartment's several blocks from here. I like running in this neighborhood. There's a lot less traffic."

"Were you here Friday afternoon?"

"No. But I heard about the murder from the news. Nothing specific just that a young woman was killed in her home."

"If you learn anything please contact the police," Quintero said.

"I will. It's good to see the police car over there. I'll be happy when the killer is caught."

Quintero and Hajek watched the jogger walk along Poplar toward the city center. They continued down Ninth Street. An individual, struggling to contain his belongings in a cart, appeared around the corner.

Still brooding about the FBI, Hajek watched the man adjust bags hanging from a grocery cart and walked toward them. He wore a black knit cap, a pea coat and looked to be in his sixties.

"It's a fine day. Blue sky. The Lord is good."

Hajek greeted the man. "Good afternoon. How ya doin?"

Quintero nodded and continued walking.

"Were you in this area Friday afternoon?" Hajek asked.

Nyland shook his head yes. "I'm here every day." Then he asked Hajek, "What day is today?"

"Sunday." Hajek ignored Quintero's look of impatience. Probably wondering why Hajek pursued this conversation.

Nyland Jones, down on his luck for several years, said, "I spend most days in this part of Charlotte. People here are kind. They don't give me any trouble."

"We're going to eat. Come with us and we can talk some more." Hajek looked at Quintero. The abrupt turn of her head and raised eyebrows registered *you've got to be kidding.*

Quintero pointed down Ninth Street. "Alexander Michael's is close." The three made their way to the restaurant.

Quintero stopped in front of a two story building.

Nyland positioned his cart close to the entrance and they sat at a table with a clear view of the street and his belongings. He sensed Quintero did not approve. He wondered what she thought but did not ask. Waiting for the daily special, chicken salad on a pita, he asked Nyland if he remembered anything out of the ordinary last Friday on Poplar Street.

Nyland whispered as he leaned toward Hajek. "A woman was killed in her home."

For a moment Hajek did not speak. He glanced at Quintero. She gave him a skeptical look.

"What do you know about it?" Hajek asked.

Nyland sat up. He took a sip of water. "She was one of those women, ya know…" Nyland paused.

Hajek hid his disappointment. "What do you mean?"

They ate the sandwiches and listened to Nyland's religious babble and his blame-the-victim theory. When they finished, Hajek helped Nyland secure a bag hanging from his cart.

"Thank you. I'm headed over to Urban Ministry Center. Have a blessed day."

The detectives watched in silence as Nyland pushed his belongings up Ninth Street.

Quintero asked, "What were you thinking having lunch with that guy?"

"It wasn't my best decision. I hoped if we got him talking he might have something useful for us. Sorry."

"Before we head back, let me tell you a little history trivia about this restaurant. In the late 1890s a mill on Trade Street produced grits. People bought them at a store in this building. In the early 1900's a man named Berryhill converted it into a grocery store. That lasted until 1940. Then it went through many reincarnations, including serving as the draft board, before evolving into the current restaurant."

"I like the windows." Hajek visualized the storefront of an earlier time. The second floor had living quarters with a balcony.

They walked along Pine to Sutter Lane and stopped in front of a massive oak tree. To accommodate the tree, a condo building had unusual angles. Hajek gazed up at the branches thick with leaves, admiring the ancient specimen. "Nice that someone thought to preserve this."

A man watched as his dog relieved itself against the huge trunk.

Quintero pointed to the huge oak. "One of Charlotte's treasure trees." She showed the dog walker her badge. "I'm with Charlotte Mecklenburg Police. Can we speak with you?"

The man stepped back and tugged the dog leash. "Is there an ordinance about peeing on historic trees?"

"Maybe, but I don't know it. Do you live near here?"

He pointed to a condo complex. "Right there."

"A woman was murdered a couple blocks from here on Friday evening. We're investigating. I'm Detective Quintero and this is Detective Hajek."

256

"Everyone's been talking about the murder. Some say the victim must have known the guy because it wasn't a break-in. I'd rather not believe it was random."

The man told the detectives that he was not home at the time of the crime. He did not know Kaitlin. He was surprised to learn that the victim did not live in Charlotte.

"Please call police if you hear anything that might help," Quintero said. The man whistled to his dog and left.

Hajek took another look at the tree. "Thanks for the tour."

They passed another condo complex. "This area is more densely populated than I first realized. Do you think officers talked to the people who live here?" Hajek asked.

"I'm not sure. I'll check. Around the bend we're back where we started."

At North Poplar Street, Quintero and Hajek stood across the street from Kaitlin's place.

"They shouldn't be too much longer," Quintero said. "For next steps, I'd prioritize visiting hotels near here and at the airport."

Ives and the FBI team came outside and gathered at the FBI's SUV. Hajek and Quintero walked over to them. Tatro turned to Ives. "How soon can you give me an inventory of the evidence you gathered?"

"First thing tomorrow."

"Good. I'd like our lab to examine the computer taken from the house and the victim's clothing. We'll need to analyze the rope to determine if it matches the others. What do we know about the victim's male friends?"

"Very little. Her parents gave us her home and work address in Nebraska," Ives said.

257

"Good. We'll have someone from our Nebraska office speak with her neighbors and coworkers. And we need to speak with Kaitlin Jenkins."

Ives turned to Hajek. "You're staying at the same hotel as the Jenkins, right?"

"Yes. If Kaitlin agrees, I can bring her tomorrow."

Tatro glowered. "Chief Ives, We'd like to question her today. Tell us where she is and we'll go to her."

"Hajek knows the family. For safety reasons he's keeping her location private. Let him speak with them and bring her to the station or your local office tomorrow."

"That's assuming she's willing to meet with the FBI." Hajek said.

Chapter 47

Once the FBI vehicle drive away. Quintero said, "Ives wants good relations with the local FBI. You risk alienating him by not cooperating."

"You're right. I need to calm down. I'll speak with the Jenkins when I get back. They'll cooperate."

"Let's see if we can find where this guy left his vehicle last Friday."

Hajek rode with Quintero to the Seventh Street Station Garage. As they took a ticket they spotted cameras at the entrance. She parked on the first level and they walked to the attendant's booth. Quintero showed her badge. "I'd like to speak with someone about surveillance data from Friday."

"You'll have to talk with my supervisor, Arnold."

"Do you have a phone number?"

"I think it's here with our emergency contacts." The man opened a drawer, pulled out a notebook and gave Quintero a number.

She called, got voicemail and left a message. They walked to an open lot across the street with a self-pay meter system.

"Somewhere there's a camera here." Hajek looked around the lot.

"Operated by E.J. Garages," Quintero read from the back of the pay and display machine. She wrote down the information posted about the parking management.

They walked to each garage and obtained information to speak with someone about surveillance recordings from Friday.

Quintero yawned. "It's late. Tomorrow's another day. I'll drop you back at your car."

"Thanks. I'll walk. See you in the morning." He retraced their earlier route and made his way back to Fourth Ward Park. As he neared the crime scene, Hajek's cell phone rang, 7:10P.M.

"Just got home. Our plane left Austin late." Snyder sounded exhausted.

"Give me a minute to get to my car." Once in his rental car he said, "The local detective and I just finished for today." Hajek summarized what he knew about Samantha's murder.

"Wow. He pursued the first victim's sister…"

"Get some rest, Otto, we'll talk in the morning."

***

Monday morning Snyder called at 7:30. "I've only been at my desk minutes but several officers have told me Wilcox is anxious to hear good news from you."

"I wish I had some. So far there are no leads. The autopsy is this morning and we may have preliminary results this afternoon. Do you know if the FBI communicated with Wilcox?"

"I don't know. Do you expect 'em to complain about you?" Snyder asked.

Hajek laughed. "They've made it clear they're in charge. Yesterday they banned me from the crime scene while they looked around."

"Don't let them get to you, Peter. Stay focused. When will you be back here?"

"Thursday morning. The service for the victim is at noon on Wednesday. I have an evening flight. I'm concerned for the safety of Kaitlin and her parents. I'll be glad when they're on a plane headed for a safe place."

"What do you need from me?"

260

"Check in with the officers on the tip line and contact the other three families. I mentioned my fear that each victim's family was potentially vulnerable. Tatro, the lead FBI guy here, dismissed me. I can't assume they notified anyone and the families need to know they may be in danger."

"I'll alert the relatives of the other three victims," Snyder said.

"Otto, I keep thinking about the two male classmates of Mrs. Jenkins, who I questioned in Connecticut."

"Don't remind me. We've never told Wilcox about that. First I'll call the people in potential danger and then I'll try to get more information on your Connecticut guys."

"Thanks. Wish me well with the FBI today."

"Behave."

***

At 7:30 the next morning, Hajek met Teresa and Vincent in the hotel lobby.

"You look tired, Detective Hajek. Did you not sleep last night?" Teresa asked.

"I'm okay."

"Let's sit down." Vincent led the way to a booth.

"How's Kaitlin?" Hajek asked once seated.

"Better. She dozed a couple of times during the day yesterday. Classmates from college texted her that they'll attend the service."

Teresa sat next to her husband. Vincent leaned forward. "Tell us anything you can."

"I wish I had something. The FBI wants to speak with all three of you today. Actually they wanted to come here yesterday but I insisted on keeping your location private."

"Thanks." Teresa fought tears. Vincent put his arm around her shoulders.

Vincent looked directly at Hajek. "Do we have to?"

"Legally, no. But it would be the right thing to do. It may even be useful."

Vincent clenched his jaw. "I hate putting Kaitlin through more interrogation. For me it's fine. I think the chances of getting the killer are better with the FBI involved."

Hajek nodded yes. "It's your decision. Don't make up your mind now. I'll call you later."

Vincent fiddled with the sugar packets. What are you doing today?"

"After we finish breakfast, I'm meeting Detective Quintero in Charlotte. We'll canvass area hotels and go over interviews that her team completed. I'll call you in a couple of hours."

***

Hajek met Detective Quintero in the police station. Chief Ives followed him into her office and asked, "When can the Jenkins family be here for questioning?"

"They're thinking about it. I'll call them later this morning," Hajek said.

"You aren't encouraging them to decline, are you?" Ives gave Hajek a stern look.

"No. Mr. Jenkins is happy to speak with the FBI. He's concerned about his daughter. I didn't speak with Kaitlin, they'll tell her."

Ives frowned. "Tatro called me an hour ago and asked when you'll bring them to his office. Set up the meeting." Ives walked away.

Quintero gave Hajek a sympathetic glance and continued working on her laptop.

"I'll be right back." Hajek pulled his phone from his pocket, stepped into an empty room, and called Vincent. The three of them would cooperate with the FBI's request for additional questioning. They settled on 1:30 as the time for Hajek to pick them up. He retraced his steps and told Ives that the Jenkins would meet with Agent Tatro at 2:30 at the FBI office on Arrowood Road.

Quintero handed Hajek a paper. "Here's a list of the Charlotte hotels we identified. A diagram of their locations is on the back. They're all close. We'll walk."

* * *

When they left the Holiday Inn, the last one on their list, Hajek said, "Pick a place for coffee. I'll buy.

"Thanks. Something Classic is on Tryon. I need coffee." Quintero smiled. "We can sit outside and talk in private."

Waiting to place their order, Hajek eyed the baked goods. "I can't resist. How about you?"

Quintero laughed. "I accept so you won't eat alone. The carrot raisin muffins are yummy."

Settled at a table in an open area between several high rise buildings, they reviewed the events of the morning. The hotels had numerous male guests from New York, New Jersey, and Connecticut. None matched the police search criteria. Hajek sipped his tea. "Wish we had more to work with."

"My team finished the transcripts of interviews. I'll go over them while you're transporting the Jenkins and see if we need to do more." Quintero removed the paper from her muffin.

"Good. I'd like copies when they're available." Hajek took a bite of his cheese Danish.

263

"Ives and I will be at the FBI office when you bring the Jenkins. There's not enough time to canvass the airport hotels this afternoon. Will tomorrow morning work?"

"It'll have to," Hajek said. "The visitation's tomorrow afternoon. Then Wednesday after the service I return to New York."

They tossed their trash in a nearby receptacle and returned to Trade Street. Outside the CMPD station Hajek said, "I'll see you later." He went to his vehicle.

Arriving at the Hampton Inn at 1:15, Hajek turned off the engine and sat for a moment. He replayed his conversations with Eugene and Harold. On a hunch he called the Larsen Roofing Company in Norwalk, Connecticut.

"May I speak with Eugene?"

"I'm sorry he's not available."

"When may I call back?"

"He's been off since last Thursday. I expect him on Tuesday. May I take a message?"

"No. I'm in town from Rhode Island. My uncle's house in Bridgeport needs a new roof. He's in a nursing home and now it's my problem. When I asked around, several people told me Eugene was the best."

"Let me have someone else here help you." The woman sounded eager to assist.

"Thanks. Unfortunately I see that my uncle's doctor's calling. I have to take it. I'll call again." He clicked off his phone. Hajek loved that giving extra information put people at ease. In exchange for nothing, the receptionist confirmed Thompson had been away from work at the end of last week.

Thinking about the call--- Coincidence…maybe…where was Thompson…should have asked…

264

There was nothing he could do now. The Jenkins expected him. Hajek walked into the lobby and met Vincent, Teresa and Kaitlin.

"You're prompt," Hajek said.

Vincent shrugged. "Let's get it over with."

"My car's right out front. Your meeting will be at the Charlotte FBI office. I have the address. It's a few miles south of the Charlotte police station."

They drove mostly in silence. Hajek replayed in his mind the conversation with the receptionist at Eugene Thompson's roofing company.

Chapter 48

Hajek left the highway at West Arrowood Road and proceeded to the FBI field office. He led the Jenkins family into the building. Quintero and Ives waited in the lobby beyond the security desk.

Having met them on Saturday evening, Quintero greeted the Jenkins once they cleared security. "Thank you for coming. I'd like you to meet Wendell Ives, Charlotte's Chief of Detectives."

"We appreciate your cooperation." Ives then nodded to a uniformed guard.

"I'll take you to the conference room." The guard started down a hallway. At an open door he stopped and motioned for them to enter. "Here you are."

Ives walked into the room first. "Agent Tatro, I'd like you to meet Vincent and Teresa Jenkins and their daughter, Kaitlin."

Tatro stood. "Thank you for coming in."

Hajek moved closer to Tatro. "Could I speak with you privately before you begin the questioning? I have some thoughts to run by you."

Tatro frowned. "Not now. Maybe later." He turned to Mr. Jenkins. "To speed things up and not keep you too long a couple of agents will help me. They're upstairs. I'll take you there. Ives, all of you are welcome to wait here."

"Thanks. Quintero and I are going back to the station. We'll talk later." Ives turned to Hajek. "How about you?"

"I'm staying. I'll walk out with you. I left my laptop in the car."

The Jenkins followed Tatro down a hallway. Hajek, Ives and Quintero exited the building. Tatro's brush off did not surprise Hajek. He considered sharing his speculation on the murderer with Ives and Quintero but decided to start with his captain.

266

Ives opened the passenger door of the CMPD car. "Give us a call when you're finished here, Hajek. Later this afternoon we'll have some information from the coroner."

In his vehicle, Hajek retrieved his laptop, sat in the passenger seat, and opened his cell phone. The screen displayed a missed call from his partner. Hajek hit call back.

"Are you somewhere you can talk?" Snyder asked.

"Alone in my car outside the FBI building."

"Good. Remember the Vietnam Veteran's website, Vetfriendship, I told you about."

"Yeah."

"Well, several messages came in while I was away. I read them this morning."

"AND…"

"The ones about the Griffin guy said things like: he's a wimp, he believed that the war's purpose was to fight communism and make a better world, He resented the drinkers and druggies, he did not fit in at all."

"When I met Griffin he made a point of telling me how upset he found the taunts of 'baby killer' when he arrived home from the war," Hajek reminded Snyder.

"Thompson, on the other hand sounds more unpredictable. I'd worry about him. Fellow soldiers recalled Eugene Thompson's unusual behavior. One said he squeaked by a court martial for making vague threats to get even with Presidents Johnson and Nixon for sending him to Vietnam. A couple others mention his reputation of being a hothead. For that he earned his squad's respect. They liked that authority did not intimidate him. One guy wrote that no one messed with him because he always gave back."

267

"This troubles me," Hajek said.

"I'll keep digging..."

"Thompson is out of town. Been gone a few days. We need to move fast. I'm calling Wilcox."

"He'll never think that's enough to act on. Let me poke around his history some more," Snyder said.

"Do that but we can't waste any time. It will take Wilcox a while to persuade the FBI. I'm calling him. Talk with you later. Thanks, Otto." Hajek disconnected the call and immediately pressed Wilcox's number.

"Captain, we may have figured out who the killer is."

"Peter, that's great. Tell me what you got."

Hajek explained his thinking and gave Wilcox the information Otto found on Eugene Thompson.

"Have you told this to the Charlotte police or FBI agents?" Wilcox asked.

"No. You're the first." Hajek did not mention that he tried and Tatro rebuffed him.

"Okay. I'm on it. Talk with you later." Wilcox voice conveyed excitement.

Chapter 49

The Jenkins walked out of the FBI building, got in Hajek's vehicle and he drove away.

"They came off as more competent than the Bethel police." Vincent said. "I'm more hopeful they'll get the guy."

"Can we pick up some food and eat at the hotel?" Kaitlin asked. "I know where to get good fried chicken."

Teresa agreed. "Sounds good to me."

"We can't go anywhere you might be known," Hajek said.

"I've only been to this place once when I was first in Charlotte."

When they arrived at Price's Chicken Coop on Camden Road, Hajek parked on the street. He saw the sign NO CREDIT CARDS. "I have cash."

Vincent and Teresa told Kaitlin to order for them.

Hajek got out of the car and went inside with Kaitlin. "You can order for me too, Kaitlin."

She smiled. "You may want to try the southern delicacies here. How about I get a bucket of chicken gizzards and two sides of chicken livers?"

He laughed. "Maybe not today." He read the menus posted on the storefront windows.

"You thought I was kidding?"

"Hoping."

"How about chicken, hush puppies, tater rounds and coleslaw."

"That'll work."

Kaitlin moved behind a woman placing her order at the counter. Hajek's phone rang and Quintero's name flashed on his screen.

"I'll take this outside." He handed Kaitlin folded bills.

"We've preliminary autopsy findings. They confirmed strangulation as the cause of death."

"No surprise."

Quintero continued. "Drug screens will take a few more days."

"Thanks for the update."

"Can you be at my office tomorrow morning at nine?"

"Yes."

"That should give us enough time to interview staff at airport hotels before the funeral visitation."

"See you then."

As he stepped back into the restaurant, Kaitlin walked toward him carrying two large bags.

"That was quick." He took one bag, opened the door and held it for her.

They secured the food in the trunk. Back in the driver's seat, Hajek asked, "Kaitlin what's the easiest way back to the hotel?"

Before she could answer Teresa asked, "Can we go to a wine store?"

"Good idea," Vincent said.

"The closest is on 6th street where I regularly shop. I don't want to go there. Let me think a minute."

Hajek heard heaviness in her voice, none of the banter of a few moments ago.

"Turn around. We'll cut across East Boulevard." They drove past businesses in former residences, strip malls and restaurants. At Providence Road they found a Harris Teeter grocery store.

"Any requests, Hajek?"

"No thank you. Water's fine for me."

When Teresa and Vincent left to select the wine, Hajek said, "How are you doing?"

"I don't know. We just spent a couple of hours answering FBI agents' questions. Now we're buying wine for dinner and tomorrow we'll be at Samantha's wake. It's surreal. A very bad dream."

Hajek sighed. "Yeah. I'm…"

Kaitlin interrupted. "If I didn't work late Samantha wouldn't have been alone. Together we may have fended him off. No job's …"

"It's not your fault."

"I don't know what I'll do. I can't stay at Professor Watson house but my job's here. My parents want me out of Charlotte."

"You don't have to decide today."

Kaitlin stared forward, lost in her own thoughts. Hajek spotted a man several feet from the entrance smoking a cigarette with his face turned away from them. He sat up. The guy appeared focused on customers entering and leaving. He wore a baseball cap. Hajek went to touch his weapon and remembered he left it in New York. A woman pushed a full cart of groceries and an infant to her vehicle. The man snuffed out his cigarette and walked toward her. His wraparound sunglasses concerned Hajek. He reached for his car door handle as the woman picked up the child and secured it in the infant seat of her Toyota. The man grabbed two bags of groceries and transferred them to the trunk. Hajek calmed down. He hoped Kaitlin did not notice his concern.

"My parents expect me to go home with them for a while. My boss thinks I'll be back on the job right after the funeral. I can't stay with them indefinitely. I also can't imagine being at work anytime soon."

Hajek shifted in his seat. "There's no easy way to cope with loss. Whatever you do will be painful."

271

"I know about your wife. I'm sorry."

"Thank you. During Francine's illness my days were busy with her care, medical appointments and the mundane tasks of living. I can't describe how awful it is for me to fill hours alone."

"I can't imagine."

Hajek continued. "There isn't a day that I don't grieve. Work helps but the slightest trigger sets off memories and stops me in my tracks. I'm forever playing scenes or hearing her voice. I wish I could be more helpful. I have no idea what's right for you."

"You think the killer won't stop until he gets me." Kaitlin's voice trembled.

"I can't read his mind. We'll protect you and catch this guy."

Kaitlin wiped a tear. "I'm the reason she's dead."

Hajek could barely hear her words. "It is not your fault."

Kaitlin looked away from Hajek. He gazed at the people coming and going until Vincent and Teresa returned to the car. Hajek drove to Interstate 85 and joined the heavy flow of northbound traffic. The dashboard clock showed 6:45P.M.

Forty minutes later they arrived at the hotel. Hajek realized the Danish had been his lunch and now he felt starved. They made their way to the Jenkins' suite, Teresa arranged chairs to create a dining area around the coffee table.

On the counter near the microwave and refrigerator, Kaitlin set out paper plates, plastic ware, and containers of chicken, coleslaw, taters and hush puppies.

Vincent opened bottles of water and a bottle of Pinot Noir. He left them near the food with the individually wrapped hotel plastic cups.

"Please start." Teresa motioned to Hajek.

272

He put a chicken leg and a scoop of each side on his plate. They settled in their seats and ate in silence. After a few bites of chicken, Hajek's phone rang. Wilcox's number flashed on the screen. He hit talk. Before he could speak, Wilcox barked, "You need to catch the next flight to New York. Be in my office in the morning."

"I'm with the Jenkins. Let me step outside." Hajek gave a 'one minute signal' to his dinner partners and headed to the door. In the hallway he said, "What's up?"

"The FBI called Commissioner Sullivan. It's clear Eugene Thompson couldn't be more innocent."

"Damn." Hajek opened the door to his room and dropped onto the couch.

The Captain's methodical speech did not conceal his anger. "This afternoon the FBI went to the Thompson residence. No one was home. Neighbors said that Thompson and his wife had been away since last Thursday and were due back today. Agents positioned themselves in view of the home. At six this evening, the couple pulled into their driveway. Tagged suitcases showed they were on an American Airline flight from San Diego airport to JFK. That was the first clue that Thompson was not in Charlotte last Friday. He cooperated with the agents and gave them hotel receipts and boarding passes. The Thompsons spent Thursday and Friday nights at Hotel Del Coronado to celebrate their anniversary. On Saturday they checked into the Ocean Beach Hotel in San Diego for an ASTM conference. He attended meetings on roofing materials."

"I'm sorry, Boss." Hajek's shoulders slumped.

"Not half as sorry as I am. I went out on a limb for you, Peter. Be in my office tomorrow morning." Wilcox ended the call.

Hajek sighed. He clicked off the phone and sat dazed. He did not want to leave Charlotte before the Jenkins but knew it was impossible to persuade Wilcox to let him stay. After a few minutes he called Otto.

"Peter, are you all right?" Snyder's concern was clear.

"I just hung up with Wilcox."

Otto groan. "Wilcox told me the FBI concluded that Thompson was innocent. He also said he's worried about you."

"And about the Commissioner and Mayor."

"He's a political animal."

"I know."

"Where are you now?" Snyder asked.

"In my hotel room."

"Good."

"I need to book a flight pronto and let the Jenkins know I'm leaving. Have you ever known Wilcox to be this mad, Otto?"

"He'll come around. The problem for him is the commissioner and the mayor."

"They must be furious."

"They want the Hanson murderer."

"See you in the morning, Otto."

Hajek got on the internet and found a flight for 10:18P.M. He booked a seat and stuffed his belongings in the backpack. At the Jenkins suite, he stopped and took a deep breath before he knocked.

Vincent opened the door. "Is everything okay?"

"That was my captain. I have to fly back to New York tonight. I'm sorry I can't tell you more. Everything will be fine. I'll speak with Detective Quintero and ask her to assign someone to transport you tomorrow and Wednesday."

274

Kaitlin got up. "Wait. I'll pack some food for you to take."

"Thanks. I don't have time. I have to go."

After checking in at the airport, he called Quintero. "My captain called me back to New York. My flight leaves in forty minutes."

"What's happening?"

"I'm ordered back to New York. I don't have a lot of detail. I'm worried about the Jenkins. I had planned to be with them for viewing and the service."

"I'll speak with the Salisbury police. And I'll go to the funeral home tomorrow and the church on Wednesday."

"Great. I'll be in touch."

Chapter 50

After a night with too little sleep, Hajek managed to arrive at his desk by 7:00A.M. An unusual quiet permeated the precinct. Taking a bagel and large tea from a paper bag, he could not stop thinking of the mess he had created for his captain.

"Good morning, Peter." Snyder settled into his seat across from Hajek.

"I really messed up, Otto. I'm sorry."

Snyder nodded. "Unfortunately for you, the mayor and police commissioner are following every step of this one."

"I may have overreacted in Charlotte. I know this killer will strike again. We have to stop him."

Snyder opened his notepad. "When I contacted the other victims' families I asked for birthdays. Roberta Cronin in Illinois told me her daughter Amy's is November 3rd. Marsha's son, Philip Rubino, in Buffalo turns thirty-five on May 28."

"Damn. That's less than a week."

Snyder looked over Hajek's head and his eyes widened. "Wilcox is coming our way," he said under his breath.

Hajek stiffened and choked down a piece of bagel.

"Peter, I'd like to speak with you in my office," Wilcox said.

They walked in silence. Hajek closed the door behind him. Wilcox sat down and folded his hands on his desk. "Peter, you look like you haven't slept in days. I'm concerned. Take the rest of this week off and next. Report back a week from Monday."

"Captain, I can't do that. This killer may strike again as soon as Monday. I can take a break when we have him behind bars."

"Peter, I have no choice. The Commissioner wants you off the case."

For a moment Hajek sat in stunned silence. "Off the Hanson case? No. It may have been a reach with Eugene Thompson, but it's not like I didn't have any reason to suspect him."

"This is not negotiable." Wilcox's eyes did not meet Hajek's. "The Commissioner believes you've lost your objectivity. He's agreeing with the FBI that cracking the Grant case was pure luck. Leave the building now and report back a week from Monday."

Hajek got up, started toward the door, and turned to make a final plea. Wilcox sat with his head down. Accepting the futility of begging, he left.

Back at his desk, Hajek stood holding the back of his chair. "Wilcox took me off the Hanson case. Put me on leave. Otto, can you believe it?"

Snyder sighed and slumped in his chair.

***

Hajek walked several blocks south without a destination. At 96th street he headed east into Central Park. He stopped and sat under a wisteria-covered trellis near a playground. His eyes filled with tears. How many times had he and Francine rested here after walking around the reservoir? She particularly enjoyed watching the children. He brushed the tears from his eyes with the back of his hand. *Francine, how can I go on without you? This is too hard. If I had you to talk with, I never would have messed up this badly.*

"Look at me," a child squealed to her mother.

Hajek watched a toddler climb onto a bright green turtle.

"My turn." A redheaded girl, four or five years old, stood next to the big creature.

You'd love those little ones, Francine. He sat for some time while memories flashed like a slideshow. Then the events of the morning and recent

277

days intruded. A potential murder in a week scared him. *The Commissioner believes you lost your objectivity.* Hajek winced remembering Wilcox's words. …haven't slept …off the case…not negotiable…report in a week. He walked further into the park.

Making his way to the path that circled the reservoir, he wondered how Wilcox could expect him to stop thinking about the killer's next move. Cold gusts hit his face as he neared the water. A steady stream of joggers and a few walkers passed him on the trail. His deliberations about avoiding another murder produced no answers. He wished he knew where the serial killer would strike. As he finished the loop, hunger interrupted his ruminating. He walked toward Columbus Avenue and found a café.

"Breakfast or lunch?" the waitress asked.

"Breakfast, please."

"Sit anywhere you'd like."

He took a booth near the window. She handed him a folded menu with stacks of pancakes on the cover. Without opening it, he ordered scrambled eggs, rye toast, and tea.

"Lemon or milk?"

"Cream please and I like the tea strong."

The woman smiled.

Hajek leaned back. His mind raced with options for preventing the next murder. Someone needed to ask the local police to protect the potential victims. Hajek called his partner. After three rings he heard Snyder's voice mail. He left a message, *call me.*

Staring at the street, he watched passersby connected to a solitary world with earbuds. Women pushed strollers. A man scavenged in a trash can.

The waitress placed a mug of tea and a bowl of creamers in front of him.

278

He fixed his tea, took a sip, and his phone rang.

"Hang on, Otto." To not be overheard, he got up and walked outside.

"I stepped away from my desk and just got your message. Where are you?" Snyder asked.

"At a café on Columbus Avenue near 83rd Street. Have you contacted the Buffalo and Western Springs PD?"

"I spoke with Buffalo PD. The FBI notified them that they have a lead on a killer and will set up a stakeout in the Buffalo Westside neighborhood. That includes Virginia Street. I'm confident they'll have Phillip Rubino's home under surveillance through May 28. I'll check with Western Springs closer to that date."

"That's good. Thanks, Otto."

"Peter, you need to stop thinking about work. Get some rest."

"I'm on my way home."

Hajek returned to his booth as the waitress brought his breakfast. Inhaling the toast aroma, he enjoyed a forkful of eggs. As he finished eating, he noticed a line forming at the takeout counter. It was only lunch time. *What would he do with the rest of this day? And how would he fill all the time before he returned to work?*

He left the café and passed a subway station on 83rd street. He intended to catch a southbound train for home as he had told Otto but he kept walking. In spite of the cool temperature, people ate lunch at outside tables. He overheard one woman tell her friend about a recent family dinner. The favorite son decided to be a stay-at-home dad, surprising and upsetting his parents.

At the southwestern corner of Central Park, Hajek walked east toward Fifth Avenue. Horse-drawn carriages waited for the next fare. From the street he watched a woman balanced on a boulder near the edge of the park practice tai chi movements. Cabs pulled up to hotels facing the park, discharging tourists and people in the city for business. He crossed the street to the Plaza Hotel.

279

For Francine's birthday three months before they married, she chose to celebrate with afternoon tea at the Palm Court. He had teased her about wishing she lived in an earlier era when such luxury was routine for a certain segment of society. From the hallway, he glanced at the linen covered tables, each holding a vase of fresh flowers. Trademark palms stood by huge windows and enormous chandeliers sparkled. He briefly let memories surface and then walked to the Fifth Avenue exit and turned right.

In minutes he looked up at the spires of St. Patrick's Cathedral. He climbed the steps, opened the door and held it for a woman leaving. Once in the vestibule he saw racks of brochures and envelopes for restoration donations next to a holy water font.

He moved inside and sat in a pew midway down the center aisle. In the familiar, spacious church his neck and shoulder muscles relaxed. Near the candle stand a man knelt, fingering rosary beads. To the right of the altar a young woman cupped her face in her palms, her shoulders slumped. He prayed she would receive assistance with her burden. Scattered about were several individuals kneeling or sitting in contemplation. Along the outer aisles tourists whispered and quietly moved about the cathedral.

Glancing up at the light filtering through the rose window, he felt certain it radiated straight from heaven. He closed his eyes and surrendered to the calming atmosphere. Oblivious to the passing of time and having no schedule, Hajek embraced the tranquility. At some point he noticed the orange glow from candles flickering in glass holders.

Reluctant to leave, he approached the rack of votive candles, deposited a five dollar bill, and lit a candle. Feeling a strong connection with Francine, he slowly walked from St. Patrick's.

***

Fifty minutes later Hajek surfaced from the subway onto a street near his home. Making his way to his building, he replayed his early morning encounter with Wilcox. The captain had started the conversation suggesting that Hajek needed rest. He had expected criticism for embarrassing Wilcox with the FBI but nothing prepared Hajek for dismissal from the case. Knowing Wilcox did not make the decision, but had to carry out orders from the police commissioner did not lessen the pain.

At 2:40 he arrived in his apartment. He hung up his jacket. Walking from his bedroom to the kitchen and then into the TV room, he felt like a bird flitting aimlessly. Finally he eased into a recliner. His body ached all over. Giving into his exhaustion, he lowered the chair back and elevated his feet. He dozed. After twenty-five minutes he picked up his head, dazed. In a few minutes he recognized his surroundings.

I dreamed about him, Hajek said to himself. I sat at Harold Griffin's kitchen table and he told me about his time in Vietnam. He sounded like he had just returned, felt hurt by public protests, and angry that government officials lied to soldiers.

With Eugene Thompson cleared as a suspect, I need to find out if Griffin took a trip to Charlotte. I will not stop working on this case.

Planning his next move, he looked up car rentals and found one three blocks from his apartment. At five o'clock he walked into Enterprise Rent-a-Car and waited for the woman to finish a phone call.

"I'd like to rent a compact car."

"How long?"

"Not sure. Two or three days."

He agreed to the daily rate, promised to return it to the Queens location, and signed the many pages of tiny print. An attendant brought the car to Hajek.

281

"Please show me how to turn on the wipers?"

"Yes, sir." The man pointed to the switch and demonstrated turning the wipers on and off.

Hajek drove the short distance to his building, checked the parking rules on a sign, and left the vehicle in a legal spot for his early morning drive. Relieved to have a plan for his first day of suspension, Hajek decided to have dinner out. He would choose a nice restaurant, bring a magazine, and enjoy a steak.

Chapter 51

In darkness, Hajek began his now familiar ride to Stamford, Connecticut. As the sun came up, he parked on Faucett Street. Commuters walking to the train or driving to work ignored Hajek as he wandered over to Griffin's beat up Oldsmobile Cutlass. *The guy had a garage but he parked in the driveway.* Hajek shook his head.

The ashtray contained a pile of butts with many more scattered on the floor. In the clutter, he spotted a jean jacket, a black windbreaker and a pair of worn out sneakers. Newspapers, candy bar wrappers and fast food containers filled the floors and seats. He took several photos with his phone. A yellow box with orange lettering grabbed his attention. He took close-ups of the shoebox-size carton, and then hurried away. Back in his car, Hajek focused on his last photo. He made out the word Bojangles and googled it. Menus featuring chicken and biscuits appeared. He searched for nearby locations. There were none in Connecticut or New York or New Jersey but Virginia and North Carolina turned up numerous Bojangles sites. Griffin had traveled some distance for chicken and biscuits.

Sitting in view of the home he now believed belonged to a serial killer, Hajek struggled to find a way to bring him in without jeopardizing the case. Lacking jurisdiction, he could not approach the guy. He could not search the car or house without a warrant. Parking his car on the street for days waiting for Harold Griffin to surface might attract attention. He could not manage a stakeout solo, but he needed to track Griffin's movements.

The logical resource for back up, local police, he dismissed. The FBI gave him full responsibility for the fiasco in Norwalk. That story would have spread to Stamford and beyond. It embarrassed Hajek that the Police Academy might use it as an example of the hazards of jumping to conclusions without sound evidence. He could not ask Snyder to defy Wilcox and help keep watch.

He scrolled through the contacts in his phone and paused at Nick Kostas' number. Maybe Nick could take a couple of vacation days and come to Connecticut. Hajek had no idea how long it would be before Griffin left his house. Hajek dismissed the idea of calling Kostas for the same reason as Snyder. Chief Wilcox was Nick's boss. He continued looking at his phone contacts. He stopped at Sloane's number. The Beacon Police Chief loved the publicity and praise his department received on the Grant Tomb bomber case. In their last conversation he told Hajek that he occasionally presented examples of real police work to law enforcement classes at the local community college. He planned to use the story of their cooperative efforts to apprehend John Gordon at the next session.

Hajek hit talk.

"Sloane here."

"Peter Hajek."

"Nice to hear from you. What's happening? Bring in that serial killer?"

"Not yet."

"I heard that he struck again in North Carolina."

Hajek shared the recent developments with Sloane, omitting that his Captain took him off the case and that the FBI insisted cracking the Grant tomb case was pure luck. "You must have also heard I messed up."

"I'm sure you had good reason to pursue that guy. Sorry it didn't work out. Any new leads?" Sloane asked.

"I'm sitting outside a guy's house that I believe is the killer. Any chance you can help me with this?"

"What do you need?"

"I don't have enough specific evidence to ask my captain to allocate officers for this surveillance task. I'm looking for a volunteer."

"I'm your man. When and where?"

"Later today and possibly again tomorrow. I'm sixty miles from you in Stamford, Connecticut."

"I have a meeting at eleven this morning. That should be about an hour. I'd say I can get to you by three this afternoon. Will that work?"

"Perfectly."

"Give me the address and I'll get back to you to confirm in about forty-five minutes."

***

When Sloane arrived at 3:20 that afternoon, Hajek slid into the Buick's passenger seat. "I can't thank you enough for helping me out."

Sloane held up a hand motioning for Hajek to stop. "What's your plan?"

He showed Sloane the photos of the car contents. "His DNA is the surest way to tell me he's our guy. We have matching DNA from two murder sites. Who does your DNA testing?"

"Our regular crime lab would be too slow and costly. I met a fellow at a conference who offered me some free testing. He wants to prove to police departments that his lab is accurate and fast. But, my friend, photos won't work. How are you planning on getting any of that stuff from his car?"

"I haven't worked that out yet. Meanwhile we need to monitor this guy." He filled Sloane in on the day and gave him a description of Griffin. "Before you take over here, I'll get your critical supplies."

Sloane pointed to a box on the floor behind the passenger seat. "I never was a Boy Scout but I'm prepared. This isn't my first stakeout."

"Want any food?"

"No. I'm good. Get some sleep."

"I reserved a room at the Yankee Budget Motel, Exit 5 off the Connecticut Turnpike. I'll be back at seven."

"Eight's fine. I got here in an hour and fifteen minutes. I'll be home before my wife goes to bed."

"I don't want her mad at me," Hajek said.

"She sends her greetings and hopes we get the guy."

With Sloane on guard, Hajek headed to the Yankee Budget Motel. As he parked, his phone rang. Nick Kostas' name appeared on the screen.

"Peter, how are you? I heard about Wilcox taking you off the Hanson case. Sorry. Let's meet for dinner. My shift ends at seven."

"I'm in Connecticut."

"That doesn't sound good. You should be home."

"I'm watching for the killer to make his next move."

"Peter, you're off the case."

"I can't let him strike again."

"Tell me where to find you. I'm coming as soon as I finish work."

"Nick, you can't get involved."

"Give me an address, Peter."

"No, Nick."

"An address."

"Okay...Call me when you're in Connecticut and I'll let you know where I am then."

Hajek checked into the motel. Nick's call upset him. He did not want Nick in trouble with Wilcox. Too many nights with less than five hours of sleep caught up with him. His brooding ceased as he fell into a deep slumber.

After he woke, Hajek stopped for fast food before returning to 9 Faucett Street. At 7:45p.m., he parked behind a van that provided cover without blocking his view of Griffin's home. He strolled to Sloane's vehicle.

Sloane lowered his window. "No sign of Harold Griffin. I'll be back by nine tomorrow morning unless something blows up in Beacon."

Back in his car, Hajek inserted an ear bud and hit the U2 playlist on his iPod. After thirty-five minutes his phone rang. He turned off the music. "Hi, Nick."

"I got a late start. I just passed Exit 5 on Route 95. Where are you?"

Hajek gave him the address and a description of his rental car.

"See you soon."

When Kostas pulled alongside Hajek's car, both men lowered their windows. "I'll find a place to park and be right over."

In Hajek's car, Kostas said, "Peter, I'm worried about you."

"The guy that lives in that small house with the broken shutters will kill again, possibly on Monday in Buffalo, unless I stop him."

"Do you have any evidence?"

"He's the only guy I haven't eliminated from my person-of-interest list. We have matching DNA from two crime scenes. I expect the results in Charlotte will give us a third."

"You're watching this guy's house in hopes of getting a DNA sample?"

Hajek pointed to the parked Oldsmobile. "That car has empty fast food wrappers from a Southern chain, Bojangles. I think he did the murder in Charlotte."

He showed Kostas the photos on his phone and explained that there were no Bojangles restaurants within three hundred miles of Stamford. "This guy's not a traveler. He wasn't in the South sightseeing."

287

Kostas sat in silence taking in Hajek's speculation. After a few moments he said, "You may be right, Peter."

Hajek explained that for the first three murders, the killer chose the mother's birthday to kill her daughter. In Charlotte he seemed to have switched to his victim's birthday. Philip Rubino, the son of one of the women, lived in Buffalo and Monday was his birthday.

"So when that car moves you're going to tail it. Is that right?" Kostas asked.

"I want to prevent another senseless death."

"You aren't planning to stop him for some pseudo traffic violation to get the items in his car?"

"No way. I'll be very careful. I know I can't stop anyone in Connecticut, especially in this rental car. When I have something specific, I'll call in the Feds and local police."

"I feel better now that we talked in person. I'll be back tomorrow. Maybe I can think of some way to help."

After Kostas left, Hajek found a talk radio station and listened to callers expound on topics ranging from health to sports to politics to celebrities. The noise helped pass the time and kept him vigilant. He alternated between music, twenty-four hour news stations, and all night talk shows.

As early as 6:30 commuters made their way to work. There were no lights on at Griffin's place. The blinds remained closed. Watching the neighborhood come alive, Hajek realized that no one paid him any attention. Focused on getting themselves and their children to school and work, people did not notice him. Around eight he thought how great a cup of hot tea would taste. Sloane arrived at nine-forty. Hajek went over to his Buick and got in the passenger seat.

"All quiet, I trust," Sloane said.

288

"Yeah. I think our guy's recovering from his long drive back and forth to Charlotte."

"And resting up for a trip to Buffalo?"

"Afraid he might be."

"If you're right, it could be a couple more days before he heads to upstate New York."

"I wish he'd surface."

Sloane tapped Hajek's shoulder. "Get going. I'm good for the day."

"Thanks. I'll be back by seven unless you call that he's on the move."

On the way back to his motel room, Hajek picked up tea and breakfast and continued to his room. Passing the desk clerk he waved. The woman never looked up from her magazine. In his room he repeated his previous afternoon's sleeping preparations, pinning the blinds together as best he could and burying himself under the covers.

***

Driving out of the hotel parking lot, Hajek wondered how much longer it would be before Griffin left his house. After picking up food again at a drive thru, he returned to Faucett Street, parked and got in the car with Sloane.

Sloane put down his laptop. "I hope you got some rest."

"I did, Darren. Thanks. Can you do one more day?"

"Sure."

"Good. One more then we'll reevaluate."

Sloane nodded. "That might do it. If he's planning a murder in Buffalo on Monday, he may want some lead time to find the victim's home and scope out his access."

"I wish I knew how this guy operates. He's very skillful or very lucky."

"Maybe a little of both. See you tomorrow."

Chapter 52

From a list of audiobooks, Hajek selected the Steve Jobs biography to listen to on his iPod. It began with the author, Walter Isaacson, explaining his surprise when Jobs asked him to write his life story. Hajek looked forward to learning more about this iconic man. Midway through the first chapter describing Steve's childhood, Harold Griffin walked to his car with a green trash bag.

Griffin opened the door to the backseat and appeared to put more stuff in the bag. Then he got behind the wheel and backed out of his driveway.

Hajek looked down until the Oldsmobile started down Faucett Street. With Hajek following a few car lengths behind, Griffin made his way north along Hope Street to the Glenbrook Shopping Center. Pulling alongside a trash receptacle, Griffin left his car idling in the fire lane while he grabbed the bag from the backseat and tossed it into the green cylinder.

Hajek clicked photos. The twilight shadows made picture taking difficult. Hoping the street lights provided enough brightness, he took a few more and then looked to see if he had captured the scene. The screen showed Griffin putting the bag into a barrel outside Target. Another photo caught the Oldsmobile with a clear view of the license plate.

Griffin pulled away from the curb. Hajek wanted to jump out of the vehicle and run to the trash container. Instead he followed Griffin across the parking lot and watched him get in a McDonald's drive-thru line.

Hajek circled back, maneuvered close to the sidewalk in front of Target, and pulled gloves from his pocket. Leaving the car idling, he got out and walked to the receptacle. Without regard for how he looked, he grabbed a fistful of bag and tugged. *How could the opening be wide enough to accept the bag but not return it?*

A boy about four years old stared at Hajek. "What's he doing, Mommy?"

"Never mind. Let's go find your stomp rocket." She took her son's hand and propelled him into the store.

Hajek reached in with both hands and compressed the contents. The container held tight. With another yank, Hajek wrenched out about a third of the bag. He repositioned his hands, compacted more, and jerked the bag through the opening. Liquid coated part of the outside of the green plastic and splashed on Hajek's pant legs and sleeves. Feeling triumphant, he did not speculate on the gooey fluid and ignored the disgusted looks from shoppers.

He dropped the bag into the trunk, took off his gloves, and chucked them next to the trash. He pulled out his phone, took several photos of the salvaged stuff in his car, and jumped behind the wheel. With potential sources of Griffin's DNA stashed in the trunk, he hit the gas with the car in park. *Calm down.* He shifted to drive and returned to find Griffin.

The Oldsmobile moved slowly beyond the food pickup window and out of the parking lot. Hajek tailed Griffin's vehicle back to Faucett Street. As he watched his suspect close the front door of his home, Hajek called Sloane.

"I got his DNA. How fast can you analyze it?"

"Whoa! I'd have to bring it to the lab first. Then we're looking at a minimum of forty-eight hours."

"I'm confident our guy's in for the night. I'll deliver the trash to Beacon now."

Sloane laughed. "Tell me what happened. I'm still five miles from home."

Hajek filled him in. Sloane agreed to alert his staff to accept the bag of trash.

"They can log in the stuff tonight when you arrive. I'll have whoever's on duty take photos and do the preliminary paperwork to assure the chain of custody. First thing tomorrow I'll bring it to the Poughkeepsie Biochemistry Lab, Inc. I'll call my contact so his technicians can begin testing in the morning."

"I'm on my way."

He checked for the best route to the Beacon police station on his phone. A tap on the passenger window caused him to drop it.

Seeing Kostas, Hajek let him in. "Shit, Nick, you scared me."

"Sorry." He picked up Hajek's phone from the car floor as he got in and handed it to him.

"I have Griffin's trash in the trunk."

"How'd you manage that?"

"Check this out." He showed Kostas the photos of Griffin tossing the trash.

"Sloane in Beacon agreed to arrange for the DNA analysis. I'm bringing it there now."

"What if he leaves while you're on the road?"

"I'm hoping he's in for the night."

Kostas pulled a silver rectangle about the size of a cigarette pack from his pocket. "In case he's not. Wait while I slip it on the Oldsmobile's bumper."

"We don't have a warrant."

"I'll be right back. Don't go away."

Hajek watched his friend move smoothly in the shadows. Once alongside Griffin's vehicle, he crouched, stretched out one arm, and quickly pulled it back. Then Kostas stood and, like a man taking a casual stroll, returned to Hajek's car.

"Now let's link that baby to your cell." Kostas picked up Hajek's phone and downloaded an app.

292

"Nick, now I'm worried about you."

"When that device serves its purpose we'll make it disappear. Simple as that. No one needs to know."

"Nick, this isn't your style."

"Sometimes we have to fudge things to get justice. If that vehicle moves, your phone will beep." He showed Hajek how to view Griffin's movements and know the exact location of the Oldsmobile.

"Thanks, Nick."

"Keep me posted. Safe travels to Beacon."

Chapter 53

There were a couple of ways to travel from Stamford to Beacon, New York. He chose the directions that took him south on Interstate 95. He turned on the radio, hit the seek button, switched stations and paused only long enough to reject the talk show or a musical selection. When he heard "God Bless the Child" sung by Billie Holliday, he settled into that jazz station.

He easily crossed the Tappan Zee Bridge. Looking down on the lights along the Hudson River, he smiled and eased his grip on the wheel, confident that the contents of the trunk would close this case. He exited Route 84 just before the Newburgh Bridge and drove the short distance to Municipal Plaza. At the top of the incline he parked near the entrance, retrieved the trash from the trunk and entered the station. As promised, the officers at the Beacon police station anticipated his arrival.

Officer LaSalle stood and greeted him. "Teaming up with our Captain again, Detective Hajek?

"Yes. We may have another big break. I sure hope so."

"Is that our present?"

"Yes. Where would you like it?"

"Follow me." LaSalle walked down the hall to a room with long tables. He pointed to one and Hajek swung the bag on top.

"We have our orders to fast track this testing. First thing in the morning the DNA experts will get the ball rolling. They'll have results on Monday for sure. If we're lucky, preliminaries will be available late Saturday."

"Tomorrow?"

"There's a chance."

"Can I hang around for a while? I'd like to see what we've got to work with."

"Sure. We're ready."

The clock in the room read 11:51P.M. The officer opened a drawer in the table and pulled out gloves. He turned on the video recorder. After untying the garbage bag he folded the sides creating a wide opening at the top.

Hajek smiled. "That drink container complete with straw should be all we need."

"Our orders are to log everything but we'll prioritize the plastic cup." LaSalle set the cup aside.

Hajek watched as the officer waded through Griffin's trash selecting possible items to analyze. Captivated by how close they were to having a definitive answer on Griffin, Hajek lingered in Beacon and assisted with removing and labeling items. Around 1A.M. he left.

Driving in silence for the first twenty miles back to Connecticut, Hajek replayed the events of the evening. The thought that the DNA analysis might not show a match with the DNA from the Illinois and New York City crime scenes scared him. Remembering Griffin had made a recent trip to the South, he dismissed any nagging doubt. During the early morning hours, he shared the highway with many trucks and a few cars. Changing from the jazz station to a classical one, he stayed in the right lane, set his speed control for sixty miles an hour, and enjoyed the peaceful darkness.

Turning onto Faucett Street, Hajek spotted the Oldsmobile parked in the driveway. Although his phone gave him the same information, he could not resist seeing for himself. He tried to imagine his suspect's next move. Possibly Griffin would wait until Saturday to travel the four hundred miles to Buffalo. If he planned a hit at the end of the day on Monday, he would have Sunday to scope out

295

the place. That seemed tight to Hajek, especially if Griffin was not familiar with Phillip Rubino's neighborhood. Maybe he would travel today and take a couple of days to study the area, plan his attack, and escape.

Deciding to trust that he could monitor Griffin from a distance, Hajek went back to the Yankee Budget Motel. His brain kept working in spite of his fatigue. Reviewing the last fifteen hours, he applauded his lucky break in getting that trash legally. He tried not to think about the analysis showing no match with the crime scene DNA. *It has to be Griffin. What other reason did he have to drive so far south?*

The bed was unmade from the previous day. His sleeping hours conflicted with the housekeeping schedule. After putting the privacy sign on his door, he took a shower and collapsed on the bed. It was 4:20A.M.

When his phone rang at 7:45 he grabbed it just before it went to voicemail. "Anything going on?" Sloane asked.

"Griffin stayed put. No movement."

"My guys told me you left after midnight. I can get to Connecticut in a few hours and spell you."

"Darren, that's not necessary. I'm in the motel. Continuing the stakeout doesn't make sense. Whether Griffin goes today or tomorrow, the Buffalo police have the information on his vehicle and license plate. If he shows up, they'll nab him. They'll keep Rubino's home under surveillance Sunday and Monday for sure. Stay on the DNA testing and call me as soon as you have any results."

"It looks like there's plenty to analyze. If we're right about Griffin, that bag will be all the evidence we need. Get some rest."

Chapter 54

Beeping like the sound of a vehicle backing up woke him. He checked the time on the bedside clock, 10:43A.M. He stretched and rolled over before realizing that the continued beeping came from his phone. He grabbed it and stared at the screen showing movement from Faucett Street. Hajek's heart pounded in an adrenaline rush. He pulled on clothes and strapped on his weapon. In his car he checked the tracking information. Griffin's car headed northbound on Route 95.

Hajek tapped the steering wheel as he waited fifth in line on the highway entrance ramp. With the first break in traffic, he moved one lane to the left and set the cruise control to the speed limit. At Exit 21, Griffin left the highway. *That was a Fairfield exit.* Hajek accelerated and moved into the far left lane. For a couple of moments, Hajek worried that instead of planning a hit in Buffalo, Griffin intended to attack in Connecticut.

Scrolling through phone numbers was not easy at 70 miles per hour. Finding Vincent Jenkins he called. "Vincent, Detective Hajek. Where are you?"

"In Massachusetts as planned. I hope you're calling to tell me you've got the guy."

"Not yet. Anyone staying at your Fairfield home?"

"No, it's empty."

"Good. Sorry to be abrupt. I'm in the middle of a few things. I'll call again."

The tracking showed Griffin's car moving slowly back and forth on the street where the Jenkins lived. Twenty minutes later, Hajek spotted the Oldsmobile parked in view of 787, the Jenkins home. Hajek continued farther down Mill Plain Road hoping he looked like a resident before pulling to the curb. In his side mirror, he watched a mail truck make its way along the street. When it did not stop at the

297

black mailbox with a cluster of faded wildflowers painted on the side, Griffin pulled out, turned around in the Jenkins driveway, and returned to the highway heading south.

Following from a distance, Hajek kept checking the tracker until Griffin's car turned onto Faucett Street and parked in his driveway. Hajek drove to Stamford and pulled over on a street near Griffin's home. The Hope Street Pizza sign reminded him that he needed food. After looking up the number, he placed an order, and waited in his car in case his quarry took off again.

After fifteen minutes, Hajek picked up his soda and meatball grinder and returned to his car. For reassurance, he drove by Griffin's home. He noticed nothing different from the app showing the parked Oldsmobile. Returning to his motel, he passed a marker for Riverside Point Park. He followed the arrow and wound by a few small shops and homes until the asphalt turned to gravel. Long Island Sound lay to the left. He continued along the road to the marina at the eastern end of the park and gazed at the Manhattan skyline.

An older couple shared a picnic at one of the tables scattered at the point. That could have been him and Francine in thirty years. Would happy couples ever stop triggering sadness, he wondered. He moved on and found a solitary spot to eat.

Although he knew any movement from Griffin's car would generate a beep on his phone, he picked it up several times to verify that Griffin's car remained in his driveway. Finished, he crushed the empty food bag, placed it in a trash can, and returned to the motel.

The sight of the rumpled bed reminded him how tired he felt. He stretched out in his clothes and fell asleep.

An hour and a half later, 1:35P.M, the sound of rapid beeps woke him. "Damn! Where's he going now?" Hajek said aloud. Sitting up he grabbed his

298

phone and focused on the Oldsmobile's route, north on High Ridge. *Shopping*? *Visiting a friend*? *Does he have any*?

Hajek knew he should move but he hoped Griffin would stop, do errands, pick up food, and then go home. As the Oldsmobile drove beyond the Stamford boundary near Norwalk on the Merritt Parkway, Hajek grabbed his weapon and ran to his car.

Looking at a Stamford map on his phone, he checked for the fastest way to catch up with Griffin. The most direct route to the Merritt Parkway involved traveling eight miles across the city of Stamford. The first few miles wound through residential neighborhoods with a low speed limit and several stop signs. Once on High Ridge Road his speed picked up. Merging onto the Merritt Parkway, his device showed Griffin on Route 7 north.

The northbound traffic on the Merritt moved slowly with cars merging at each entrance. Several yards shy of Exit 39, movement slowed. As he considered getting off the highway and taking an alternate route, the car in front of him accelerated. A couple car lengths later, Hajek saw the sign for a right lane closure. Edging his way to Exit 39, he hoped to do the speed limit on Route 7 but it proved even slower when it changed from four lanes to two with frequent traffic lights.

Unfamiliar with this part of Connecticut, Hajek could not guess Griffin's destination. He kept driving. Another time, he would have found the villages and rural landscape pleasant. Griffin's car stopped in Kent. Thinking that place sounded familiar, Hajek struggled to recall why. He had never been there but for some reason it stayed in his memory. Who mentioned it? What was the association?

Hajek's speed increased when Route 7 merged with Interstate 84 near Danbury. That lasted about four miles and he exited I-84 to continue on Route 7 north. In about ten miles the road dropped to one lane in each direction. Hajek estimated that he was twenty miles behind Griffin's car on Route 7.

Kent Falls. Hajek recalled that the Jenkins picnicked there on the way to their home in the mountains when the girls were small. The memory caused Hajek's heart to race. *I need to call for back up. First Jenkins.*

Hitting talk, his phone redialed Vincent Jenkins number.

"What's going on?" Jenkins asked.

"Vincent, I'm concerned our suspect is on his way to your place in Great Barrington. I have to assume he knows about your second home."

"The bastard. You have to stop him."

"We need cause. I'll alert the Great Barrington Police and ask them to post an officer in your home. All of you need to stay inside. I'll get back to you."

Before Hajek set the phone down, a siren caught his attention and he spotted the swirling blue light in his rearview mirror. He pulled over.

"License and registration," The officer requested.

Hajek complied and included his NYPD badge.

"Listen, Detective. You're in Connecticut and you need to follow our laws. This state forbids cell phone use while driving."

"Sorry, Officer. I'm actually working undercover and needed to convey some information."

The officer gave a look that suggested he doubted the truth of that statement. "I'll take your word."

"Thank you, Officer."

Hajek drove another mile before looking at his cell phone while holding it lower than the dashboard. He found Griffin's location three miles south of Canaan, Connecticut. Hitting the button for speaker, he then called Sloane.

"Peter, you'll love this. The analysts told me they have at least three good DNA samples. We may have something definitive soon to check against the DNA from the Illinois and New York City crime scenes."

"Listen, Darren, I'm following Griffin in northwestern Connecticut. Earlier today he drove to the Jenkins home in Fairfield. I think he knows they have a second home and that's where he's going."

"Not Buffalo?"

"Doesn't look that way. I need to notify the Great Barrington Police. Can you look up that number? I've already been stopped for cell phone use while driving." Hajek pulled a pen and index card from his pocket and continued driving.

"Got it."

Hajek jotted down the number as Sloane gave it to him.

"And a number for the Massachusetts FBI?"

"Sure."

"Thanks, Darren. Call me when you know the DNA results."

Hajek pulled over in the parking lot of a store that sold bird supplies and placed his first call. When an officer answered at the Great Barrington police station, Hajek asked to speak with the person in charge.

After a brief pause on hold, someone picked up. "Sergeant King here."

"My name's Peter Hajek. I'm a New York City detective. I believe a serial killer is on his way to Great Barrington and I need your help to prevent a murder."

King remained silent.

"This may sound unbelievable to you but it is true. NYPD and the FBI are pursuing a killer of young women. Last week he hit at the home of Kaitlin

Jenkins in Charlotte, North Carolina and murdered her friend. We believe Kaitlin was the target and he's going to her family's home in Great Barrington."

"You're working with the FBI on this?"

"Yes."

"What do you need from me?"

"Please send someone to the Jenkins home at 13 Lake View Road in Great Barrington. Keep your patrol cars out of sight."

"Will do. Stay on the line."

King returned. "I've dispatched an officer to Lake View Road. Give me what you know about this suspect."

"His name is Harold Griffin. He's driving a gray Oldsmobile Cutlass with Connecticut plate H654B32. Griffin is a white male, in his sixties, medium build, short curly dark hair with streaks of grey."

"I'm on it. Thanks for the heads up."

Hajek disconnected and immediately called Vincent Jenkins. He told him that the Great Barrington Police would be at his home soon and FBI agents would arrive later. Cars whizzed past Hajek while he remained parked and entered the number for the FBI in Massachusetts.

"Good Afternoon, Federal Bureau of Investigations, Agent Bronson speaking."

After identifying himself, Hajek explained the reason for his call.

"You need assistance in Great Barrington with a serial killer?"

"That's right. This killer has crossed jurisdictions. He's hit in New York City, upstate New York and North Carolina. I have an address I believe he's headed for right now."

"This Boston office is more than two hours from western Massachusetts. Albany, New York is closer. Give me the details and I'll call them."

Hajek gave Harold Griffin's name, the address and phone number for Vincent Jenkins, and added that he had also alerted the Great Barrington police.

Before edging back onto the highway, Hajek checked Griffin's location, Canaan, CT. He could gain on him if he picked up the pace.

Winding through the center of Kent, Hajek thought about stopping for a Coke. He rejected the idea. Not wanting to take even five minutes from the pursuit. In a couple of miles the scenery turned to rock formations abutting the left edge of the road and on the right, trees stood along a river with several people in fishing waders

The app showed Griffin's car now in Sheffield, Massachusetts.

Hajek's phone rang. Nick Kostas' name appeared on the screen.

"Where are you?"

"According to your gadget I'm thirty-three miles south of our suspect."

"You're chasing Griffin?"

Hajek filled his friend in on the events of the afternoon.

"What do you have to arrest this guy?" Kostas asked.

"Nothing yet but I can't let him get near the Jenkins. Sloane is close to a confirmation."

"Or elimination."

"I refuse to believe that's possible," Hajek said.

"Listen, Peter, no one can find that tracking device. You have to get hold of it first. Call me when you can. Good luck."

Griffin's car stopped again, Sheffield, Massachusetts. Hajek pressed on.

Twenty minutes later he answered a call from the Great Barrington Police. "Detective Hajek, where are you?"

"Near a Cornwall covered bridge."

303

"We pulled the Oldsmobile over for a broken brake light and told Mr. Griffin our database indicates he has outstanding fines and brought him in for questioning. He's cooperating. It won't be easy to detain him for long. Please come directly to the police station."

"Did you bring the car?"

"No reason. Without a warrant we couldn't search it." King's casualness angered Hajek.

"What's the station address?"

"Main Street. Stay on Route 7 and as you enter Great Barrington we're on the right. You can't miss the station."

"How are the Jenkins?"

"One of our officers is with them and an FBI agent is on the way."

Chapter 55

The app showed Griffin's car stopped on Castle Street. In fifteen minutes, Hajek passed the police station, turned left on Taconic Avenue, right on Castle and pulled behind the unattended Oldsmobile in the train station parking lot. Three cyclists rode in, leaned their bikes against the station and pulled snacks from their packs. One consulted a map and reassured the other riders they were on course. After waiting for them to leave and ride out of sight, Hajek reached under the right back bumper. Feeling nothing there, he stood. A passenger in a passing car looked his way. He walked around the car before checking the left bumper and knocking Nick's device to the ground.

He retrieved it, jumped back into his car, and tossed it into the glove compartment. While deleting the tracking app from his phone, Hajek thought about calling Kostas with the good news, but eager to see Griffin in custody he decided to wait. He made his way back to Route 7.

At 4P.M, Hajek arrived at the door of the Great Barrington Police Station. A man in a dark suit greeted him. "Are you Detective Hajek?"

"Yes."

"I'm Agent Bloom. Come with me." The Federal agent appeared to be about thirty-five. He led Hajek into a room at the back of the station and introduced him to Sergeant King. The Great Barrington man stood six feet, had light brown hair and brown eyes and looked about forty-five.

Hajek shook King's hand. "Please to meet you. Thanks for apprehending Griffin."

King turned to FBI Agent Bloom with a questioning look. "Detective Hajek, please surrender your weapon to Sergeant King."

Hajek stiffened.

Bloom repeated, "Your weapon, Detective."

Hajek complied. King took it, placed it in a cabinet, and locked it.

"Now empty your pockets," Bloom said.

He placed his cell phone, badge, a few crumpled bills, change, hard candies, and a credit card case on the table.

Bloom continued. "Sergeant King brought in Mr. Griffin as you requested. He's in a room down the hall. You understand that we cannot arrest him without cause. We have spoken with agents in Connecticut and with Captain Wilcox."

Looking directly at Bloom, Hajek had a pretty good idea of what was coming next.

King looked down as Bloom spoke. "Wilcox removed you from this case and asked us to detain you. He's not happy that you ignored his orders. This is not the first time you've suggested a suspect. We need to follow procedures. That's how we'll solve this case."

Hajek's phone rang. Before he could pick it up, Agent Bloom answered it. "Hello." He looked surprised, "I'm Agent Bloom with the FBI. Who are you?"

"Beacon police?" Bloom paused. "Yes, you're calling Detective Hajek's phone. What's this about? Oh…Okay I'll put you on speaker." He hit the button.

"Put Hajek on the phone," Sloane shouted.

"Hi, Darren I'm glad to hear from you. I'm in the police station in Great Barrington, Massachusetts. Agent Bloom took my phone. He thinks I'm crazy for pursuing Griffin."

"Well you're not. Griffin's DNA matches DNA from the Illinois crime scene and the Manhattan case."

Bloom looked bewildered.

Hajek smiled.

306

Another phone rang. Bloom pulled his cell from his pocket. "Bloom." He turned from the others as he listened to the caller. "So it's legit. There's a confirmed DNA match. We'll book Griffin and make arrangements to transfer him to New York City." He put the phone back in his pocket. "King, give Detective Hajek back his weapon and his personal belongings."

Chapter 56

Hajek returned to his rental car parked outside the police station. After taking several deep breaths, he resumed normal breathing, and slowed his rapid heartbeat. Not wanting to consider the dismal options if Sloane had not called, he quickly got in his car, drove two blocks, and parked.

He pressed the number for Nick Kostas.

"The killer's in custody."

"Way to go. When's the press conference?"

"I don't know. You are not going to believe what happened. An arrogant FBI agent ordered me to turn my weapon over to the Great Barrington Police."

"Shit. They found the tracker."

"No, it's secure. The idiots had Harold Griffin and would have released him but they had to deal with me first. Wilcox asked them to detain me. I feared they would send me to a psych unit."

"How'd you slip out of that?"

"Timely news from Beacon."

"Sloane got DNA results from the trash and they matched?"

"Yes."

"That's great, Peter. Where are you now?"

"In Great Barrington, Massachusetts."

"When will you be home? We need to celebrate."

"I'm stopping at the Jenkins next. They have a home here. Then I'll drive back to Connecticut. I left stuff in the motel. I'll be lucky if I got back to Stamford by eight. Could be later. I haven't had much sleep for days so I'll probably crash at that dumpy motel and drive to Queens in the morning. I'll call you when I'm home."

When Hajek arrived at the Jenkins home, a police officer waved and walked toward him. "I'm Jason Bartlett with the Great Barrington Police. Are you Detective Hajek?"

"Yes." They shook hands. "How's everything?"

"Agent Bloom reported that the serial killer is in custody."

"Is there still an agent with the Jenkins?"

"Yes, Anderson's inside. The family's relieved to learn the good news. They're looking forward to seeing you. Nice work."

"Thanks for your help, Officer Bartlett."

Vincent Jenkins opened the door and greeted Hajek with a shoulder hug. "Come in. We're happy to see you."

From the entranceway, Hajek looked over a spacious living and dining area with a wall of windows revealing a small yard, evergreen trees, and a hint of water in the distance.

Vincent motioned toward a leather couch, a rocker and wing-backed chairs on a rug in front of a fireplace. "Please have a seat."

Teresa entered from the right and gave Hajek a warm hug. "Detective Hajek, you have been so good to my family. We're all grateful for your work."

"Thank you, Teresa."

"You look tired. Are you okay?"

"Yes."

"Let me get you something. You probably haven't eaten all day."

"I'm fine."

Teresa looked askance. "We had chicken salad for lunch. I'll fix you a sandwich."

Hajek smiled. "Thank you."

Vincent sat on the couch. "The FBI said that you were way off base and they needed to keep you from messing up their investigation. I can't tell you how much that offended me."

Agent Anderson moved his eyes away from Vincent toward Hajek. "I'm afraid The Bureau misjudged you." He cleared his throat and added, "We obviously had wrong information. No insult intended."

"None taken."

Vincent glowered at Anderson. "I overheard you telling the local police officer earlier that your superiors in the FBI thought Hajek should be committed to a psychiatric facility…"

Hajek shifted in his seat. "Vincent, it's okay. We got the guy."

"The day you came to my house after Angela's daughter was murdered, I didn't believe you'd find Maura's killer. But you impressed Teresa. When you kept talking about high school classmates, I thought that was a reach but seeing you piece things together amazed me. My family owes you."

Hajek shrugged.

Kaitlin walked into the room and stood by the large table with chairs for eight. After a moment, Hajek caught her eye. "How are you, Kaitlin?"

"Drained." She placed her hands on the back of a chair.

Vincent looked lovingly at his daughter. "Please sit with us."

Kaitlin took a few steps and stopped with her back to the fireplace. Looking directly at Hajek she said, "When my Dad told us the killer was coming to Great Barrington, I felt sick. I wanted to run into the woods. I know the trails here. The killer would never find me. But Dad convinced me to follow your instructions and stay inside."

Hajek nodded. "I can't imagine the terror you felt today. We hoped this would be a safe haven for your family."

Teresa placed a tray with a sandwich and a glass of water on a small table next to Hajek. "I've put the kettle on for your tea. Can I get you anything Kaitlin? Vincent?"

"I'll have coffee, dear," Vincent said.

"Mom, I'll get Dad's coffee and myself some tea."

Teresa sat next to her husband, who put his arm around her and said, "Detective, I intend to tell the NYPD how lucky they are to have you on their staff. You risked your career to bring this killer to justice."

Hajek's phone rang. He pulled it from his pocket. With a surprised look he answered it and rose to his feet. "Detective Hajek, this is Patterson, FBI Agent-in-Charge in Manhattan. I appreciate your part in the team effort that apprehended Griffin."

"Thank you. I'm glad he's in custody."

"We have a search warrant for Griffin's Faucett Street home. Could you join the staff there?"

"I'd be happy to. I can be there in about two hours."

"What was that all about?" Vincent asked.

"An invitation to participate in the search of Harold Griffin's home."

"They've finally got it." Vincent smiled.

Hajek took a bite from the sandwich. "This is delicious. Thank you."

"We'd love to have you stay for dinner, but we understand the FBI needs your help in Connecticut. Someday we hope you'll visit and let us show you this beautiful area," Teresa said.

"I'd like that." Hajek finished eating. "I do need to go." He stood, hesitated, and walked over to the windows. Gazing at the row of hemlocks and scattered colorful flowers he did not know the name for, he felt transported to a foreign land.

"It's so peaceful here and I have memories of many good times. I don't know how I can go back and live in Charlotte." Kaitlin spoke softly standing next to him.

Hajek looked at branches bent and woven into a seat. "Where did you find that bench?"

"A local artist made it. My parents bought it years ago."

"Someday I'll be back here."

"I hope so. Look at this." She walked over to a 3 foot by 4 foot map mounted on a board. "This is Berkshire County."

Hajek stared at the map. "There's a lot of undeveloped land."

"Sadly, our open spaces are under attack. There are plans to put a high-pressure, gas line across Berkshire County and the entire state of Massachusetts."

"I saw *stop the pipeline signs* as I drove here."

"The environmental and health risks are enormous. Look, here's where it will cross the Appalachian Trail." She pointed to a spot on a dotted red line.

"The one from Georgia to Maine?"

"Right."

"Never been on it."

"I've hiked it south to north in Massachusetts and in parts of Connecticut and Vermont."

"I'm impressed."

Vincent came over and stood with Kaitlin and Peter. "The AT has spectacular scenery, diverse terrain and I hate that a greedy corporation wants to ruin it."

"I hope you can stop it. I really have to go."

312

Chapter 57

When Hajek approached Faucett Street, he found the local police had blocked all traffic from the street. He identified himself to an officer.

"Just a minute. I'll call someone."

Hajek saw a TV news van parked nearby and a crowd of people gathered near it.

A tall man wearing a tweed jacket made his way toward Hajek. "I'm Agent Pilarski. Pull your car up on the sidewalk and I'll escort you inside."

Once in the house, they picked their way through the cluttered hallway into the kitchen. Dirty dishes filled the sink. Cereal boxes lined the counter top. Layers of grime on the linoleum floor made the original color unidentifiable.

Pilarski shook his head. "Housekeeping was not a priority. Let me introduce you to the others."

After meeting two FBI agents and three crime scene investigators working in the house, Hajek asked to look around.

"Feel free. The photographers are almost finished and the investigators are checking for any other evidence."

In a bedroom the odor of dirty clothes assaulted him.

"Want a mask?" A woman wearing one asked as she searched the contents of a dresser drawer.

"I'm okay." Hajek bent his right arm and covered his nose.

In a pile of old mail and spiral notebooks on top of the dresser, he recognized a slim book with a textured green cover, Stamford Catholic High's 1965 yearbook. He flipped to Teresa's photo. "This is the mother of the first victim."

Pilarski picked up a paper that fell to the floor. "Teresa October 3rd"

"Her birthday," Hajek said.

Together they looked at the birth dates for Roberta, Marsha and Angela. Envelopes stuffed inside the back cover held yellowed newspaper clippings. One fell out. Hajek picked up an article in *The Catholic Transcript* and read the caption under students dressed in their school uniform *Four Crusaders against Hunger*. He recognized Teresa. Looking back at the yearbook he saw that the other three were Roberta, Marsha and Angela.

Flipping through the rest of the news articles, Hajek found engagement and wedding announcements. He handed the yearbook to an investigator. "You'll want to keep this."

Hajek located a photographer in another bedroom that looked untouched since Griffin's mother died. Her clothes hung in the closet. Rings nestled in dust on the dresser along with a stack of prayer cards and white rosary beads. A wedding picture, probably Griffin's parents, hung on the wall over the dresser.

The photographer showed Hajek a catalog of security devices and a box of padlocks and combination locks. "Was the father a locksmith?"

"I don't know. He entered secured homes without leaving a trace. Maybe he practiced with this stuff."

"I have photos of all this."

"Good. Can you shoot these news clippings before I add them to our evidence collection?" Hajek asked.

"Sure." The photographer took four sheets of paper from his clip board and placed them on the quilt-covered bed.

Hajek laid out the newspaper clippings. He smiled when he recognized that Teresa's engagement picture showed a strong resemblance to Kaitlin. After the photographer shot all the announcements, Hajek returned the fragile pieces to the envelopes.

"Detective Hajek, check this out." Pilarski stood in the doorway holding a large plastic bag with a coil of rope.

"Where was that found?"

"I'll show you." They walked through the kitchen to a door that led to a small screened porch.

"Right here." Pilarski pointed to the floor in the far corner.

Hajek noticed a pulley still attached to the outside. At one time a clothesline had extended to a tree in the back yard. "That rope looks like the segments left at other crime scenes."

The agent from the bedroom stood waiting for him in the kitchen. "You'll want to see these."

Hajek opened a folder filled with Stamford Catholic High Alumni newsletters. Circled or starred were the birth announcements of Teresa, Roberta, Marsha and Angela's children. The dates for each were underlined in red ink. "You've already photographed them?"

"Yes."

"Agent Pilarski, I'm calling it a day. It's been a long one."

"We'll let you know if we find anything particularly interesting. I'll walk you out. We really appreciate your help."

Outside on the opposite side of the street two men holding dogs on leashes talked with a Stamford police officer. Vehicle access to Faucett Street remained limited to residents.

Making their way from the Griffin house, Pilarski asked the Stamford officer standing at the end of the walkway, "Anything new out here?"

"Several of our officers interviewed the neighbors. They're baffled. Griffin's arrest for murder stunned them."

"Did anyone know the family?"

315

"The old-timers who knew his parents described them as good decent people who would be horrified if they were alive."

"No one remembers anything strange about Griffin's behavior?"

"Everyone said he never caused any trouble…mostly kept to himself. No interests or hobbies…kind of an enigma."

"Thanks. Good night." Hajek returned to his car.

A man approached. "Who are you?"

Hajek gave the reporter a tired look and reached for the door handle.

"I saw you leave the Griffin home. I'm with NYOne. Can you give me an update?"

"The investigation is ongoing. The FBI have everything under control. No one's in danger." Hajek got in his car. Driving back to the motel with his brain still churning with the day's events, he decided to check out and go home. If he left in the next half hour, he would be in Queens by midnight. His phone rang as he gathered his belongings.

"Captain."

"This is the first chance I've had today to call and thank you. Great work, Peter. You were ahead of the curve on this one. I hope you realize the pressure the higher ups put on me."

"I understand."

"We're cool, right?" Wilcox asked.

Hajek smiled. "We're cool, Captain."

"Good. I spoke with Commissioner Sullivan. He, Agent Patterson, and the mayor have scheduled a press conference tomorrow at 2P.M. They'd like you there."

"Okay. Where?"

"The FBI offices downtown. Get some rest. See you then. Oh, Peter, the DOJ agreed to a plea deal with John Gordon, two years in jail and five year probation. Congratulations."

"I don't know how much I had to do with it."

"A lot."

Chapter 58

At 1:20 Hajek walked into 26 Federal Plaza. Agent Bloom caught up with him after he cleared security.

"I'm not carrying my weapon," Hajek said deadpan.

Bloom grimaced until Hajek laughed. "You might want to hear about Griffin's ride from Massachusetts to New York."

"I do. Tell me."

"Let's find a quiet spot." Bloom walked past the elevators to the end of the hallway. "Not much action here on Sunday but I don't want to be overheard."

Hajek nodded.

Bloom rocked on his heels. "Griffin talked nonstop. Everybody had a better deal than him. Girls he liked in high school wouldn't go out with him. His father died right after he finished high school and his mother struggled financially. He expected to be honored for his military service. When he came home from Vietnam, protesters said the war was senseless. They called the soldiers baby killers."

"He said all that?" Hajek asked.

Bloom nodded. "Several times I suggested he might want to remain silent. I told him again he had a right to an attorney. He ignored me. He gave a detailed description of Teresa Collins Jenkins refusing to dance with him at a mixer on Valentine's Day in 1965. Seems to be his justification for killing her daughter Maura."

"Taking her daughter's life is excessive payback," Hajek said.

"When he saw Teresa laughing with her girlfriends he thought they were making fun of him. All these years he has obsessed about revenge," Bloom said.

Hajek interrupted. "After his mother became ill, he acted on those crazy thoughts. The first killing in Bethel, Connecticut happened about a year before Ursula Griffin died."

Bloom ran his fingers through his hair. "Some people remain stuck in the past. We should go upstairs."

With the FBI logo prominently displayed on the wall behind him, Special Agent-in-Charge Patterson stood at the podium before rows of seated reporters, agents, and police officers. Positioned to his immediate right were Commissioner Sullivan and Captain Wilcox. Hajek joined his captain standing at the edge of the platform.

TV cameras panned the room and then focused on Patterson. Photographers moved around clicking shots from various angles.

At exactly 2P.M., Patterson began the press conference. "We have captured the serial killer, Harold Griffin, of Stamford Connecticut. This arrest is the result of the joint effort of the FBI, the NYPD, and several local police departments in New York, Connecticut, Massachusetts, Illinois, and North Carolina." Patterson looked directly at the audience. "Special thanks go to NYPD Detective Peter Hajek."

For the next ten minutes, Patterson explained that the series of crimes occurred over a seven year period in four states. When Patterson finished summarizing, he introduced Police Commissioner Sullivan.

Commissioner Sullivan praised Captain Wilcox, applauded the investigative talent of all members of the team and thanked them before citing Peter Hajek's critical role in capturing the serial killer. "In early April, Hajek began investigating the Hanson murder in Manhattan. During his investigation, he found similarities with a seven-year-old Connecticut murder. His persistence linked five murders to the same killer."

319

When the live feed ended, Hajek walked off the raised platform toward Otto Snyder.

Snyder smiled and slapped Hajek on the back. "Big guys went from singing, 'rein him in, he's crazy…to he's a skillful problem solver…"

"Keep it down, Otto." Hajek whispered. Feeling his phone vibrate, he pulled it from his pocket. Two missed calls—Nick and Vincent Jenkins. Later. He turned it off.

Looking toward the officials, Snyder said, "Wilcox is waving to get your attention, Peter."

Hajek turned and saw his captain motioning for him to return to the front of the room.

"I'll be right back."

Wilcox stood tall. "Photo opp time."

For the next three minutes Hajek posed with Mayor Lockhardt, Police Commissioner Sullivan, Captain Wilcox, and Agent Patterson. He forced a smile and shook their hands.

Returning to Snyder, he filled him in on Bloom's report of Griffin complaining about his hard life and justifying his murders.

"Much crueler to kill a daughter." Snyder shook his head. "With Griffin's confession, the Feds have it easy. Do they want anything from us?"

"No. Well maybe our silence about their behavior."

"Of course." Snyder laughed.

"I'm going to see my mother. I'll be in tomorrow."

Back in his apartment, Hajek turned on his phone and listened to his missed calls. Nick said, "I was on patrol during the press conference but Camille filled me in. Nice job. How about a celebratory dinner on Wednesday?"

Next he played Vincent Jenkins' message. "We watched the press conference and we're delighted you got the credit you deserve. We plan to be here the rest of the week, if not longer, and we'd love to have you as our guest."

Chapter 59

At the nursing facility, Peter wheeled his mother to a sheltered patio. Wearing a sweater and with a blanket over her legs, she breathed deeply.

"Isn't the cool air nice?" Peter pulled over a chair from a nearby table. Holding her hand, he wondered how she managed to cope when his father died after decades of marriage. After four years with Francine, he found it difficult to remember life before her. He felt the loss every day.

"Fred, are we going to that little place near Jones Beach for supper?"

"If you'd like." He smiled at his mother calling him by his father's name.

"They have the best fried clams."

His mother gazed straight ahead. She looked content. He accepted that she had no idea who he was and he took comfort in her serenity. At the same time he had never felt so alone.

His eyes filled with tears and he blinked them back. I could not help my wife. I can't do much for my mother. I miss both of them terribly.

They sat looking at the daffodils and tulips for a few more moments.

"I cracked a big case, Mom. I saved a young woman."

***

Hajek sat in his living room. The city noises of traffic, people talking on the street, horns, and airplanes overhead created a familiar backdrop. His thoughts jumped from his mother to Francine to the Jenkins family.

Kaitlin's close call upset him on several levels. Effortlessly he had established rapport with Teresa and enjoyed their discussions. He found her motherly interest and concern for him endearing. Once he met Vincent, they easily connected. He could not imagine this couple enduring the loss of another daughter.

Back in April during his telephone interview with Kaitlin, Hajek heard a vivacious person with a sense of humor. He remembered laughing when she said, "I was an older sister's nightmare, a real brat." Silly how that sentence stuck in his mind. Her ability to move on after her sister's death gave him faith that with time he would pull through.

***

Monday morning Wilcox fell in step with Hajek as he entered the precinct. Beaming with pride he waved the folded newspaper. "Great coverage of the press conference. New York Times front page above the fold."

"I saw."

"Peter, I know it's useless to talk with you about taking time off so I won't bother. Get your notes from the last week into the file, and our record will be complete if the FBI wants anything."

"I'll take care of that right away." Hajek continued to his desk. The voicemail light flashed. When he accessed it, the robot announced *your mailbox is full*. Returning calls required more energy than finishing paperwork. He started on his notes.

While Snyder attended Griffin's arraignment, Hajek worked alone in their corner nook. He recorded the final events of obtaining Griffin's trash, observing him near the Jenkins home in Fairfield and following him to Great Barrington. He included pictures: Griffin dumping a green plastic bag, the now public trash in the rental car's trunk, and the same garbage bag folded open on a table inside the Beacon police station.

He summarized his thoughts on the yearbook, news articles and rope found in Griffin's home. Knowing the FBI had a detailed inventory, he hit save and closed the file.

323

Finished, he pulled up the Internet on his phone and entered two words. Noting an address, he walked out the back of the precinct to the closest subway stop. He traveled south and exited onto Spring Street in SoHo.

Inside the store, the selection overwhelmed him. "Can I help you, sir?"

"Yes, please."

Hajek's phone rang. Seeing it was his friend Nick Kostas, he gave the clerk a one minute gesture.

"Peter, I just stopped by the precinct. Where are you?"

"Soho's Outdoor Gear."

"What are you doing there?"

"Buying hiking boots. I'm taking a few vacation days to log some miles on the Appalachian Trail."

The End

Acknowledgements

I cannot express enough thanks to Joyce Hunsucker for being my writing buddy throughout this project. I particularly appreciated Joyce's close reading, her consistent, honest, feedback, her eagle eye for things misplaced, and her excellent sense for dialogue and rhythm.

I am sincerely grateful to Sergeant Robert Angelo for answering my questions and for being an example of a police officer making a difference in his community. Any errors in my description of law enforcement individuals or their work are mine.

I also thank the following:

- Lauren Bier for sharing her knowledge of living in uptown Charlotte
- Dr. Thomas J. Cahill for his insight on the various ways grief impacts individual behavior
- Cheryl D. Nelson for her caring and astute criticism
- Kathleen Kelleher for her input on the cover design
- Patrick J. Cahill, Pauline T. Lancaster, and Aaron A. Toscano for technical support
- My husband, Edward, for his loving encouragement and belief that this story would be told
- Ulysses Grant for providing a physical location

My deepest gratitude to all.